Safe Passage

Black Flag, Book 1

Rachel Ford

ISBN: 9781099218392

CONTENTS

CHAPTER ONE

"I'm sorry," he said, "we don't have room."

"You had room five minutes ago," I reminded him.

But the captain of the *Night Runner* just shrugged, an unconcerned grin spreading across his weathered features. "You know how it goes. I got a better offer."

"I'll pay more," I insisted. "Name your price. Please, I need to get off of this rock."

"I don't think you could match this one. And even if you could, I'd rather not piss off the people paying to keep you here." Now, Captain Ebert's expression hardened. "Which you didn't mention, by the way, when we made our deal."

"Please," I implored. "I've been here six months. I need to get back home."

But Ebert was unpersuaded. Neither my offers of emptying my savings nor my protests that he'd given his word made an ounce of difference. The captain brushed past me, ambling up the gangplank to his old freighter, and sealed it after him.

Then, I heard the hum of the engine startup procedures, and had to back away before I ended up crispier than a side of hopper legs. I watched, fury and fear competing for supremacy, as the *Night*

Runner blasted off. Another ship, another captain, another failed flight; it had been six months and countless tries since my "temporary" layover on Trel began.

I cursed myself for having been such a fool. I cursed myself for taking the job in the first place, much less for having believed anything one of the Conglomerate's pilots said. If I'd never taken the bank job, I wouldn't be here. If I hadn't gotten off the ship when we detoured so suspiciously on the way back, I wouldn't be here. *Delousing? God, I'm an imbecile.* How could I have fallen for a story like that?

Now, I was a prisoner in everything but name, a prisoner light years from civilization, stuck on a dusty rock in the middle of nowhere. Oh, the Conglomerate kept me well enough, I supposed. I had money for food and entertainment – what passed for it here, anyway. But I wasn't a fool.

Well, not all the time, anyway. There was a reason the Conglomerate cordoned me off from the rest of humanity. There was a reason they kept me on a planet they owned. And it had nothing to do with the feeble excuses they'd offered in those first weeks, when they still took my calls. It wasn't a matter of an overtaxed fleet.

I was the engineer behind the Conglomerate's new Deltaseal bank security. It was a masterpiece, the first and only of its kind: an integrated combination of digital checks and physical balances, that incorporated all the best of contemporary security – the high-tech locks and biometric scanners – with the best of more traditional technology – armed battle bots and the highest end old-fashioned vaults. To break it, you would need a team of vault crackers, code breakers and soldiers.

Or me. That, of course, was the piece the Conglomerate feared. I knew Deltaseal's secrets, because I built it. Not that I planned to use them. I didn't violate my clients' trust, even when I suspected they might work on the wrong side of the law. Since the business on Echo Prime, I took work where I could get it. A job was a job. But that didn't mean my professional standards had lapsed, even if my judgement had.

And this time, I'd miscalculated. My ask-no-questions policy that had seemed so smart at the time put me right in the Conglomerate's crosshairs. The fact was, the only reason I was still drawing breath was because the system hadn't been running long enough for them to kill off the brains behind it.

But the grains in my hourglass were slipping away. I could feel it. My last so-called furlough paycheck had been a week and a half late. This week's hadn't come at all. A six-month had passed since Deltaseal went live. As they learned their new system – my system – my value to the Conglomerate was fading.

It wouldn't be long, now, before I had an unfortunate accident, or wound up the victim of a random and unexplained death on the streets of Trel. No one would ask questions. No one would care.

And I'd be dead.

I started as a hand touched my shoulder, and spun around. I found myself face-to-face with an old man. He cracked a gap-toothed smile. "Woah there, miss."

I blinked, feeling a little ridiculous. "Sorry, uh, can I help you?"

"Maybe we can both help each other."

"Oh?"

"I heard your conversation with Ebert there."

"Oh." I could feel a scowl forming just at the memory.

"Sounds like you need safe passage off this rock?"

"That's right." I looked the old man up and down. He wasn't particularly clean, and I got the impression that that was a matter of habit. I had taken him at first to be a freighter hand. Now, I reconsidered. "You got a way to get me out of here?"

He grinned again. "See that ship over there?" He pointed to one of the freighters in port, some half a dozen ships from us. "That's the *Lady Louise*. She's my bird, alright."

It was a small ship, meant for cargo runs rather than human transport. But I wasn't about to be picky. I'd have gone in a space capsule at this point, if someone had one available. I nodded eagerly. "I can pay," I said. "I just need to get to another port. It doesn't even matter where, as long as it's in Union territory."

He nodded. "I don't usually take passengers. But you seem like you're in a pickle." He shrugged. "Tell you what. I've got some business I've got to wrap up now. But, you know a place called Tully's?"

Tully's was a little eatery and bar in Trel's main settlement. It tended to attract shady clientele, but, then, so did everything on this planet. "I do."

"Good. Meet me there, say…oh, eighteen hundred hours. We'll talk about getting you out of here."

"Thank you," I said. "I'll be there."

"Good. And I'm Captain Joe Billers, by the way. People call me Captain Joe, though."

"Kay," I said, extending my hand, "Kay Ellis."

"Nice to meet you, Kay." He grinned again. "I'll see you tonight, then."

I was waiting before six o'clock rolled around at a table in the back of Tully's. I'd spent the afternoon wondering in turns if I was walking into a trap or if my luck had finally changed. Was I getting out? Or was I getting fitted for a pine box?

He arrived at two past, and threw a glance around the room. Spotting me, he flashed his signature grin, and ambled over. "Miss Kay," he said, sidling into a seat next to me. "Good to see you again."

He was a little closer than I would have preferred, and the smell of tobacco and engine oil was strong. But I said, "You too, Captain Joe."

He turned in his seat, so that he was facing me, and I mirrored the movement. I wanted to be able to see his facial expressions. I still didn't know if I was dealing with a Conglomerate contractor, or a good Samaritan, after all. "So, you're in a bit of a bind?" he said.

"I need a ride off world," I said. "My last ship bailed while I was on layover, and I'm behind schedule." It was all more or less true, though I'd skipped some of the more pertinent details.

He nodded. "Bad bit of luck."

"Yeah."

He glanced me over, up and down, and I found something I didn't like in that gap-filled grin; something I hadn't noticed before; something that made my skin crawl. But in a minute, he'd turned to flag down a waitress. "What's your special, honey?"

"Fried hopper legs and cheese sauce."

I cringed. Of course it was hopper legs. Hoppers were just

about the only thing that was native to this damned rock, and there were so many of them it seemed Trel was permanently under the curse of the second plague of Egypt.

"Great. I'll take a platter for two. And a Keldian sunrise, one for the lady and one for me."

"Coming right up."

"So," he said, turning back to me. "Where are you headed?"

His tone and expression were solicitous enough that I found myself relaxing a degree. Whatever I'd thought I'd seen, I decided, I had imagined. "Back to Union space." Trel, like most Conglomerate territory, was just outside the established borders of the Union. It meant the law applied less here. Technically, all Union citizens were bound by Union laws, wherever we went. But with no one to enforce them, technicalities meant little. "It doesn't much matter where, I just need to get to a port in Union space."

He nodded. "You got family there?"

The question surprised me. "A brother." It didn't seem necessary to mention that Jake and I hadn't spoken in five years.

"No husband?"

I blinked. "What?"

He moved a little closer and lowered his voice. "Can't imagine a fine woman like you, sleeping alone at night."

I pushed back in my own seat. "Captain Joe," I said, "please. I'm just here to arrange a ride home."

He scooted to the edge of his seat, so that he was again near me. "All work and no play makes Jack a very dull boy." He grinned. "We wouldn't want that, would we?"

Mercifully, the waitress reappeared now, a platter of sizzling hopper legs drenched in thick orange goo. "Here you go. Drinks are on the way."

"Thank you, love."

"Anytime, Joe."

My head was reeling. I had the impression that I'd made a terrible mistake. It should have been a relief, I supposed, that Joe wasn't there to kill me. But the something very different he had in mind was not much better. I decided I needed to make my escape.

As if he sensed my growing unease, Captain Joe eased over to his own seat, away from me. "Well, dig in, Kay," he said. "You don't get better hopper legs than at Tully's."

"I think I should go," I said.

"Go?" He paused from chewing, a hopper leg hanging out of his mouth. "We haven't even discussed passage."

"I…I think I made a mistake coming here."

He frowned. "Was it me?"

I blinked at the question. Of course it was him. What else would it have been? But I said, "I'm just looking for a ride home, Captain Joe. Nothing else."

He stared at his plate of hoppers, then nodded. "Alright. Well, you can't blame a man for trying. Let's eat now, and talk after." I hesitated. "Come on. You can't expect me to eat all these hoppers by myself."

Good sense told me I should go. But the memory of six months of failed escape attempts, of six months of being turned away from every ship that touched down at Trel's port, combined in my head with the thought of that missing paycheck, with visions of a Conglomerate assassin arriving on one of these ships. "Alright," I said in a moment.

"Good, good." He passed me a plate. "Dig in."

Reluctantly, I did. I didn't care for hopper legs. They had a chewy texture that rather turned my stomach, even when battered and fried like these ones. The fact that hoppers – fried, boiled, steamed, baked, grilled and even pureed – had composed the bulk of my diet since landing on Trel only solidified my stance. I detested the damned things.

But if Captain Joe meant what he said, that the shenanigans were really over, I didn't want to offend him. So I ate. I did not, however, drink when our Keldian sunrises arrived, despite his few hints on the point.

He did, working his way through three of the mixed drinks and then a Coratian ale. Finally, his appetite sated, he sat back. "So, about passage…"

I pushed my plate away, grateful to be able to call it quits. "What are your rates?" I asked. "I can give you twice standard." I could, in truth, afford a lot more than that. Hell, I'd have cleaned out my bank account for safe passage out of here. But twice standard rates was a good starting point for negotiation.

He nodded. "Twice standard. Hm." He seemed to consider. "Alright."

My eyes widened in surprise. I hadn't expected him to be that easy to convince. "Oh."

"Twice standard," he repeated, "and tonight."

"Tonight?"

He grinned. "You know what I mean, Miss Kay." He slipped a hand onto my thigh.

I pulled it off, with some difficulty. "I thought you said no more of that?"

"I never said that. I said we'd talk after dinner." He was grinning ear to ear now. "And here we are, talking."

"Please," I said, "I'm serious. I need passage out of here."

"And I need a good, long fuck," he said.

"That," a third voice sounded, "is why God gave you two capable hands."

We both started, and I looked up to see a woman. She was tall and thin, and wearing a long coat that made her seem a little taller and thinner than she probably was.

Captain Joe swore. "What in God's name do you want, Landon? We're conducting business here."

"Nah," she said, plopping heavily onto a bench opposite us. "You're done. The lady heard your terms, and, surprising no one, rejected them." A cross between arrogance and self-satisfaction had settled on her features, but it did nothing to diminish her beauty. The twinkle in her green eyes, the flush to her cheeks and the confident smirk on her lips rather enhanced it. With her flame-red hair and trim figure, she was the kind of woman, I thought, who might have been a model or a senator's wife, if she'd been interested.

"This doesn't concern you," the freighter captain countered.

"Go." Her tone, now, was mirthless. "I'm not asking, Joe."

His eyes flashed and he offered a whole litany of swears. But he went.

"Dammit," I said after he'd gone. "What are you doing? He was my ride out of here."

She'd been sifting through what was left on my plate during Captain Joe's farewell tirade, and now, pausing from chewing a hopper leg, she shook her head. "The kind of ride you'd have gotten from that old bastard isn't the kind you're interested in."

I could feel my face flush, as much from anger as embarrassment. "I would have paid."

She looked me up and down with a gaze so free that I felt myself color again. "Nah. He'd get better money, by weight, for felka berry. That is his preferred cargo, I understand." Felka berry was grown on some of the desert planets, and when dried it was a powerful narcotic. Its use and transport were illegal throughout the Union, but that, of course, didn't stop either.

The newcomer was continuing, "Trust me, Katherine: men like Joe aren't your ticket out of here." She leaned back and cocked her head to the side. "Now, me on the other hand? Well, I may be just what you're looking for."

I rather doubted it, and let an eyebrow creep up my forehead just far enough to convey my skepticism.

She laughed. "The thing is Kate – you don't mind if I call you Kate, do you? Anyway, the thing is-"

She hadn't slowed down long enough for me to say that I did mind, but now another thought crowded that one out. "Hold on. How do you know my name?"

She grinned. "Oh, that's easy. I came here to find you."

I felt my heart sink. This was it, then: the assassin I'd been expecting. The Conglomerate had finally decided I was no longer worth keeping around, and they'd sent this irreverent scrap of a woman to do me in. "For the Conglomerate?"

She smirked. "You can't be naive enough, Kate, to think that they're really sending someone to rescue you from the exile they've imposed? They want you here, where you're safely out of the way – where they can reach you if they need and dispose of you when they decide they're done."

I could feel my hands trembling. I tried to force a steadiness to my tone. If I was going to die, I was going to do it with my boots on. "So you're here to kill me?"

She laughed. "Don't be ridiculous. I wouldn't join you for dinner if I was here to kill you." She shrugged. "Anyway, assassination isn't my style."

"Then what do you want?"

"The same thing they're trying to keep safe." She leaned across the table and tapped a forefinger against the side of my head. "The secrets buried inside that brain of yours, Katherine Ellis."

CHAPTER TWO

"Wait," I said, "you want me to cross the Conglomerate? Are you nuts?"

"Yes, and…" She shrugged. "Most days, also yes."

I frowned. Her levity was almost as disturbing as the proposition. "You can't be serious."

"I'm completely serious. You give me what I want, I give you what you want. Everyone wins. Except the Conglomerate." She grinned. "But they're overdue for a few losses, I think. Don't you?"

"You're insane."

"We've already established that," she said airily. She was, I thought, positively enjoying herself. "But it's not relevant." She poked through my plate, pulling out a fat, meaty leg. "I'm on the clock, Kate. I need your answer."

"My name's not Kate," I snapped. "And it's a no. Of course it's a no. I'm not suicidal."

She chewed the fried hopper thoughtfully, then shrugged. "Your neck, I guess. If you want to sit around waiting for a Conglomerate bullet, that's your call."

I scowled at her. "I'll find another way."

She laughed. "Maybe you could try Joe again, see if his offer still stands." She scrunched up her nose. "I'd make it a delivery first, payment later deal, though. Can't say I trust old Joe."

"Go to hell." My cheeks were flaming.

"Come on, Kate," she said. "You and I both know there's no way off this rock for you unless it's in a body bag – or my ship."

"Who the hell are you, anyway?" I demanded. "A Landon-something?"

"Ah. Where are my manners. I forgot, we hadn't been introduced. Magdalene Landon, captain of the *Black Flag*, at your service."

"*Black Flag*?" I pulled a face. "A pirate?"

She frowned at me. "A privateer, Kate. Everything I do is legal."

"Other than blackmail," I pointed out.

"This isn't blackmail. I'm offering an exchange of information for services. Nothing illegal about that."

"It's exploitation," I fumed.

She shrugged. "That's kind of my business." She reached over and took my yet untouched Keldian sunrise, sipping it appreciatively. "Not quite how they make them on Kelda Prime, but still…damned good."

"Look," I said, deciding to take another approach. "You're obviously not afraid of the Conglomerate."

"Only an idiot is unafraid of the Conglomerate," she said.

"But you're willing to cross them."

"Of course." She grinned. "Only an idiot would let fear keep them from that much gold."

"My point is," I persisted, "you're willing to take a chance for a payout. I've got six months of furlough paychecks. They're all yours if you get me out of here. That's all you got to do: get me out of here, drop me off at a port in Union space."

"I'm not here to negotiate, Kate."

"I'm not Kate," I snapped.

She frowned at me. "What should I call you, then?"

"My friends call me Kay. You can call me Katherine."

A grin replaced the frown. "Alright then, Katherine." She effected a superior tone as she said the word. She drained the glass of Keldian sunrise. "But come on. I really am on a schedule. What do you say? Do you stay and wait for death, or join the *Black Flag*?"

"If I give you information about Deltaseal," I said, "I'm as good as dead anyway. Even in the Union."

She considered for a moment. "Maybe," she said. "But you're definitely dead if you stay. You've got a chance on the run."

I scowled at her. "So death now, or death later?"

"And," she said, ignoring my question, "I'll even cut you a percentage. Say, five percent, if we get out clean."

I blinked. "Five percent?" It was my turn to laugh.

"Five percent of Deltaseal's gold is a lot of gold, Kate. Don't be greedy now."

I sat up a little straighter. "You wouldn't get a red cent without me, Maggie."

I saw with a measure of pleasure that her eye twitched at the appellation, and she corrected, "Magdalene."

"Whatever. My point is, you could spend the rest of your life trying to crack those vaults and computer systems, and you wouldn't get anywhere. Not that your lifetime would be very long after you set foot there anyway. Our worst test runs gave thieves about forty-five seconds before the drones and battle bots reached them." I smiled, crossing my arms. "So if you're asking me to put my life on the line, to cross the Conglomerate for your damned crazy plan, Maggie Landon, you better talk a hell of a lot more than five percent."

She crossed her arms in turn and leaned back in her seat. Then, she smiled. "Alright. I'll raise your cut to seven percent. Not a penny more."

I laughed out loud. "Fifty," I said. "Or find yourself another fool."

"Fifty?" Her eyebrows raised in surprise, and she laughed. But there was less amusement to her tone than there had been earlier. "You're new to this, I see."

"Maybe," I agreed. "But from where I'm sitting, I'm a dead woman anyway. I've got nothing to lose. But you?" I shrugged. "There's trillions of credits sitting there in Deltaseal's vaults. And the only way you see a penny of them is through me."

She gritted her teeth. "Ten."

"Forty-five."

She snorted. "You're insane."

"Maybe."

"I'll give you fifteen, and nothing else. I've got an entire crew to split this between."

"And I've got a life on the run to fund. Forty. And that's undercutting myself."

She scowled at me, and I fought to repress a grin. I had the impression that Magdalene Landon wasn't used to losing, and didn't care for it. She pushed her seat back and got to her feet. "I'll give you twenty-five percent, Kate Ellis. And that's my final offer. I mean it."

I believed her. "Done," I said. "It's a deal." I stood and extended my hand. "Pleasure doing business with you, Maggie."

She took the hand with a scowl, reminding me, "Magdalene."

We shipped out within the hour. I was insane. I knew that. No one in their right mind got involved with pirates. No one in their right mind crossed the Conglomerate. But, then, they'd crossed me first, hadn't they? And it wasn't like I had options left.

The truth was, I would have taken the five percent. If she'd pushed her case hard enough, I probably would have done it for nothing, as long as it meant getting off Trel. But some part of me, as I walked up the gangplank, thrilled at the idea of all the gold in the bank of Deltaseal. I wondered how many trillions of credits a quarter of Deltaseal's holdings would be.

We wouldn't be able to take it all, of course. We'd be limited by how much we could haul. The matter-resynched bars would be easiest to move, since their mass had been shrunk. The solid gold would be the most difficult.

The credits would be easy enough to download to credit chips. Easy enough for me, anyway. That would be a good security measure, in case Captain Magdalene got any ideas about double-crossing me. Hopefully she wouldn't be the kind to sacrifice trillions of credits for a little petty revenge.

The crew of the *Black Flag* was waiting for us as we embarked, and viewed me with unabashed curiosity. They were as motley a band of ne'er-do-wells as I might have imagined. About half of them were human. The rest seemed mostly to hail from West Alfor. I saw representatives of at least three of the humanoid races from that planet, and one young man who looked to be a cross of Alfor's arctic Tulians and sub-equatorial Esselians. He had the thick, silver hair of a Tulian, and the copper skin and violet eyes of an Esselian. Landon introduced him as Corano, the *Black Flag*'s tactical officer.

Most of the other bridge officers were less remarkable. Drake Sage was the ship's engineer, a human on the young side of middle-age. He grinned as we were introduced, saying, "Well, well, looks like you talked her into it, Captain."

The ship's navigator was another Esselian called Kereli. She was an older woman, the coppers of her skin having progressed into a mature green. She shook my hand without much interest.

It was the *Black Flag*'s helmsman, though, who really caused me to do a doubletake. He stood a head taller than anyone else on deck. It wasn't his height, or even the fact that he was as wide across as two humans. "You're Kudarian," I said, catching myself a moment too late. It was unusual to see a Kudarian on a human-run vessel, even all these years after the Kudar wars. I'd met a handful of his species throughout the years, but it was not a common occurrence.

"F'er ark inkaya," he said. "My friends call me Frank. And, yes, I am Kudarian."

"Well, uh, it's nice to meet you, Frank."

We moved on, until I'd met everyone. There were sixteen personnel, not including myself, on the *Black Flag*.

"Quarters are back this way," Captain Landon was saying,

leading me down a steel-gray passageway. "We run a lean operation, as you can see."

I scoffed. "Lean? It's a skeleton crew."

"It works for us."

"Have you ever done anything like this before? Taking on Deltaseal, I mean?"

"Not quite. But we don't play it safe, either, Miss Ellis."

"There's a world of difference between scavenging smugglers and taking on the Conglomerate."

She frowned at me. "If I was planning on 'taking on the Conglomerate,' that might be a good point. But I have no intention of sieging the planet. I wouldn't need you for that suicide run." She shook her head. "We're going in quietly, getting the stuff, and getting out long before the Conglomerate knows we're there."

She turned to stare at me pointedly. "If, that is, you're worth the trouble to get you."

CHAPTER THREE

I'd watched Trel disappear into the void of space with a measure of relief and fear. I was relieved to be off that damned prison, finally. I was afraid of what lay ahead. The Conglomerate was an organized crime syndicate so ruthless, so effective, so bloody and brutal that it made the organized religion of yesteryear seem like child's play by comparison. It existed almost outside the law.

This was due, in part, to the Conglomerate bosses' acquisition of planets outside the official borders of Union space. But even that pointed to corruption. Unless territory belonged to a recognized ally, the Union had to approve charters for colonization. How crime bosses managed – and kept managing – to get their hands on entire planets was what people would term *a real mystery*. Meaning, of course, it was no mystery at all. It was done the way things were always done: the right bribes to the right people at the right time.

Then again, who the hell was I to criticize those avaricious civil servants? Hadn't I done more or less the same when I took the bank job in the first place?

Not exactly the same, my mind argued. I'd taken the job because I didn't have a choice. It doesn't matter how good an engineer you are. There's no coming back from some mistakes, and on Echo Prime, I'd made the mother of all mistakes.

Seven billion dollars of terraforming washed away. I cringed at the choice of words. It was apropos in a dark sort of way. It had been my mistake with the water cycle generator that had put Echo Prime underwater before the project was…well, underwater.

Forgetting to carry your decimal point'll do that. Of course, so will fifty-six hours without sleep. But the board didn't take that part into consideration. They didn't take into consideration that I'd been working two and a half days straight on their orders. They didn't take into consideration that they'd lost their last engineer two weeks before go-time because they'd pulled the same crap with him.

He'd been smart, and bailed. I was stupid, and stayed. Last I heard, he was still working profitable gigs.

Me? I was blacklisted. No one wanted to touch the genius behind the Echo Prime disaster. No one dared. No insurance company would cover a project I ran after that. No investor would drop money on my work.

No one, that is, until I started getting contracts from a client just outside of Union space. *Rex Henderson.* A businessman, allegedly, working on small projects for his investors. It started with a security system for an off-world home, one of the new floating mansions the rich liked to clutter planetary orbits with.

Did I know he was Conglomerate? No. Did I have a very strong suspicion, bordering on a fair degree of certainty? Yeah. Of course I did. But I was desperate, and they were paying well. And the jobs kept coming.

Until, of course, they didn't – and I was stranded on Trel, waiting for death. Now, I reflected that I'd made something of a career of bad decisions since taking that job with Henderson. Crossing the Conglomerate and signing on to a pirate ship was just the latest in a long, unbroken chain of idiotic choices.

What did I know about Landon, anyway? Not a damned thing, except that she was a privateer. Privateers were essentially licensed pirates, free to prey on raiders and smugglers, to exercise salvage rights, and engage in acts of piracy against enemies of the state.

And that's what they were permitted to do *inside* the law. Everyone knew privateers in general picked and chose what laws they'd follow, and when.

Even I, who made a career of being an imbecile, wasn't imbecile enough to take a pirate and lawbreaker at her word.

So here I was, then, about to go to war with the most ruthless crime syndicate in the galaxy, and relying on a professional cutthroat to keep me out of harm's way. That was a level of stupid that outdid even my history of stupid to date.

I'm a dead woman, I thought glumly, my satisfaction at escaping Trel all but gone in light of this realization.

"Hey," a voice said. "You eat yet?"

I turned. It was the Kudarian, Frank. "What?"

"Anyone show you where the mess hall is?"

"No," I said, shaking my head.

He gestured for me to follow him. "Follow me, then."

"I already ate," I said, feeling my stomach heave a little as I recalled the mess of hopper legs and slimy goo.

"Hoppers aren't real food," he declared.

I frowned. "How'd you know it was hoppers?"

He raised an eyebrow archly. "Is there anything else to eat on Trel?"

"Good point," I agreed. "Alright. I suppose I could use something light. Settle my stomach a bit."

"So," he said as we walked, "how long were you on Trel?"

"Six months."

He shook his head and grimaced. "Enough to drive someone out an airlock, six months of hoppers."

Despite myself, I laughed. "I think you're the first person I've met who doesn't like the damned things."

"Kudarians don't eat them," he said simply.

"Oh. Well, I don't know many Kudarians."

It was his turn to laugh. "I could tell."

I felt my face color. "Sorry about that. I didn't mean to be…well, rude, earlier."

"It is no matter," he said. He turned a grin my way. "On my last ship, the first officer called me Cannibal."

I blinked. "You mean…because you're Kudarian?"

"Of course. Your people are very sensitive about our history. Very insecure."

I studied him for a moment. He was, as I had already seen, huge, with broad shoulders and a height that dwarfed most humans. But for the pallor of his skin and lines of ridges that ran down the length of his nose, though, he might have been a giant man. Except, that was, when he smiled, as he was doing now. Then, his mouth full of fangs gleamed in the light.

I had to repress a shudder. "I don't think it's insecurity," I said. "Your people did eat mine, not so long ago."

He nodded. "But I did not."

"I know," I said.

"And it is prohibited, now, to eat the flesh of sentient beings. Even," he grinned again, "lesser ones, like humans." I frowned. "I joke, Kay Ellis."

"Oh," I said. "I knew that."

He laughed again. "I trust you are a better hacker than you are a liar." I would have protested that I wasn't lying – a lie in its own right – but we'd reached the mess hall now. He gestured for me to go first. "This way."

He was, I thought, surprisingly gallant for someone who spoke so casually about eating human flesh. "Thanks."

We headed to the line, and I grabbed a tray. I'd done a fair bit of traveling for my jobs – back when I got work, anyway – so I knew what to expect when it came to mess hall food: very little. In this regard, the *Black Flag*'s cook didn't disappoint, although by any other standard, his efforts would have done nothing but disappoint.

For entrees, I was faced with the choice of a lumpy soup, a colorful sludge of pasta and – presumably – meat, and a tofu-based concoction that defied description. For sides, he assured me, I could pick any or all of what was available.

"I'll take soup, please," I decided. "And a glass of water." Staring at the buckets of pale, limp corn kernels, runny, reconstituted mashed potatoes and suspiciously perky broccoli, I added, "Pass on the sides."

He plopped a bowl of slop and a pale roll on the tray beside an empty glass. "Water's at the end."

I moved on to the water station. I heard Frank behind me

say, "Two servings of everything."

I thought, at first, this was a joke, and turned around to make a crack about Kudarian appetites. But he wasn't joking. He carried two trays, and the galley cook was piling them with plates. "You can really eat that much?" I wondered, astonished.

He glanced up. "Of course. Kudarians metabolize about six times as much food as humans. We need a lot of protein."

I shivered, remembering our topic of earlier. The Kudar wars had ended a hundred and ten years ago, give or take a year. But the images of Kudarian soldiers feasting on the corpses of human enemies were preserved in textbooks and documentaries – preserved and seared into the minds of new generations. I had rarely met a Kudarian in my lifetime, but the fact was, the long-banished practice of eating the flesh of so-called lesser races was the first thing that came to mind when I did.

He seemed to sense my discomfort, for he flashed a toothy grin and said, "Which, of course, is why we no longer eat your kind. Your meat is fatty, and the proteins are of poor quality."

"Don't mind him, Kate," a voice said. I started. "Frank fancies himself a comedian."

"Captain Landon," I said. Somehow, she'd snuck up again without me seeing her, this time materializing at the end of the line.

She nodded, turning for a moment to the cook. "I'll take the – what are we calling that?" She pointed at the colorful pasta concoction.

"American chop suey," he said.

She shivered. "Right. Okay, load me up with the chop suey, David. And wow, that corn looks great. I'll have some of that and the potato soup."

"Mashed potatoes."

"My mistake."

CHAPTER FOUR

"Well," Landon was saying, "what do you think, Kate?"

"Katherine," I reminded her. "And about what? The soup?"

"No. But, wow, that looks disgusting. What are those lumps?"

I sighed. "I have no idea."

She shivered, but then shook her head, as if purging it of the thought. "Anyway…about the bank. How do we get in?"

"I don't know," Frank said, "I think the soup is pretty good." We both stared at him, and he shrugged, slurping down another spoonful. "Good dumplings, too."

"These aren't dumplings," I said. It tastes like clumps of flour."

"The bank," she reminded us both. "How are we going to get onto Deltaseal without getting blown to pieces before we even touch down?"

I frowned. "That's a good point. They're not going to let a pirate ship into atmosphere."

"Privateer, Kate. Privateer."

"Katherine," I said.

"I thought you were Kay?" Frank wondered.

"I am," I admitted. "Or Katherine. But not Kate."

"I keep forgetting." There was an impish look in Landon's eyes that led me to believe that the oversight was deliberate.

"That's okay," I said. "I'll keep reminding you. Maggie."

Frank glanced between us, then snorted. "Maggie?"

"Magdalene," she corrected.

"Oops," I shrugged, moving my spoon through the lumps in my bowl. "I keep forgetting."

"O-kay," the Kudarian said. Then, "Damned good soup, though, eh?"

His efforts to change the topic were, in a fashion, successful. Landon returned to the topic of Deltaseal. "How do we get into orbit, without getting shot out of the sky?"

"We'll have to mask our id codes," I said.

"That's illegal."

I felt an eyebrow raising. *An ethical pirate? How's that for a contradiction in terms.* Out loud, I opted for, "So is running a crime syndicate. But we'll be outside Union space, and we can switch our codes back as soon as we're done. We just need to look like a civilian vessel while we're there."

She frowned in thought. "Alright. I think I know where we can get a forged set of codes."

There's a surprise, I thought. *So much for the hand-wringing about legality.*

"So we fly under false papers to get planet-side. Then what?"

"I don't know." The truth was, I hadn't put much thought into it. We'd only been underway for an hour or so, and I'd spent that time…well, wallowing in self-pity.

She nodded. "Well, we'll need to figure it out. For the id's, we'll be heading to Kraken's Drop. That's about three weeks away. If we need anything else, I'd like to get it en route or there."

Kraken's Drop was a water planet, run by an aquatic race of vaguely humanoid, vaguely piscine sentient mammals, called the Sciline. In the language of the Sciline, the planet was known simply as 'the great sea.' To everyone else, though, it was Kraken's Drop, so named by the first Union starship to discover it. It was within Union space, but reputed to be a hotspot for smugglers and illegal trade due to the heavy dampening effects on sensors of the ocean cover. I'd never been there – a choice most people would have deemed wise. *Add another stupid decision to the list*, I thought.

"We'll need a terminal, too," I said. "My old accounts will be gone, but I'd be willing to guarantee they didn't get rid of the local accounts I set up." Despite the situation, I grinned at that. The Conglomerate was smart, and they would have taken steps to thwart any attempts at sabotage. But I was smarter.

"How do you know?" Landon asked.

"Because the system hasn't crashed." I shrugged. "They're the accounts that run the security protocols, that feed the battle bots their updates, that monitor planetary traffic. If they deleted those accounts, the entire system would stop working."

"Maybe they switched them out," she pointed out. "Created new ones."

I scoffed. "That's why you hardcode things, Magdalene. Job

security. In this case, life security."

She grinned. "Well, remind me never to piss off the nerds."

It was decided that we'd convene at oh-six-hundred hours in Magdalene's ready room. It was an ungodly hour, but she'd pulled a face when I complained. "Civilians," she'd sighed.

"I didn't realize pirates were such early risers." In my mind, I suppose, I envisioned them singing with parrots and drinking rum to the wee hours of the morning and rising at noon, like some old home world flick. This crew, though, seemed to keep a normal shift rotation. And there wasn't, I saw with a disappointment, a drop of rum or parrot anywhere to be seen on the ship.

"I learned that in the service," she'd answered dryly. "And we're privateers, Kate."

Mercifully, there was at least coffee waiting for us in the ready room. I remarked as much when I fell on the pot, pouring a steaming mug for myself.

"You're not kidding," Frank said. He emptied what remained of the pot into a thermos.

"Dammit, Frank. Get another pot going," Magdalene called from the front of the room.

"Aye aye, Captain," he grumbled.

We took our places. I found myself pulling up a seat beside the Kudarian. His questionable sense of humor notwithstanding, we seemed to get along alright. If nothing else, he was one of the few members of the crew that I had actually spoken with so far; and he, at least, got my name right.

"Alright," Captain Landon said when we had all taken our places. "You all know the mission: break into the bank on Deltaseal, clean it out, get out alive.

"You've met Kay Ellis. She's going to be in charge of…well, all of the above: the 'break in,' the 'find everything,' and the 'get out alive.'"

A few grins were aimed my way, and here and there a *welcome to the team.* Frank said, his tone low enough for my ears only, "We're going to die." He was grinning too, though, so I ignored him and tried to project an air of confidence.

I wasn't feeling it, but, then, the coffee hadn't kicked in enough. I was too tired to really indulge self-doubt either. So I nodded a bit apathetically, and it must have come near enough the confidence I'd intended, because Magdalene seemed satisfied.

She smiled and continued, "Kay's the brains behind Deltaseal. She knows how it's built and, how we break it. She's already identified a way for us to get on planet without the automated defenses kicking in." She looked to me. "You want to tell us?"

I didn't, but she seemed to expect me to. "Uh…sure." Captain Landon nodded and took her seat. I stood. "So, uh, there's a safety protocol built in. In the orbital defenses. The, uh, command center automatically scans incoming vessels, and runs the id codes against every registration database in the Union." I shrugged. "And, maybe, a few lists that aren't so easily attained."

"Maybe?" Landon wondered.

"Maybe," I said. "That part won't bother us. But if you're a lawman from Algeron, you're not going to be happy." I grinned – Algeron's databases were practically undecipherable to human eyes, but I'd made it work anyway – and she frowned. "Anyway, if you're a flagged ship, you're going to be warned to turn away. If you don't, the automated systems will destroy your vessel."

"Flagged?" Frank asked. "What ships are flagged?"

"All known pirates, to start with." I caught myself before she did. "Privateer, I mean."

"So we won't get into Deltaseal airspace," Magdalene concluded. "Not with the *Black Flag*. Not unless we disguise her."

"Falsified id codes?" Corano guessed, his violet eyes gleaming with appreciation.

"Exactly."

"I can install 'em," Drake nodded. "It'll take a half day or so, to get it right."

"I can help," I offered. "There's specific things Deltaseal Air is looking for; I know what they are, so I can help us avoid them."

"Deltaseal Air?"

"The planet's air control system."

"Ah."

"That's good, Kay," Magdalene said, nodding appreciatively. "Okay, so Drake and Kay will handle the codes once we get them.

"As for that, I've got a contact on Kraken's Drop. I reached out to him this morning. He says he should have something for us by time we reach the planet."

"You trust him?" I asked.

She glanced over. "I don't trust anyone. But…" she shrugged. "I've done business with him before. He's always come through."

I nodded slowly. "Okay. Because this is our calling card. If the system calls our bluff here, it's game over. We're lucky to fly out."

"He knows better than to double cross me, Kay."

I nodded again. "Alright. The other thing we're going to need is a terminal with access to the planet's network."

"How the hell are we going to get that?" Frank wondered. "They're not likely to just let us walk up and use a bank computer."

"No," I said. "They're not. But we don't need a bank computer. We just need a computer that's got access to the network." The Kudarian – and most of the crew – stared at me, uncomprehending. "Another Conglomerate machine. So when we boot it up, it jumps on the network immediately." I spread my hands as I explained. "My network account isn't going to work. I can promise you that; they'll have disabled it already.

"So I won't be able to remotely log in to anything. And even if I could, they'd have it flagged – they'd know as soon as I logged in, and the gig would be up.

"I'm going to need a physical device that's a part of the network, so when I boot it, I can log in with the local admin account."

To judge from most of my new compatriot's expressions, I might as well have been speaking Greek. But Magdalene nodded and said, "Alright. So a Conglomerate device. Anything specific? Or can we pinch any terminal?"

I shook my head. "No. Nothing public-facing will work. Their access has been locked down to specific functions." I didn't feel it necessary to mention that I was the genius behind that particular move, back when Henderson had first hired me on. It was part of their security upgrade – a public-facing terminal with access to the entire network was a huge security risk, I'd pointed out, and we promptly locked those devices down to the specific access that was needed.

It had been the right call from a security standpoint, of course, but right now I could have used a little security risk.

"We need something with full access to the network," I finished.

"Okay. Where do we get that?"

I considered. "Any Conglomerate 'shareholder' will have full access." Shareholder was the syndicate's term for the bosses. It had probably started tongue-in-cheek, but no one blinked at it now. Bosses were shareholders. Clients were investors, if they were involved in a financial scheme, and consumers, if they'd hired the Conglomerate to run them something not legally available. Crimes were products and services. Hostile takeovers of other gangs were acquisitions. They had their own language, with all its own nuances. I'd picked up on some of it in my time working for them, but there were still terms that baffled me.

"So we got to hit a mob boss?" Frank's nose, ridges and all, wrinkled at the idea. "Isn't that risky? What if they get wise that something's up?"

I considered. "There's a guy we can target. It's not unexpected for him to go dark for weeks at a time. It's part of what he does. They call it a 'client account manager.'"

"What the hell's that?" Magdalene wondered. "Sounds like some kind of paper pusher."

"Yes," I nodded. "In a sense. He mostly manages client relationships, makes sure their projects are going according to plan, that they're getting what they paid for and all that. He works with new contractors too. He spends a lot of time off the radar, and no one wonders when he doesn't check in."

"And he'll have access to the network?"

"Oh yes."

She nodded. "Alright. Who is he and where do we find him?"

I smiled as I named him, the son-of-a-bitch who had got me into this mess in the first place. "Rex Henderson. And unless he's on a new project, he'll probably be working out of his 'home office' in Santa Valentina."

CHAPTER FIVE

Santa Valentina was a small, tropical planet on the edge of the Dacu Sector. It was just inside Union space, and was famed for its beauty and allegedly miraculous waters. It was a popular destination for New-Agey tourist types and fat cats with too many credits to burn.

It was also where my Conglomerate handler had chosen to set up shop, in a great, orbital mansion overlooking the planet.

"Santa Valentina's on the way to Kraken's Drop," Magdalene reasoned. "We'll stop there first. If Henderson's home, we'll nab him. If he's not, we'll try to find out when he will be back, and nab him on the return trip."

She made it sound so damned easy I almost believed her, until I remembered we were a crew of sixteen – seventeen, when I counted myself – and that I'd been the one to install the security system for his floating monstrosity. "He's well protected," I cautioned. "There's sentinels on the ground, biometric scanners…you name it."

"Well," she shrugged, "it'll be a good test run, won't it?"

"Good one-way-ticket to the morgue."

She grinned. "You need more confidence in your own abilities, Kate."

"I built the damned system. It's my abilities I'm worried

about, Maggie."

It was two days before we reached Santa Valentina, and we were eating breakfast in the mess hall. Landon joined me, as she often did in the week and a half we'd been under way – her or Frank. I had the sense they were keeping an eye on me. Not that I minded particularly. I wasn't an active member of the crew, so there wasn't much to do. Conversation now and again was just about the only thing that kept me from pondering just how insane our suicide run of a mission was.

She shook her head. "Now that's something," she said, "I don't quite understand."

"What?"

She looked me over with a curious gaze. "How you ended up working for a syndicate like the Conglomerate. All your talk of pirates, and yet you sign on with organized crime?"

I felt my cheeks flushing. She had a point. "I didn't know they were organized crime."

"Come on, Kay. You're not stupid, and neither am I. You're trying to tell me you had no idea Henderson worked for the Conglomerate?"

My cheeks burned a little hotter. "I had an idea," I said. "But nothing solid."

She scoffed. "'See no evil?'"

"I didn't have a choice," I protested.

"Didn't you?"

"No." I frowned at her. "As a matter of fact, I didn't. I was out of work-"

"There's always jobs."

"Not for me."

Her brow creased. "What do you mean?"

I hesitated. It really was none of her business, I thought. And yet, I supposed, she did have a vested interest – I was working for her. *Through no choice of my own*, my mind kicked in. Who, after all, was a pirate to judge my life choices?

When I didn't respond, she asked, "You mean, after the Echo Prime business?"

I blinked in surprise. "You know about that?"

"I did my research. I don't just let people into my crew without knowing who they are."

"Well, then," I said, and there was a bitterness to my tone that I'd not anticipated, "you know what an imbecile you're dealing with."

She smiled, but it wasn't her usual mocking grin. "If I thought that, you wouldn't be here now, Kay. None of us would."

I wasn't sure how to respond to her. My gaze fell to my plate, and for a moment I picked at my food.

"So," she said in the next, and her tone was brisk, "Henderson's mansion…provided he's there…how are we getting in?"

It was the sixty-four-thousand-dollar question, but the longer we thought, the fewer our answers. "The only way to get around the security is to deactivate it. But you have to be on the network to do that."

"And we need his terminal before we can get on the network."

"Exactly."

"It's like the chicken-egg paradox: which came first, the terminal to shut down security, or shutting down security to get the terminal?" Frank sighed. "Speaking of chicken, though…anyone else hungry?"

We had no epiphanies en route, and we were as much at a loss for what to do as ever when we approached the Santa Valentina docks. Here, at least, Magdalene's ingenuity came into play. When air control asked her purpose, she nonchalantly stated, "A little R-and-R for my crew."

"Carry on," the air controller said, "and welcome to sunny Santa Valentina."

"Well," she decided, "first things first. We need to establish if Henderson's even on-world. We can worry about what to do if he is after that."

A little reconnaissance, then, was in order. For the first time since I'd boarded the *Black Flag*, I was excited. Santa Valentina was gorgeous, with clear green waters and vast blue skies, with sun and shade trees and warm sand. All I needed was a bit of sunscreen, I thought, and the day would be perfect.

Magdalene, though, had other ideas. She saw me join the party to disembark, and she caught me by the arm. "Kay, what are you doing?"

"Going with you."

She frowned. "You can't."

"Why?"

"Henderson knows you. You've been here before."

"Henderson won't be planet-side," I said. "Not unless it's at one of the private resorts." We were planning to scope out some of the public areas. The orbital residences and their residents were of great interest to those below, so we had no concerns about getting our intel. The floating spheres were our era's version of the old gated communities: a distant, elevated way of life, always in sight and always out of reach, where the rich could look down on the poor. In this version, the looking down on was just a little more literally. *The miracles of technology.*

But Magdalene wasn't persuaded. "No."

"Come on," I protested. "You can't leave me on this damned ship. Not here."

"Sorry, Kay," she said, and she seemed to mean it. "But it's too risky."

"So I'm going to be stuck here alone, while you all are exploring Santa Valentina?" My tone, admittedly, had something of petulance to it. But the injustice of being confined to a ship while on one of the most beautiful planets in known space was rather hard to tolerate.

"I'll stay too," Frank decided. "Too much sun out there anyway."

Captain Landon threw him a curious gaze then acquiesced, and I scowled. "Got to keep an eye on me, eh?" I said after the others had disembarked. "Maggie put you up to it?"

I'd meant it when I said it. His and Landon's hovering seemed, in my anger, indicative of sinister motives. I felt in the moment not much better than a captive, cajoled into service, kept under surveillance, and forced out of sight, a kind of spacefaring

Cinderella locked in my tower. *Or was that Rapunzel?*

But Frank's expression drove these facile wonderings away. He stared at me for a moment in surprise, and then glanced away, a combination of ruddy embarrassment coloring his cheeks and offense touching his eyes. "Don't worry," he said, "I've got plenty of work. I won't bother you."

CHAPTER SIX

He was as good as his word. I didn't see him for the rest of the day. If I was of a more philosophical bent, I might have convinced myself that my own time was spent reflecting on my situation. Self-pitying though I might have been, I was not self-deluding. I spent my afternoon sulking.

I'd been in the wrong. My explanations and excuses, one by one, fell away, and I faced that truth. Frank had given up his R-and-R on a vacation world because he'd felt sorry for me. And I'd reacted by accusing him of being a spy. I'd taken my anger at being left behind out on him.

When evening approached, and the crew trickled back, laughing and joking about their adventures, I felt rather miserable. I still hadn't seen hide nor hair of Frank since morning.

David headed to the galley to whip up something with a fresh batch of groceries he'd acquired. I wasn't enthusiastic about the end result, but at least it would be different. There was only so much chop suey a person could eat, after all.

I followed a little while later, cringing at the fishy odors that emanated from the mess hall.

"Grab some baked beans," he called as I entered. "Chowder still has a bit to go."

I shuddered at the idea: baked beans and fish chowder. As pairings went, I couldn't think of a worse one. Still, in fairness to David, he'd had the beans heating all day. He didn't know what he'd find at market.

So I took a scoop and a fork, and thanked him. Then I found a table in the corner and picked away at my plate.

I was focused on my beans when Frank entered. He avoided my gaze, heading for the line and helping himself to a full platter. Then he found a seat on the other end of the room.

I glanced back at my plate. Then, I gritted my teeth, got to my feet, and headed over. He stared at me as I approached, and I felt very stupid standing there, dish in hand. "Can I…uh…join you?"

"Aren't there other tables free?" He glanced down at his food.

I swallowed, then, impulsively pulled out a chair opposite him and sat. "I'm sorry, Frank."

"For what?" He still wasn't looking at me.

"For being an asshole." He glanced up at that. "I know you were trying to be nice. And I was…well, an asshole. I'm sorry."

He shrugged. "It's fine."

"It's not. I really am sorry. I'm sorry you missed going with them. And I'm sorry I was such a jerk."

He scrutinized me for a minute, then shook his head and laughed. "You humans have volatile tempers," he said. "I should be used to it, by now."

I took that to mean that he forgave me, or that he would forgive me anyway. "Well," I said, "I shall endeavor to keep mine under control."

He grinned. "Or at least give me fair warning next time."

"Alright," I agreed, smiling in turn.

It was now, with the pair of us grinning like idiots, that Landon found us. "There you are," she said, pulling up a seat of her own.

Uninvited, I noted. I was contrite where Frank was concerned, but I hadn't forgotten that it was Magdalene Landon who had banished me to the ship – who had stoked my temper in the first place.

"So, did you two have a good day?" Her eyes were twinkling, and I scowled. That seemed to me insult on top of injury. She knew well enough how much I'd wanted to go, and that it had been her call that I couldn't. "Find anything to occupy your time?"

Frank nodded. "I got the nav system recalibrated. Been putting that off for two months."

"Sounds exciting."

"It wasn't. But it had to be done."

"What about Henderson?" I asked. I wasn't in the mood for Magdalene's sarcasm and small talk.

"He's here, alright. Been here for the last two weeks."

"Great," Frank said. "Now all we have to do is figure out how to get him."

"Kay'll figure something out," she nodded.

"Yeah," I muttered, "I'll just wave my magic wand."

"Oh, and Kay? I got you something since you couldn't be with us. You too, Frank." She had a bag slung over her shoulder, and she paused from her beans to pull it forward. For a moment, she fished through its contents, then she extracted two parcels. The first was large and seemed heavy; it went to the Kudarian. The second was small and light, and this she handed to me.

I took it suspiciously. "What is it?"

"Open it and you'll see."

I did, gingerly, and found myself holding a plain gray rock strung on a cord of some manner of leather.

"Well?" she asked.

I glanced between her and the stone, wondering at first if this was another of her jokes. She seemed earnest in her expectation that I'd recognize it, though. "What is it?"

"It's an Esselian water stone. Corano found it."

"A water stone?"

"Yes," she nodded. "It's a symbol of luck." She stretched out her hand. "May I?" I handed the rock back, and she took it in one hand and Frank's glass in the other. The latter she tipped, so that water poured out in a steady stream. Then, she set the glass back, and handed me the rock. "You see? It's not wet."

It wasn't. A droplet remained here and there, but the rest had all run off into a puddle on her tray. The stone was as dry as it had been when I'd handed it to her in the first place.

"They're nonporous. Whatever you throw at them, it all runs off. They don't absorb anything." She smiled. "That's why it's a symbol of luck. It's moving forward, shaking off the waters to stand in sunlight."

"Oh," I said.

"I thought of you when he showed me it." Another time, in a different tone, I would have thought she was mocking me. But her smile was genuine, and her eyes kind. "And the mission. Getting back at the Conglomerate."

"Thanks."

"Of course." Then, she shrugged. "Of course, if they had another of Frank's pies, I would have got you that instead. Delvanian meat pies beat an Esselian water stone any day."

"Pie?" Frank turned his attention from the rock I held to his own parcel, and he unwrapped it with a measure of haste. He grinned as the wrappings fell away to reveal a great, golden pie. "Damn," he said. "To hell with chowder. I'm having pie for dinner."

CHAPTER SEVEN

I toyed with the stone that hung from my wrist. I wasn't one for necklaces, but I'd braided the cord into a good bracelet length. Now the Esselian water stone dangled above my hand. It was, objectively, not a pretty ornament. It wasn't ugly, exactly, but it was plain and common looking.

Still, I rather fancied it. It was the symbolism, I supposed. Maggie had chosen well. This mission was my chance to move on, to let the water of past mistakes roll off me; to move forward, from the flooded shores of Echo Prime to the sunlight of a new life. A new life, with trillions of credits in my pocket.

I could get used to that idea, I thought.

Of course, all of that hinged on my ability to break my own security systems and get to Rex Henderson. At the moment, I did not share Maggie's confidence that I'd figure something out. I'd done a good job on Rex's home security. My Deltaseal designs were built, in part, off that early work, but he had something going the bank didn't: fewer points of entry.

Deltaseal was an entire planet, which, while heavily protected, could be entered from anywhere. Rex's floating monstrosity was an orbital station, with exactly two entry and exit ports. Both were locked down tighter than a politician's donor lists.

"Well," Landon was saying, "maybe you should try your

network account."

"If I do," I said, "they'll know we're here. They'll know *I'm* here. And they'll know something's up."

She nodded. "There's no way to break in?"

"Not with the firewalls I've got in place. You'd need a team of hackers, and there's no way they'd get in without being detected first."

"Dammit, Kay," Maggie sighed. "You were *too* good at your job."

I nodded glumly. "I don't know how we're going to get in."

"If we can't break in," Frank suggested, "we've got to figure out how to get him out."

"Or," Corvono offered, "how to get ourselves *invited* in."

"Invited?" I repeated. "Rex is suspicious. That's the whole reason he put the security in place. He won't just ask random pirates in."

"We would need to offer something he valued more than he feared for his safety," Maggie pondered.

"Some*one*, perhaps," the Esselian suggested. I realized, now, that his purple eyes were fixed on me. So were Maggie's green ones. In fact, the entire ready room had turned, of one volition, in my direction.

"Wait, me? As bait?"

"It's a good idea," the captain declared.

"It's a terrible idea."

"He will have heard you got off Trel," Frank shrugged. "That won't sit well with the bosses."

"No," Corano agreed. "And you said he's the one who recruited you. Your disappearance will probably come back to him."

"That's true. But none of this," I said, "points to using me as bait."

"All of it does," Maggie countered. "He'll be feeling pressure from the – what did you call them? Shareholders? It's going on two weeks now. They're not going to be any closer to finding you since you haven't been to any ports, so they'll have been no sightings of you. He's going to be feeling the heat. So when someone shows up with a lead…" She grinned. "He might just leap before he looks."

The rest of the day was spent in planning. Drake and I went over the locking port seal details. One of several features designed to keep a trespassing ship from escaping, the port seals could hold most commercial and some military classes of vehicle in place until they were released. And the seals were on both entry hubs. There was no getting onto the orb without Henderson anchoring you down – without an airtight seal, the multiple checkpoints beyond the docking port would remain barred. And there was no getting off the orb without Henderson releasing you – not without long, vulnerable wait times, anyway.

"There's not going to be a fast getaway," I explained to the rest of the crew, once we'd hammered out the technical details. "The seals can be cut with a laser cannon, but it'll take just over five minutes per generator."

"And there's five generators," Drake put in.

"We may not have half an hour to wait," Magdalene said, her

brow creased.

"No," I agreed. "As soon as Henderson finds out he's been played, he's going to turn everything he's got against us."

"Which means," she continued, "we need to subdue him before he realizes he's been had."

"Yes – but," I said, "the system is operated by voice command as well as manual input. It's programmed to respond to Henderson's voice. So if he can speak, we're fucked."

"Then we stun him," Frank shrugged.

"You can't bring weapons onto the sphere."

"No weapons?" Corano's eyebrows rose. "Is this an abduction or a suicide mission?"

"If you bring weapons, it'll be a suicide mission," I said. "You're scanned as soon as you step off the ship. You'll be ordered to disarm before you're allowed to pass the first mantrap. If you do, it unlocks, you proceed to the second. If you don't…" I spread my hands wide, to simulate broad dispersal. "Poof. He hits you with the laser pulse. There's nothing left but ash."

"Jesus, Kay," Magdalene said. "I get taking pride in your work. But did you have to make this dirtbag a floating bunker?"

I flushed at her words. "That wasn't me," I protested. "He already had the checkpoints, and the drones. I just…well, beefed it all up."

She shook her head, but said no more. I could feel my cheeks burning at the criticism, the little that had escaped her lips and the lot implied by her reproachful eyes. Not for the first time, I felt my ethics being questioned – and found wanting – by Magdalene Landon. And the idea of being judged for choices I'd made in desperation by someone who chose in ease to ply the trade of pirate rankled.

I'd chosen to work with Henderson for the same reason I was working with Landon: I'd run out of better options. She had a ship and a crew, and all the options in the world. And yet, from safe behind her glass walls, she was very good at casting stones my way.

"Well," Frank said, "if we can't bring weapons, then we have to physically overpower him."

I tried to focus on the discussion, and not my own discomfort. "Easier said than done. Henderson's not a lightweight."

The Kudarian grinned. "Neither am I."

I considered, then nodded. Frank, of everyone here, would be capable of silencing Henderson. "Okay, so we get past the mantrap. We reach his office. You grab him, and shut him up. I get the terminal."

"How do you know the terminal will be with him?"

"It's always with him. Especially if he's about to conduct business."

"Alright," Magdalene nodded. "So you get the terminal."

"Now I've got to power down the bots. They're equipped with body language interpreters. If they detect distress, they will come to Henderson's aid." She frowned, but made no comment. I continued. "Then, we take the terminal, and get the hell out of there."

"I say we just kill Henderson," Corano declared. "It'll be easier than trying to manage him on the way back."

"Kill him?" I felt my eyes widen in alarm. We hadn't talked

about killing anyone.

He shrugged. "He's Conglomerate. Even if he hasn't directly killed anyone, he's got buckets of blood on his hands."

"That's murder," I protested.

"There's a fine line between murder and justice," he said matter-of-factly. "When it comes to a Conglomerate stooge like Henderson, it'd be justice."

"Yes," Magdalene said. "It would be. But we can't kill him. If he turns up dead, the Conglomerate knows someone's after their men. If they get wind that Kay's involved, everything she's ever touched is suspect. We need him to drop off radar, not die."

"We could still space him," Corano offered. "Wait until we're in the deep." He opened his hands, as if he was releasing something. "Let him meet his maker."

"Not a bad idea," Frank nodded.

I shuddered at the casual way they talked about killing, and the focus on the Conglomerate. Where, I wondered, did their self-appointed judge, jury and executioner routine begin and where did it end? Did it end with the Hendersons, the syndicate's high-level paper pushers? Did it reach the contractors like me, who took credits to protect those paper pushers? Was I at risk of being spaced by this crew the instant my own use to them ran out?

Magdalene was watching me, and now she shook her head. "No. We'll keep him alive. When we're done with the mission, we'll drop him off somewhere. Let him deal with his beloved shareholders."

I swallowed, and my throat seemed very dry. That was, of course, a sentence worse than death. The others seemed satisfied, though, and moved on.

"So we get him back to the ship," Frank said. "What about the seals? He's not going to release them for us. And if we start cutting them off, we're sitting ducks if he's got any other defenses."

"Yes," I said, recalling myself again to the business at hand. "He does. But if we get the terminal, I can take care of that."

"Good," Magdalene said. "So this is a fairly straightforward extraction mission. A few nuances, but if we all play our parts right, we'll be fine."

"And if we don't," Corano offered, "we'll be charbroiled."

"So we win, or we're too dead to notice," Frank grinned. "Sounds good to me."

CHAPTER EIGHT

Our deliberations for the day had wrapped up, and everyone had gone to dinner. Everyone, that is, but me. I was in a nook by a porthole, one of the few spaces on the *Black Flag* reserved for something other than stark function. There was a bench there, and I was sitting on it, my face pressed against the glass. I watched the sun set and night fall, toying absently with the stone that hung at my wrist.

Santa Valentina was as lovely in the evening as it was during the day. Somehow, though, the sight did nothing to improve my mood. It seemed to have the reverse effect. The higher the moon rose, the more the breeze danced and the waters shimmered, the lower I felt.

"Hey," a voice said, and I started. It was Frank. "I didn't see you at mess hall."

I turned, and saw that he was carrying a tray of food. There was a bowl of something white and creamy, with pale lumps floating in it. *Yesterday's leftover chowder.* If the goal was to find a way to make fish chowder even less appetizing, leftovers was certainly the solution. "I'm not very hungry."

"You should eat," he said, pushing the tray toward me. "You need protein. You cannot afford to be weak tomorrow."

Frank's concern was so practical, so mission-oriented, that

despite myself, I almost laughed. "Fine." I accepted the tray. "I'll eat."

He nodded, and took a seat beside me. "Are you frightened?"

"What?"

"Of the mission, tomorrow."

I shook my head. "No. You weren't far off the mark earlier, when you said we'd either succeed or die." I shrugged. "There's not much room to be frightened there. Whatever happens, happens."

I turned my back to Santa Valentina, and concentrated on the chowder. My nose wrinkled as I spooned through it, pushing the fish and sodden vegetables and mystery ingredients this way and that.

"Is it Henderson, then?"

I blinked, glancing up at him. "What?"

"Were you…?" He seemed at a loss for words, and I was in no position to assist. I had no idea what he was getting at.

"Were we what?"

He flushed and diverted his gaze. "I'm sorry. It's not my business."

It was my turn to color as I understood, now, his attempts at delicacy, ham-fisted though they'd been. "Good God no," I said sharply. "Me and Henderson? I'd have sooner spaced myself."

He was watching me now, and laughed at my vehemence. "Alright, alright. I'm sorry."

I shivered. "I might have been desperate for a job, but not *that* desperate. Jesus." Is that, then, what they thought of me? That I was a syndicate pawn, fucking my way up the chain of command? I felt my anger rising, and I decided to call him on it, right there and then. "What would even put that idea in your head?" I demanded.

He shrugged. "I don't know. You picked him out, as the mark. It seemed…personal."

I frowned at him. "The son-of-a-bitch left me stranded on Trel to be killed. It doesn't get much more personal than that."

"Yeah, but earlier you were defending him." It was said nonchalantly, but I could feel the weight of suspicion behind the words.

"Defending him? You mean, because I didn't want to see him murdered in cold blood?"

He frowned at my answer. "It's not murder, Kay. He's a murderer."

"I know," I said, "because he worked for the Conglomerate. I guess that makes me a murderer too." I fixed him with a piercing gaze. "Are you going to space me too, Frank? I set up their vaults. I made his 'bunker', remember? Once this is all said and done – maybe when it comes time to divide the credits – are you going to rationalize killing me too? Or maybe handing me over to the Conglomerate?"

He blinked at the vehemence in my words. "Shit, Kay. Of course not. Is that what it was about?"

"You sure?" I fired back. "Because you were all pretty happy to justify getting blood on your hands earlier."

"That's different. You're nothing like Henderson."

"Aren't I?" I felt my cheeks burn, with rage and shame and fear. "I took a paycheck from them, the same as anyone else."

"Yeah, but you weren't involved with killing people, Kay.

Henderson manages the clients and contracts. You worked with robots and computers. He sets up killings, and kidnappings, and God knows what else."

"My robots and computers kept them safe," I said rather miserably, "while they did their killings and kidnappings and God knows what else." The fact was, for all my protests about being judged by a pirate, I was as guilty as Magdalene implied. I wasn't much better than a man like Henderson. My hands might be, by degrees, a little bit cleaner, but my pay had been in blood money. Every credit of it. I probably deserved to be spaced; and that was the part that scared me more than the fear that Frank and the others would rationalize throwing me out of an airlock.

He considered this for a minute, then nodded. "Yes. But…" He shrugged. "Everyone fucks up, Kay. When you're desperate, you can rationalize just about anything. And what you did? It wasn't good. But it was a lot better than it could have been."

I scoffed. "That's some consolation."

"No. But it's true. And in our business, you need to be able to see the shades of grey." I scoffed again, and he smiled, saying, "So, if you don't mind some advice from a lowly pirate: let it go. Learn from it, but let it go."

"I thought you were privateers, not pirates?"

"We are. But that's not black and white enough for you, is it?"

"I don't see a difference, if that's what you mean."

"We operate within the law."

I rolled my eyes. "Legalized piracy is still piracy."

"It's the same thing as with Henderson, Kay: targets matter.

Is it murder if you kill a murderer? Is it wrong to rob a thief?"

"So you're thieves with honor? Isn't that a contradiction in terms?"

"Maybe. Or maybe we've just expanded the definition of the terms a little."

I wasn't convinced, but I wasn't going to argue either. "Well," I said, "as long as you can convince that captain of yours not to space me, I suppose I'll accept your suspect rationalizations."

"I don't think you have to worry about Landon spacing you."

I snorted, remembering her expressions and comments from earlier in the day. "She'd be the first in line to push the button, I think."

He grinned, then leaned over to tap the stone that hung at my wrist. "And how would you 'move forward to stand in the sunlight,' if she put you out an airlock, Kay?"

CHAPTER NINE

My palms were sweating, and I wiped them nervously against my pants now and again. I couldn't stop thinking of facing Henderson.

"Hold still," Magdalene said. "Or this is going to smear."

She'd decided I needed a few fake bruises for our chat with Henderson, and she was painting them on with eye shadow.

She opened another tiny vat and sighed. "Dammit, Ginny, don't you have anything without sparkles?"

The young woman, Ginny Olson, shrugged. "I like glitter." I found that somewhat hard to imagine, since I'd never seen the engine tech in anything but thick layers of grease.

"And pink?" Magdalene was continuing as she opened another one. "How am I going to use that for a bruise?"

Again, Ginny shrugged. "You said to bring my eyeshadow. I did."

The captain shook her head. "Fine, fine. We'll have to stick with mine. I was hoping for a little color variation." She picked up a palette of smoky purples and rust browns.

She dipped the brush in a panel of eggplant browns. I watched her eyes as she trained them on my hairline, and I found myself wondering, absently, what those green orbs would look like, lined and shaded, their long lashes lengthened by mascara. They were pretty eyes already; very pretty. She'd look like a film star, I supposed, from one of those old black & white Earth movies, perfect and distant and not quite real. But, then, no makeup would hide the twinkle that snuck into her gaze or the smirk that crept onto her lips, those giveaways that she was real and tangible. *And so beautiful.*

I frowned. *Where the fuck did that come from*?

"Stop moving your face, dammit."

"Sorry."

"Don't talk. That's moving your face."

I sighed, and Frank laughed. He was sitting, arms crossed, watching the entire spectacle with unreserved amusement. "It could be worse, Kay," he advised. "She could have decided you need real bruises. For authenticity's sake."

"Shut up, Frank," she grinned. "Or I'll give you some real ones. For authenticity's sake, of course."

He laughed again. "Henderson's not going to pay that much attention, you know. This is just wasted time. He's not going to even notice them."

As much as I wanted to agree, I couldn't. If I showed up looking as if I'd been a guest onboard the *Black Flag*, he might just notice. "He's paranoid. He might."

"Hush," Magdalene chided. "Every time you talk, you move your face. And you can it too, Frank. Nobody wants to hear from the peanut gallery."

"You're a tyrant," I sighed.

"You're talking again..."

After a few minutes, she set down the brush, stood back to observe her handiwork, then nodded.

"Thank God," I said, getting to my feet.

She put a hand on my shoulder to stop my escape, though. "One more thing."

I groaned, but she ignored me. My hair was pulled back into a tight ponytail. She leaned close to lift a hand to my head and slipped her fingers among the tied down locks. She ran them backward from my forehead to the tie, loosening the hair as she went and now and again dislodging a piece.

I was again keenly aware of how beautiful she was. The realization didn't surprise me. I'd seen it the first time we met, back on Trel. I'd have been blind not to notice it at a glance. Still, I felt oddly uneasy. My stomach was regretting that I'd complied with Frank's insistence to eat a full breakfast. My palms were sweating again, and my pulse was racing. "I don't want hair in my eyes," I protested.

"Stop whining. You're supposed to have spent a week in the brig. You need to look like it."

I swallowed my discomfort and said no more. *So much for having a handle on my nerves; so much for being ready for the mission.*

Finally, mercifully, she took her hands off of me.

"There," she said, handing me the palette of eye shadow with its tiny mirror. "What do you think?"

I focused on my reflection. She'd done a good job. It wasn't so theatrical as to raise suspicion, but I looked roughed up and bruised, like I'd put up a fight and lost. "Looks good." I smoothed down my hair. "For what we're going for, anyway."

"Good. Alright, now for the cuffs."

I shook my head. "You geniuses better not get me killed. I'm going to be very pissed if I die handcuffed and wearing fake bruises."

Magdalene laughed, and her eyes twinkled. "You better hope your plan's a good one, then, Kay."

"*You* better hope so too," I reminded her.

I rose and Corano slipped the cuffs on with an apology. Our impromptu makeup studio was swept away. Then, Magdalene took my place in the captain's chair, and I was moved offscreen. People took their places around me.

"Alright…everyone ready?"

"Damned right," Frank said.

"Alright people…on the count of three."

"Lights," Frank put in, "camera, action."

"One," she said, shaking her head, "two, three." Then, she punched a few codes into her control panel. A loading screen appeared on her display, with a black background and white text reading, "Initiating call…"

For a moment, the call remained in this state. Then a pinched face appeared onscreen. "Rex Henderson's residence. Andrew Esser speaking." Esser was the gatekeeper for Rex and several other Conglomerate men, a kind of secretary and remote bouncer in one. He managed the low-level administrative duties and kept the undesirables away. He was actually stationed on Earth, but he managed to run his various operations as smoothly as any ten secretaries might be expected to do.

"Mr. Esser," Magdalene said, her tone easy. "My name is

Magdalene Landon, captain of the *Black Flag*. I need to speak to your boss, Mr. Henderson."

He wrinkled his nose. "A pirate vessel?"

Despite the situation, I threw Frank a triumphant glance. He rolled his eyes. Magdalene, though, just laughed. "If we were, you can't think I'd own up to it, Mr. Esser. But, no, we're lawfully licensed privateers."

Esser's expression didn't soften. "I'm afraid Mr. Henderson is very busy, *Captain* Landon," he said, with a hint of sarcastic emphasis on Maggie's title. "If you leave a message, of course, I will see what can be done, but I can make no guarantees."

She leaned back in her chair, as if we weren't all on edge, and laughed. "Alright, Mr. Esser. Tell your boss I've got the architect of Deltaseal on my ship. Tell him I'm heading out in half an hour if I don't hear from him." Andrew's expression remained neutral, but there had been a temporary flash of interest in his eyes at the mention of the bank. She grinned. "Something tells me we'll be talking soon."

Then, she terminated the connection with a press of a button, and loosed a breath.

Frank whooped with delight. "Well done, Captain."

"Yeah, let's just hope that did the trick."

It did. Not even five minutes had passed before the line rang. This time, the screen read, "Incoming call…" Maggie accepted it with the same casual air she'd affected in the previous call. "*Black Flag* here. Landon speaking."

Esser's pinched features appeared, and he said, "Thank you for picking up, Captain. Please hold to be connected with Mr. Henderson."

Maggie grinned, and so did Frank. I tried to ignore the heavy thudding of my pulse in my ears. *This is it. This is go time.*

Then, Henderson's face materialized. It was funny, in a way. There was nothing extraordinary about Rex Henderson. There was no cartoon villain-esque aura of evil to him. His features were plain but not homely, his age was somewhere north of young and south of old. His hair had started to thin, but he still had plenty of it left. He seemed as ordinary and unremarkable a businessman as ever I'd met.

And yet, staring at that face, I felt a well of hatred in my soul. I'd given him my best efforts, and would have kept the Conglomerate's secrets forever if he'd not crossed me. I'd ignored my moral qualms and better judgment to do it. And yet, I'd been as disposable to this mild-mannered account manager as an old shoe. Just a line on a form, a checkbox waiting to be checked.

I remembered Frank's words, and the fact was, in the moment, I could have spaced Henderson myself if I'd had the option. But, I was bound, and playing the role of a captive. There was no time to indulge fantasies of retribution. I had to get into character. I was the worm set out to writhe on the hook to lure the eel out of hiding.

A fitting role, I thought, *for the pair of us.*

He, meanwhile, was projecting a professional disinterest, much belied by the haste of his returned call. "Esser tells me, Captain, that you needed to speak to me? I believe you were in something of a hurry?"

Maggie eased back into her chair and smiled. "A pleasure to speak to you face-to-face, Mr. Henderson. I am on something of a schedule, so I'll make this brief. I believe you're acquainted with a Miss Katherine Ellis?"

"Perhaps. May I ask what this is about?"

Maggie's grin broadened. The eel was slipping out from behind his rock. She gestured to Corano, and he pushed me forward. When we reached the captain's chair, he gave me a shove to push me onscreen, and I had to catch my balance. He was playacting a little too well, I thought.

Still, I threw myself into my own role, and cast terrified eyes at the monitor. Henderson smiled at me. "Well, well, little miss Katie. There you are."

He was circling the hook, now. Maggie cocked her head to one side. "I thought you'd be interested. But, Mr. Henderson, this little acquisition cost me a pretty penny."

He waved this away. "Name your price, and let's get on with it."

"One trillion credits."

Even I nearly blanched at this figure. Henderson laughed out loud. "You must be joking," he said, "or insane."

"I think it's a fair price," Maggie shrugged. "With what this one knows about Deltaseal, I'd have thought you'd be willing to pay five times as much."

Henderson's eyes narrowed. "You understand, Captain, that the shareholders would not care for such talk."

It was Maggie's turn to laugh. "That's more your department, and problem, than mine, Rex."

"It can be your problem," he answered evenly. "I promise you that."

"Not before it's yours."

He held her gaze for a moment, and then seemed to decide

on a different tactic. "What do you want? Really, Captain? You know a trillion credits is absurd. Even if I had it to give you, I wouldn't."

"Maybe." She grinned and sat up straight in her seat. "But it is in your power to write contracts, isn't it? To sign new charters? To take on new ships?"

"Ah." His eyes lit up with understanding, misplaced though it was. "I think I understand."

"Good. Then let's talk conditions."

"I'm all ears."

"In person. I don't do business unless I can look a man square in the eyes."

He hesitated. "Are you suggesting you don't trust me, Captain? That's a poor footing for a business relationship."

"I don't think you'd want to do business with someone who trusted you, Mr. Henderson."

He smiled in turn. "Alright. Esser will send you coordinates to dock at my station."

"No," Maggie said. "I'm not meeting on your turf. Somewhere neutral."

He sighed, saying, "Captain, I've been very obliging so far. But my patience is not unlimited. Esser will send you the coordinates. If I don't see you in half an hour…well, we'll have to work this out a different way."

The call cut off, leaving a "Call terminated" screen. Maggie laughed out loud, and Frank whooped again. Even I was excited – but not too excited to say, "Alright, get these damned cuffs off me."

CHAPTER TEN

"Katie, eh?" Magdalene asked, her eyes twinkling. "Haven't heard you called that before."

"That's because people who want to live don't call me it."

She grinned. "I'll keep that in mind, Katherine. Alright, you ready?"

I grimaced. We were standing on the bridge as the *Black Flag* approached Henderson's base. "Let's get it over with."

She nodded and slipped the cuffs back on. "They're going to be tight," she said, "to make it look real. But remember, if you need 'em off, pull. Hard."

"Yeah, yeah. Just don't screw this up."

I'd seen this approach dozens of times when I was working on the sphere's security. Still, there was something that never quite got old about it, some sense of wonder and mortification. These new orbital homes were a marvel of technology, self-contained spheres that could withstand the onslaught of space debris. They were virtually self-sustaining, with recycling facilities for water and air, processing plants to convert waste to energy, and self-contained ecosystems. Most relied primarily on solar energy to power the adjustment thrusters and meet the inhabitants' needs.

Of course, self-sustaining on paper wasn't quite the same

thing as self-sustaining in practice. The spheres took tens of millions of credits to build, and usually the residents who could afford a multi-million credit home in the sky weren't about to drink recycled water or power their station on waste gasses. They'd pay absurd fees to have water shipped up from the surface and waste taken away.

But, in theory, anyway, these monstrosities could clutter the skies of a planet for thousands of years without needing external intervention. I watched Henderson's base grow larger and larger before the *Black Flag*. From a distance, it seemed a great, smooth, silver sphere. On closer approach, the metal ribs of a complex three-dimensional polygon emerged, with flat panels connecting these ribs. Some were transparent and others solid, depending on the amount of light the sphere was admitting at the moment.

The greens of the massive garden were visible on our approach, situated just south of the port. Whether Henderson had any true affection for growing things, I couldn't guess, but he certainly believed it to be a distinguishing mark of a great house to have a great garden. He employed two on-staff gardeners, and often, during the early days of our acquaintance, fell to boasting of the varied flora he'd imported from every sector of known space.

Frank eased us into port, and the nuances of the sphere fell away; we were staring at solid, silver metal. The hiss of seals attaching to the gangplank sounded a moment before a communication reached the bridge.

It was Esser. "You're clear to disembark, Captain."

Magdalene flashed us a grin that didn't quite hide her nerves. "Alright, people. You ready?"

"As I'll ever be," I said.

"Frank, you and Corano are with Kay. I'll go first. Everyone else…well, if this thing goes south and we end up cooked or otherwise dead, just get the hell out of here. Kereli, you're in command. Alright, move out."

The Kudarian placed a gentle hand on my shoulder as she passed to indicate that we could move, and Magdalene rolled her eyes. "She's a prisoner, Frank, remember? Not a china doll."

Corano grinned and grabbed my arm brusquely. "Move it."

"That's better," Magdalene nodded.

"Bastards," I said to the pair of them.

We made for the gangplank, and she palmed the access panel. The door slid open, and we stepped into the clean, gray, airtight space beyond. A digital voice asked, "For your safety, please place all weapons in the indicated locker. They will be returned on your exit."

Now, a kind of drawer slid out of the far wall. "Do as it says," Magdalene ordered.

"When you are finished," the computer droned on, "please confirm disarmament by vocal input. Say 'done' when finished."

"Done," she said after the three of them had surrendered their hardware.

"Confirmed. Please note that any attempt to bring weapons onto the station will result in your immediate, violent death. Thank you and have a great day."

I grimaced. Rex had gotten a kick out of that verbiage, and the flat monotones of his system's delivery. He practically giggled when we got to it as he ran me through his security set up the first time. He'd insisted on keeping it, too. *You have to have a sense of humor, Kay*, he'd said. Well, we'd see who laughed last now.

The door at the far end of the chamber opened to another

similarly grim room. This, of course, was where that immediate, violent death would occur, if you chose to proceed with weapons. Predictably, as soon as we entered, the door closed behind us and a rush of light flooded us.

I caught my breath. The thought had occurred that here, now, would be a perfect time for Rex to end us all – to dispose of the troublesome engineer who knew too much, and the pushy pirates who demanded too much.

Fortunately, even in his business, reputation was everything. Rex had given his word, and if he murdered a captain who had come to parley with a fugitive he sought in-hand, that might dissuade future captains who found themselves positioned to help him. And, we were in the belly of his beast, in the fortress he'd constructed to keep him safe.

Whether these were the considerations that prompted him to spare our lives in the moment or not, I couldn't say. But no ray of death consumed us. The scan ended, and the far end of the chamber slid open. We proceeded.

We were met by a robot. This was an older series battle bot, repurposed into a domestic. Rex had a few of them. They were another product of his questionable sense of humor. Battle bot butlers, he called them.

They were fairly useless. They were outclassed, now, by the new battle bots, and had been for the better part of a decade. As domestics, they were an absolute nightmare. Battle bots were designed to be large and lethal. Rex had started routines to convert these clunking metal beasts into household helpers. When he'd hired me on, he'd had me clean them up – which consisted of a full redesign and rewrite, as Henderson's skills did not lie in coding. Even my work, though, was not particularly effective. Sure, they broke less, and he could trot them out for demonstrative purposes. His guests seemed to delight in the sight of a battle bot dusting or cleaning the floor. But their work was sloppy and incomplete. They didn't have the motion and range to do it well. They were designed to kill, not clean.

"Welcome to the Henderson estate," this one said, its tones even and metallic but – was I imagining it? – lightly accented. "I am Sydney, and I will be taking care of you today. This way, please."

I rolled my eyes. *Nope, that's definitely an accent.* A British accent, of all things, on a battle bot. Henderson was getting cheesier.

The bot – Sydney – turned on his track, rolling toward the hallway that led to Rex's office. I didn't move until Corano prodded me. I was, after all, supposed to be a prisoner, and if Henderson was watching – and I was sure he was, as there were surveillance cameras all through this section of the house – nothing would be as good a giveaway as me eagerly marching to my supposed doom.

"I hope your trip was pleasant," it was continuing. "Nothing quite like Santa Valentina this time of year."

When no one responded, Sydney repeated, "I hope your trip was pleasant."

This time, Magdalene said, "Yes, thank you. Very."

Rex's coding is as good as ever, I see. I would have been willing to bet that he'd built a single, global conversation routine, probably based on the command input method I'd programmed in. After thirty seconds of no response, it would repeat the query up to two times. He'd probably applied the same logic to conversation.

Somehow, such an annoying approach to small talk seemed more absurd than the idea of a robot engaging in small talk at all.

"Did you have time to enjoy the sights?"

"Uh…yeah."

"Excellent. Personally, I prefer the sulfur baths of South Valentina. But I hear the geysers of central are in fine form this year."

I'm going to kill Rex myself, I thought, listening to Sydney prattle on in his fake, metallic accent. *With my own hands.*

CHAPTER ELEVEN

Sydney ushered us into Henderson's office. "Right this way, ladies and gentlemen, right this way."

Henderson was seated behind his great wooden desk, the terminal right beside him, where I knew it would be. His bland features turned our way as we stepped inside, set with his typical serenity.

He did, however, allow himself a smile as he saw me. "Oh Katie." He tutted. "That's some nasty bruising. You would have been so much better off just cooperating on Trel."

"Go to hell, Rex."

"Quiet," Corano said behind me.

Henderson turned now and smiled at Maggie, with all the charm of a serpent. "Take a seat, please, Captain."

She did. Frank and Corano stayed by me as she sidled into one of the chairs opposite Rex.

"You've done me a favor, Captain. And I always repay my debts."

Magdalene's face was largely obscured due to the angle, but I saw her ponytail bun bob. "That's what I wanted to hear, Mr. Henderson."

He smiled again, this time with a more patronizing air. He saw a low-level criminal with grand ambitions before him. He saw someone too big for her britches, perhaps, but definitely manipulatable. I could tell it in the certainty in his gaze: he thought he had her all figured out, like he'd had me all figured out. Like he was used to figuring people out.

I had to bite down on my cheek to repress the grin that threatened to spill over. In all his years of managing criminals and fools, Rex Henderson hadn't met a Magdalene Landon before. This was going to be a pleasure to watch.

"But," he said, "where are my manners? Can I get you anything? Something to eat? Something to drink? Tea, perhaps?"

She hesitated. "Sure. Tea sounds great."

He smiled. "Sydney, get our guests some tea."

"Right away, sir."

He glanced my way as the battle bot trundled away. "You see, Katie, I've made some improvements to Sydney." He spread his hands. "No one, I'm afraid, is so valuable that they can't be replaced." He turned back to Magdalene. "But to business. You have done the Conglomerate a turn, and demonstrated your own capabilities in the bargain. So, you want a contract?"

"I do," she lied.

"Doing what?"

She shrugged. "I'm flexible. Running cargo, locating and transporting 'guests' like Miss Ellis here – as long as the pay's good, *Black Flag* is game."

He nodded. "I am curious about one thing."

"Oh?"

"How did you find her?"

I could see the hint of a grin on Maggie's turned face. "That's my business."

"Hm." He steepled his fingers. "Because, I did a little digging myself, Captain. I do know that your ship put down anchor at Trel during the timeframe that Kate disappeared."

Shit. I felt my heart hammer in my chest. Had I underestimated Henderson?

She, though, leaned back in her seat with a casual air and laughed lightly. "So my secrets are not so secret after all."

Henderson smiled coolly. "It's my business to know secrets, Captain. Especially a potential employee's. So tell me, what were you doing at Trel?"

"I thought you knew."

"Tell me."

"Biding my time." She shrugged. "Secrets may be your business, Henderson, but you're not as good at keeping them as uncovering them." His jaw tightened at that. She continued as if she hadn't noticed. "I knew about Katherine. I knew she was trying to make a break for it. I knew she had a ship lined up." She spread her hands. "I knew it was a matter of time before she got off world. We just made sure she got on the right ship when the time came." She was grinning again. I could tell by the tone of her voice.

He smiled too. "Very clever."

She shrugged. "Ingenuity is the name of the game."

"Well," Henderson said, "I won't compensate for your

'ingenuity.' But…I will give you the contract. You'll be on a retainer, and we'll call you in for special deliveries. You will, of course, be on a trial period." He fixed her with a hard stare. "And Captain? Don't try to be clever again."

She shrugged. "Alright. How much do you pay per job?"

"It depends on the job. But you will be compensated well."

"What's the retainer? What kind of frequency are we talking?"

He handed her a pad with a figure on it. Magdalene let out a soft whistle. "I can deal with that."

"I thought you might. As far as frequency, that depends entirely on what our clients need. That's why you get the retainer, because some months you'll be sitting in dock more than anything else."

She nodded. "Like I say…I think we can live with that."

He smiled. "Good. Then give me Ellis."

She glanced back at us now. "You heard him."

Frank walked me forward, but Henderson put up a hand. "That's close enough, Kudarian."

"Ma'am?" Frank asked.

"You heard him."

This was a development none of us had planned for. I hesitated, and Frank said, "Move." There was a note of concern in his tone that, I hoped, didn't reach Rex's ears.

The worry was misplaced, though. Henderson was grinning at me, taking my hesitance to be fear rather than indecision. I stepped forward.

When I reached his desk, he nodded and turned back to Magdalene. "So," he said, "shall we discuss details about your future with the Conglomerate?"

I glanced at Frank. The Kudarian nodded, ever so faintly. Then, I pulled on my bonds. At first, nothing happened. I pulled harder, straining to remain silent as I did so.

All at once, the joint gave, and the cuffs flew apart. My arms, now free, swung wide with all the force I'd been exerting on the cuff. Rex drew back in his seat, throwing a startled glance in my direction. Frank flew forward.

I had been anticipating the need to step in, to do something to occupy Henderson's attention while the Kudarian reached him. I'd been overthinking things, it turned out.

I had never seen someone move as quickly as Frank did after my bonds snapped. It seemed to be done in the blink of an eye. He covered several strides before Henderson had gotten to his feet. Before the syndicate man could utter a sound, he was pinned to the desk, Frank's hand wrapped around his mouth and his knee in his back. He was bent at so sharp an angle that it practically hurt just to behold. He didn't dare resist.

"Now that doesn't look very comfortable, Rex," I said. I slid into his seat, moving a bit to the side, out of Frank's way. Henderson did struggle now, but only for an instant. In the next, whimpering, he fell still.

Rex was logged in, but the terminal was locked. I brought up the account input screen and chose *alternate user*. Then, sucking in a trembling breath, I entered the local admin account name and password.

I hit the enter key, and held my breath. A loading screen appeared, and I didn't loose it until I saw the familiar icons and menus populate. “We’re in.”

CHAPTER TWELVE

Magdalene was on her feet. "Nicely done, Kay."

"Good job," Frank agreed.

"Hurry this up," Corano put in.

I didn't need the urging, and told him as much. One by one, I powered down the security systems. "Turrets down. Drones offline. Security bots down. Weapons grid offline." I glanced up, grinning and trembling at the same time with sheer excitement. "We are good to go."

"Then let's get the hell out of here," Corano instructed.

"You got Henderson?" Magdalene asked.

"Roger that," Frank grinned.

She smiled too. "Then like the man says…let's get the hell out of here."

I closed the terminal, snapping the external shell shut, and got to my feet. Magdalene clapped a hand on my back as I rounded the desk. She was smiling ear to ear. "Well done, Kay. Really well done."

I preened the tiniest bit but shrugged. "I'm just glad it worked and-" My faux modesty was interrupted by the office door opening.

Frank, still behind us, swore. So did Corano. So did I.

"Fuck."

It was the robot, Sydney, rolling into the room with a tray of tea and biscuits pinched between the fingers of one of his metallic appendages.

I'd shut down the battle bots on the surveillance network. I'd forgotten about the damned domestic ones. "Fucking fuck."

Sydney, meanwhile, dropped the tray in a clatter of shattering glass and ringing metal. "Hostile forces detected," he declared in his clipped British tones, even as he retracted his more humanoid arm and exposed one of the laser arms. His tracks bore down on the shattered china and disbursed biscuits, grinding them underneath him. The red dot of a laser targeting system appeared on Maggie's forehead. "Initiating purge protocol."

I stepped forward, putting myself between her and the robot. I was driven more by instinct than anything else, because I was practically blind with fear. I screamed, "Override protocol."

Sydney froze in place. "Facial recognition accepted: Ellis, Katherine. Please confirm override code."

I licked my lips with a dry tongue, praying like hell that I remembered the sequence of numbers and letters I'd built into the units' base program. "Alpha-alpha-three-one-beta-zeta-niner-eight…" I trailed off, my mind racing. Seconds ticked by. I was close to hitting the timeout. "Juliet-tango-five," I finished. It was jt5, or kt5, and for the life of me, I couldn't remember which.

"Input confirmed. Purge protocol aborted. Please specify alternate protocol."

"Defend protocol."

"Input confirmed. Please identify target."

"Uh, me."

"Confirmed. Defending Ellis, Katherine."

"But, uh, weapons hold, Sydney." Knowing what I knew of the domestic bots, I wasn't about to risk the crew's life on Sydney's interpretation of hostile intent.

"Weapons hold. Confirmed."

"And disable all access for Rex Henderson. His authorization to your program is revoked effective immediately."

"Confirmed. User 'Henderson, Rex' no longer authorized to offer input or interact with this unit."

"Good. Okay, Sydney, we're heading back to our ship. Can you cover us?"

"Of course, Katherine. I hope your stay was a pleasant one, though?"

"Uh…yeah, great."

"Excellent."

We reached the *Black Flag* without incident. The drones had nestled to the ground quietly, the battle bots powered down without incident. The turrets sat motionless and the surveillance cameras looked on unseeing.

I'd never seen Henderson's mansion so quiet, its opulent halls and ostentatious rooms missing that familiar whir and whine signifying an ever-watchful mechanical presence. It was like a ghost town, and it made me shiver.

Esser was, I knew, probably having a conniption fit trying to figure out why he'd lost connection and trying to power everything back up. And sooner or later, he'd succeed. We couldn't have him getting the cameras back on in time to see us kidnapping his boss.

Twice during our retreat, Henderson attempted to wriggle free. After the second try, Frank exerted pressure at the right points, and the syndicate man turned a shade of purple I hadn't seen in a human before. After that, he abandoned his efforts at escape.

When we reached the ship, Magdalene caught me by the elbow and signaled for Corano and Frank to go ahead. I braced myself as they passed for the reckoning that was about to come. I'd missed the repurposed battle bots. After all my cautions to her not to screw up, I'd gone and screwed up.

"Kay," she said once they'd stepped inside the ship.

"Yes?" I couldn't look at her, but I tried not to cringe at least.

"That stunt with the robot?" I swallowed and glanced up. To my surprise, she was beaming. "That was damned gutsy, Kay."

"It was?"

She nodded. "And not just because you saved my ass, which you did. But that was quick thinking, and damn brave." She rested a hand on my shoulder, and I felt something like a flutter in my stomach. "Thank you."

"Of course," I said. "I'm just sorry I missed him in the first place."

She shrugged. "Shit happens. Especially in this line of work. It's what you do when it all hits the fan. It's how you roll with the punches that determines if you live or die." She smiled at me again, and there was an appreciation in her eyes that made me smile too. "And today? We lived because you rolled with the punches."

"Thanks, Magdalene."

"Call me Maggie," she said. Then, she added, "Just…not on the bridge."

"Alright," I grinned. "Maggie."

She smiled too and turned toward the ship. "C'mon."

I followed her up the gangplank but paused at the entry. The whirring of wheels and the steady *clack-clack-clack* of tread had followed me. I turned to find Sydney on my heels.

"Pardon me," the battle bot said. "I hope I did not startle you."

"Uh, no. But…what are you doing?"

"Following mission parameters: defend 'Ellis, Katherine.'"

"Mission accomplished," Maggie said.

"Unrecognized user. Input rejected."

She rolled her eyes. "You tell him, Kay."

I frowned. "Actually, Maggie, maybe we should take him."

"You're kidding, right?"

I shook my head. "If anyone comes to check on Henderson, they'll be able to tell he's been tampered with."

"Well, can't you reset him? Clear his history or whatever?"

"No. Not with all the customizations loaded into him." I grinned. "Anyway, come on. It'll be fun to have a mechanical bodyguard around the ship."

In the end, Maggie relented, but only on condition that we

were going to leave Sydney off at the first port we reached. I figured we'd fight that battle when we reached it, and agreed.

As soon as we were onboard, I released the seals from the *Black Flag* and we left orbit to a round of whoops and cheers from the rest of the crew. "Damned fine work, Captain," Drake said.

Even Kereli managed a, "You didn't get everyone killed, so that's something, I suppose," in my direction.

Frank alone of the party was sullen. For my own part, I felt a little too dazed to wonder at that, much less join into celebration with the same vigor as everyone else. It was the brush with death, I supposed. It had put things into perspective and made me realize just how close I'd come to being no more.

But as we stood on the bridge, Maggie telling the story of how I'd saved them all – and leaving out the part where I was the idiot who nearly got us all killed in the first place – I realized that it wasn't true. It wasn't the brush with death.

It was Maggie. That same strange, heady sense flooded back every time she turned those twinkling green eyes my way. I could feel my pulse race as they softened, losing a little of the edge of merriment and gaining something of respect.

The fact was, I liked her. I liked her a lot. I liked her smile and her eyes, and her sarcastic sense of humor. I liked her confidence and her insolence. I liked *her*.

The realization damn near bowled me over. I'd had crushes before, of course. I'd had boyfriends and lovers. But they'd always been men. That wasn't the part that bothered me. It surprised me, sure. After a few decades of living, you think you know everything there is to know about yourself. At least, I did.

And then, along comes Maggie Landon. My head reeled a little at the idea, but it didn't bother me.

But Maggie was a pirate. Sure, Frank talked about honor and choosing targets wisely and all that. But rationalization was a powerful tool, and it was too easy to excuse just about anything. I knew firsthand just how easy.

I watched her, listening to the pulse of blood in my eardrums. She seemed to feel my eyes on her, because she turned my way and smiled. I smiled too, my heart racing.

God, I'm a moron. Apparently, getting involved with the Conglomerate hadn't been lesson enough. Now I'd gone and gotten myself involved with pirates – and all I could do was sit there thinking how much more involved I wanted to be, with a certain pirate. *What the hell is wrong with me*?

CHAPTER THIRTEEN

We stored Rex in the brig until we'd left Santa Valentina far behind, and hit deep space. Then came the task of convincing him to reach out to his minions and set their minds at ease.

This, of course, was going to be a task easier said than done. And every minute he resisted, Esser would be frantically assuming the worst.

There was already an email in his box from Esser, demanding a status check. I didn't dare respond, because I knew that the next message would be a demand for a visual status check.

And Henderson was having none of that. He laughed out loud when Maggie told him. "Certainly, Captain. Go ahead. Put me on the line with Esser," he'd taunted.

Maggie smiled. "I don't think you understand, Mr. Henderson. You're a captive. And bad things happen to uncooperative captives."

"Bad things happen to people who cross the Conglomerate."

"I'd worry more about yourself, right now. Whatever may or may not happen to us, you're not going to be around to enjoy it if you make yourself too disagreeable, Rex."

"What?" he asked. "Will you set your pet Kudarian on me again?"

Frank grinned. It was the first time I'd seen him grin since we got onboard, and it was a broad, full grin, with his teeth bared. Rex perceptively shivered.

"You know," Maggie said, "there's an ancient belief among some tribes of Kudarians, that eating the flesh of a living animal imbues you with its strength. The more you eat while the heart is still beating, the more strength you take from it. It's called the ritual of assumption."

Rex snorted. "You don't frighten me, Captain." His skin had adopted a very strange pallor, for a man who wasn't frightened.

"My great grandfather served in the Kudar war," Frank offered. "In the First Division. You may have heard of the First Division?" I guessed, based on the way Henderson was sweating, that he had. "They were famous – infamous, to you humans – for performing the ritual of assumption on captured prisoners. They got quite good at it. They could eat a man's limbs and pick most of his torso clean before he died of blood loss."

"Go to hell," Henderson said. "You need me alive, or else you would have killed me already."

"No, actually, Rex," I put in. "They don't. They just need you out of the way. So you can cooperate, and we'll drop you off after we're done with – well, that's not your concern. Or you can not cooperate, and…" I shrugged, and Frank grinned again.

"Don't cooperate," the Kudarian urged. "Please."

"I wish you would," Maggie sighed. "It's a messy business. And Frank is so gassy afterwards."

Corano shivered. "He clogs every toilet on the ship too. Disgusting."

He knew we were enjoying his discomfort. He was visibly

struggling to tell, though, how much of what we said was true, and how much was invented. In the end, he decided to counter bluff. "Go to hell," he said again.

Frank glanced at Maggie, and she shrugged. Then he lunged for the syndicate man, his jaws wide and parted. Saliva trickled down his chin.

I think everyone on the bridge turned pale with fright at the sight. I'd never seen Frank – or anyone – look so terrifying.

But neither had Henderson. He leaped back, tipping the chair into which he was cuffed. "I'll do it," he screamed. "God, I'll do it. I'll do it!"

Frank didn't stop, though, falling upon the figure as one might a juicy steak. He only relented when Maggie called, "Frank, stop. Frank, don't you dare. Frank!"

Then, eyes gleaming wildly, he pulled away, panting. "You said I could." Henderson lay whimpering in a puddle of urine.

"He's going to cooperate."

Frank growled. "We don't need him."

"Dammit Frank. Get it together."

The Kudarian threw the bound man a poisonous look. "And if he doesn't?"

"Then he's yours."

Frank passed a sopping wet tongue over the tips of his fangs.

Henderson was given a change of pants, and then set up in a seat on the bridge. He wasn't allowed access to his terminal, but he did dictate the response message. I typed, "On the *Black Flag*. Long story. All is well. H."

About half a minute later, the expected, "Visual confirmation requested," popped into his inbox.

"Remember what happens if you screw us over," Maggie warned.

Frank smiled. He shivered. "Open the connection."

We dialed Andrew Esser, and the man's features appeared even more suspicious than usual. "Mr. Henderson?" he inquired.

"Here," Rex said. "Satisfied?"

"No sir. What happened?"

Rex shifted in his seat. "Someone got a little smarter than they should have."

"Oh?"

"It's under control." Henderson's tone was firm and final. "I'm a little busy, Esser. Anything else?"

"I need more details than that, sir, or I'm going to have to send someone to the home."

Rex rolled his eyes. "You're a worrying old woman, Esser. One of the pirates tried to get into my office safe. The power drain caused a short circuit in the surveillance feed." He smiled. "And what a smell. Poor bastard practically melted. I trust none of your crew will be that stupid again, Captain?"

"No sir," Maggie said through gritted teeth, as if she resented every syllable.

"Satisfied?" When he didn't respond immediately, Rex

shrugged. "Really, I don't care. Send someone if you want. But I'm busy."

Now, Esser nodded. "Forgive me. Just following up."

Henderson waved it away. "I know, I know. That's what they pay you for." The line was terminated. "Satisfied, Captain?"

"I think so."

Frank growled.

"Take him to his cell, Corano."

Frank's performance had been the highlight of the day. Before long, word of it spread around the entire ship. We were in the mess hall eating dinner, and it seemed like every other minute someone stopped by to congratulate him on a job well done, or comment that they'd remember not to piss him off in future.

"What you said," I asked after Ginny left, "about your great grandfather and the First Division…any of that true?"

He grinned at me. "Why? You worried?"

"No. Just curious."

"It's true about the First Division, and the ritual of assumption. But…" He shrugged, grinning again. "My great granddad was a pacifist. He didn't believe in the war. He spent five years in prison rather than serving."

I laughed. "I'm pretty sure Henderson will be having nightmares about him for the rest of his life."

He nodded. "Maybe."

"But Frank?" I'd been leading up to this all this time, cringing at every interruption.

He glanced up from his third plate. "What?"

"I'm sorry. I know you're pissed at me, for screwing up at Henderson's house, with Sydney." I'd thought about it as the day wore on, and it was the only conclusion I could reach.

He, though, shook his head. "I'm not mad at you, Kay."

"Yeah you are."

He sighed. "Maybe a little. But it's not about screwing up."

"Then what?"

"I don't like it when people play hero. It ends up getting people killed."

I blinked. "What do you mean?"

"The thing with Sydney, and the code."

"But…I saved Maggie's life."

"This time," he agreed. "And you were lucky. But luck runs out. And people who do stupid things relying on luck end up dead."

"It wasn't planned, Frank." I was incredulous. The criticism struck me as decidedly unfair. "It was the only play we had in the moment, though."

He sighed again. "I know, I know. I just…" He shook his head. "You're impetuous, Kay. You've got to be careful, that's all."

CHAPTER FOURTEEN

I'd been in something of a huff with Frank since our conversation. Part of me argued in his favor that I had been the one to insist on an answer. But another part protested that his anger at me was unjustified. I hadn't been playing hero, and I resented that he'd assume I had.

I had mostly forgotten about it, though, by our third day underway. Something of this was attributable to Frank's affinity to Sydney. The battle bot, with its ridiculous accent and clumsy manners, had aggravated me at Henderson's house. But following me around the ship offering up inanities, annoying everyone in our path as it jammed the narrow walkways with its huge metallic frame, I found my opinion shifted rather.

Sydney, I decided, was hilarious. In this, I was joined by a lone ally: Frank. The rest of the crew were at best indifferent, and at worst, outright hostile. "I'm going to space that monstrosity," Drake threatened when the battle bot had crushed a wrench in its tread.

"Come on, Syd didn't mean to. You shouldn't leave your tools lying around, if you're worried."

"I'll space you too, Kay."

"Analyzing threat," Sydney piped up.

"Stand down," I said quickly, my own amusement replaced

temporarily with fear that the *Black Flag*'s chief engineer would be gunned down over a joke. "He's only joking, Syd."

"Affirmative."

Drake glared daggers at us both. "Get out of here with your murder bot."

Frank damned near busted a gut when I told him about the encounter. We were in the mess hall, and he was downing enough casserole-of-suspect-origins to feed an army. Or more accurately in this case, poison an army. David's work was particularly foul today. It was a sludge that seemed to be comprised of beans, pasta, tomato sauce and quite possibly leftover fish. He was calling it simply "the lunch special."

"Hey Drake," he called. The engineer was a few tables over from us. "I hear we almost got rid of you."

He scowled at the pair of us. "I put in a formal complaint with Landon," he said. "I want that damned thing off this ship."

Frank belly laughed for a full minute.

"It's not funny," the engineer sniffed. "It's going to kill someone one of these days."

"Don't be a baby," I sighed. "Anyway, David's got the killing us part down with these 'specials.'"

"You're always welcome to cook for yourself," he shrugged from behind the counter. "Otherwise, shut the fuck up and eat what you're given."

We all scowled now. "What the hell is this, anyway?" Drake wondered.

"It's what's for lunch. And you better eat hearty, otherwise, if

I've got leftovers, it's what's for dinner too."

It was now that Maggie walked into the mess hall and cast a curious glance at her scowling crew. "Am I walking in on a mutiny or something?"

"We're thinking about it," I said. "But against the cook, not the captain."

She grinned but checked the expression as she turned to the line. "I'm sure whatever David's put together is delicious," she declared.

"Famous last words," Frank offered.

A glance at the entrée quickly laid Maggie's forced optimism to rest though. "Uh, what is this, David?"

"Lunch," he declared sullenly.

"And dinner," I informed her, "if there's too many leftovers."

"Better dig in, Captain," Frank grinned.

"'Eat hearty,'" Blake quoted.

Maggie dutifully loaded a plate with goop, then joined us. She took one skeptical forkful and shuddered. "I expect you all to get seconds," she told us.

Groans of protest met this directive, but she added, "I didn't say eat them. I said *get* them. You can toss 'em out after that. But there's no way I'm eating this for dinner too."

"I can hear you, you know," David scowled.

"Sorry, Dave," she said, "but this is a little too adventurous. Even for me."

"Hey," Frank said suddenly, grinning, "that bot of yours, Kay…you think you could program it to cook?"

"I don't know," I said.

"I'd be willing to withdraw my complaint," Drake offered, "if it can. Even if it kills me, it'll be quicker than this."

Since leaving Santa Valentina, we'd been underway for almost a week. "We'll be at Kraken's Drop inside of two days," Maggie said, leaning against the bulkhead as I caught my breath.

We'd been running laps on the deck. It had been her idea. "Since we haven't been off ship in a while, it's good to stretch your legs." She'd asked me if I'd wanted to join. Normally, from anyone else, that would have been a hard no. I hated running. But the way I felt about Maggie hadn't changed since the raid on Henderson's place. As ridiculous and cheesy as it was, I felt butterflies in my stomach when I was around her. And all I wanted was to be around her.

Even now, with a stitch in my side and my lungs burning like they were underwater. I nodded, sucking down enough air to ask, "Hey Maggie?"

"Yeah?"

"When this is over…when we get the credits and all that…you still going to do this? Privateering, I mean?"

She considered. "I don't know. I don't tend to plan that far ahead." She shrugged. "Making plans that hinge on outcomes that may not happen? It's just a path to disappointment."

"But if it did," I persisted. "Would you still do this?"

"I don't know. Maybe. I like the work. I like being in the sky." She grinned at me. "I like the weird characters you run into in this business."

I smiled at that. "You wouldn't retire, though?"

"What would I do?"

"I don't know…see the galaxy?"

"I do that already."

"Yeah, but…you wouldn't have to worry about pissing off people like Henderson. You wouldn't have to worry about dying."

"Civvies die too, Kay," she said. "Just because you're not wielding the sword, doesn't mean you won't die on it."

I blinked at the grimness of her tone.

"What about you? You going to go into a comfortable retirement?" She grinned. "Maybe build yourself a house like Henderson's, set up house with that robot of yours?"

"I don't know," I said honestly. Then, "None of that, of course. But I don't know what I will do."

"You've got family, don't you? You could spend time with them."

"My mom and a brother," I acknowledged. "But…my mom is busy with her new husband, on a tour of the Union. As for Jake, well, we don't talk anymore."

"Oh. Why?"

The question surprised me a little, but I shrugged. "We fought."

"Sorry," she said, "that wasn't my business."

"No, Mags, it's fine. He…he liked to gamble. I found out he was putting my name on securities, for gambling credits."

She whistled. "Son-of-a-bitch."

"Yeah. I threatened to have him arrested if he didn't get into rehab. He said I was a…well, a lot of colorful things." I smiled reflexively, to hide the hurt. "We haven't spoken since."

"I'm sorry."

"Don't be. Shit happens."

She nodded slowly. "One of the reasons this life is nice. A lot less drama."

"What do you mean?"

"Well, in this line of business, you have to keep your ties to a minimum. The more you have, the more leverage someone has over you." She shrugged. "You leave a wife and kids at port, they're going to be the first target of any smuggler or raider you cross. Safest thing you can do – for everyone – is not have that tie in the first place."

"Oh," I said. "Still, that sounds awfully lonely, Mags."

She glanced at me, and for a minute held my gaze. I could hear each beat of my heart in the interval, my pulse crashing in my ears. My heartbeat was so loud I was half sure she could hear it too. "Sometimes," she acknowledged. Then, she looked away. "But it's easier that way. Less drama, no worries." She stood up, pushing off the bulkhead behind her. "But come on. We've still got five rounds to go."

CHAPTER FIFTEEN

I blinked into the flashing overhead lights. It was early – it couldn't have even been five yet. *What the hell?*

"Code red," the ship's overhead was saying. "Code red in the brig."

The brig? I struggled to free myself from sleep's lingering grasp. What the hell could be going on in the brig? Then, of course, it hit me. *Henderson.*

"Unauthorized cell access."

I was out of my rack in a second, my heart hammering in my chest. "Shit." Every muscle in my calves and thighs seemed to ache – compliments of Maggie's brutal run last night – but I paid no heed as I dashed on my clothes.

You never realize how damned long it takes to get dressed until you know, instinctively, that lives are on the line. *Bra. Shirt. Jeans. Boots.* Part of me felt an idiot for bothering. There were lives on the line…what did it matter if I was in pajamas or not?

But Henderson scared me, and the idea of him on the loose terrified me. I wasn't going to meet him in my pajamas. I was going to die with my boots on, if that's what it came down to.

I punched the access panel on my door and sprinted out, only to collide head-on with a bulky metal form. Sydney's bulky metal form, in point of fact. "Shit," I cried, grasping my nose. It felt like I'd broken the damned thing. My knee didn't feel much better. "Sydney, what the hell are you doing here?"

The bot whirred to life now. "Standby aborted. Resuming operation. Assessing situation. Ellis, Katherine sporting superficial injuries. Unknown assailant."

"Good God, Sydney," I said, my voice muffled because of the hand I was still applying to my nose. "There's no assailant. Get out of my way. Henderson is on the loose."

"Henderson, Rex," Sydney answered. "Unauthorized user confined to the brig for malfeasance."

"I know he's an unauthorized user, dammit. He's out of the brig, and I need to find out what's going on. Now get out of my way."

"Wouldn't you be safer inside, Katherine? If Henderson, Rex is dangerous, you should stay far from him."

"Dammit Sydney, I'm not going to tell you again: get the hell out of my way."

"Affirmative." The great bot trundled a foot and a half to the side, then pivoted to face me again. "But your safety is my primary objective, Katherine."

"Then follow me," I said.

"Affirmative."

"And for the love of God, keep it down."

"Keep what down?"

"Don't make noise."

"Unable to comply. I do apologize for the inconvenience, Katherine, but I am not equipped with stealth runners. However, such options do exist for my model. For a full range of stealth upgrades, contact a Via Robotics salesperson or a licensed seller."

"Shut up!"

"Affirmative. Switching communication mode to silent."

We raced down the hall, me in the lead and Sydney rolling along after me. He kept apace with my steps without issue. Our haste, though, meant that each new section of his tread impacted with the metal grate flooring a little bit sooner and with more force than usual. His normal noisy trundling was downright cacophonous now. Henderson, I thought, could probably hear him from the other end of the ship.

We were nearing the brig when we ran into a group of the crew. Maggie was there, pistol in hand, and so were Frank and Corano. On the other side of the hall, their heads jutting out from an open doorway, were Drake and Kereli.

They all looked over as Sydney rolled up. Corano put a finger to his lip and Frank hissed, "Shh!"

"He doesn't have a silent mode," I whispered.

Maggie gestured me over. She'd taken up position across from Drake and Kereli. "Stay down," she said, her voice low. "He's holed up in there." She gestured to a storage closet a few doors down from the brig.

"What's he doing in there?"

"Hiding. He was trying to make a run for the shuttle bay, but Corano spotted him before he got far."

"Hey," Frank said. "Do you have a gun?"

"No."

"Hell, Kay." He frowned at me. "What are you doing out here without a gun?"

"I've got Syd," I reminded him.

"Great, so you can rest assured your death will be avenged."

"Frank, focus," Maggie said. "Jesus."

His frown didn't ease, but he fell silent.

"Here," she continued, handing me her pistol. "Take mine."

"What about you?"

"I always carry a spare." She reached into her boot and drew out a second gun. She was wearing, I saw, an ankle holster.

Somehow, that didn't surprise me. "Thanks."

"Don't shoot anyone," Corano grimaced.

"Other than Henderson," Frank put in. "If you see that son-of-a-bitch, put a hole in him."

"Do we have any reason to think he's going to come out?" I asked.

"Not any time soon. And when he does, he's not going to be cooperative. He got a gun from Ginny."

"Ginny?" I said. "Is she alright?"

"She's probably got a concussion, but she'll be fine. She's in medbay now."

"Why don't we send Syd in?" I wondered.

"The robot?" Corano asked, a silver eyebrow raised. Maggie pulled a face. Even Frank seemed skeptical.

"I'm serious," I said. "The domestic stuff aside, he's a battle bot. Breaching a storage closet door? That's small potatoes for one of these guys. They're built to take on bunkers."

Maggie considered. "That's actually not a bad idea," she said. "It'll be a hell of a lot better than trying to wait him out." She turned to her tactical officer. "What do you think, Corano?"

He grimaced. "I hate to say it…but I recommend trying it."

She nodded. "Alright. You'll have to give him the order, Kay. He doesn't listen to any of us."

I smiled at the annoyance in her tone. Mags wasn't used to her commands being ignored, and I had the impression that she didn't care for the sensation. "Alright." I turned to Sydney, who had planted himself in the hallway in front of me. "Sydney?"

He made no response.

"Sydney?"

"Is he ignoring you now too?"

"Sydney, answer me, dammit."

"Affirmative. Silent mode deactivated."

I groaned. I'd forgotten that I'd told him not to speak. I'd forgotten, but he obviously hadn't. "Listen, Sydney, Rex Henderson has locked himself into the storage closet there."

"Confirmed. Infrared sensors detect the presence of Henderson, Rex, in designated space."

"Any chance you can get him out?"

"Affirmative."

When he made no move to do so, I asked, "Okay, *will* you?"

"Yes. Shall I proceed now, Katherine, or would you prefer I wait until a later hour?"

"Now, please."

"Confirmed. Extracting Henderson, Rex."

He trundled over to the door, his humanoid appendages folding back into his torso. Out came a breaching drill, its laser bit flaring a reddish orange. Sydney turned the drill on the door, and a shower of sparks flew this way and that. The stench of melting metal assailed my nostrils a moment after the hiss and sputter hit my ears.

The battle bot worked for a few minutes, cutting the door out of its frame. Henderson's voice sounded now and again as the barrier fell away. "Goddamned treacherous hunk of metal: get the fuck out of here."

A few blasts of laser fire flared through the cuts Sydney had made, dissipating before they could do any harm. "He's definitely not in a cooperative mood," I observed.

"Hostile, potentially lethal action detected. Permission to use force, Katherine?" Sydney called from the doorway, still cutting away at the metal.

"Uh, we want to take him alive, Syd."

"Copy."

Finally, he'd bored out a handhold for himself, and severed one half of the door. The drill retracted, and the humanoid appendages returned. He reached for the hole he'd carved, and, his fingers finding purchase, he rolled backward.

A terrible shrieking of metal sounded, and the door bent outward. At the same time, Henderson darted out of the opening and past Sydney. The robot was still occupied with the door, and the Conglomerate man was firing in our direction. We all ducked out of the incoming volley as blasts sailed overhead and underfoot, landing in the walls, singeing the floor panels, charring the ceiling. After the third or fourth shot, the lights flickered and went dark.

"Shit," Maggie swore.

Sydney, meanwhile, declared, "Target Ellis, Katherine in extreme peril. Aborting secondary functions. Resuming primary mission."

A fearful mix of noises reached us a moment later. It sounded like metal impacting with something soft and pliable. It sounded like the snapping and breaking of solid things. It sounded like a billow being forcibly deflated.

The gunfire stopped. Sydney followed up his prior commentary with, "Threat neutralized according to parameters established by Ellis, Katherine. Target's safety assured."

CHAPTER SIXTEEN

A few spindly beams of light from flashlights lit our path as we stepped into the hall. Henderson was lying in a pool of blood, still as death itself. I felt a chill run up my back. "Sydney," I said, aghast, "you killed him."

"He had it coming," Frank shrugged.

"Negative, Katherine. I merely incapacitated him."

I glanced between the unmoving form and the great bot. I shivered a second time. Sydney was still holding the piece of door he'd wrenched free from its frame. But the steel was slick with red blood.

Maggie, meanwhile, reached Henderson, grabbing his gun first and then patting him down for weapons. When she was satisfied that he was fully disarmed, she checked for a pulse. "He's right," she said in a moment. "He's definitely alive."

"Affirmative," the battle bot declared. "My scans indicate that he has sustained several injuries of moderate to critical severity, but he is alive."

"How moderate?" I frowned. "How critical?"

"He stands a ninety-two-point-five chance of survival," he answered.

"Oh," I said. That wasn't so bad, then.

"The subject may experience lesser symptoms than death, however, including blood loss, blurry vision, lower lumbar pain, broken bones, headaches, possible blindness and temporary or permanent paralysis."

Even Maggie was horrified by this prognosis. She glanced up at Sydney, then at me, mouth agape. "Jesus, Syd," I said. "Paralysis? Blindness?"

"Affirmative. Based on the force and location of cranial impact, I calculate a three percent chance of blindness. However, I am not equipped with the medical database upgrade. This estimate is provided as a courtesy only. Via Robotics makes no guarantees for the accuracy of any diagnosis made by a unit without proper licensing."

"That's great, but what about paralysis?" Frank asked.

"My projections show a one percent chance that Henderson, Rex will have sustained spinal bruising sufficient to cause long term paralysis."

"I told you we didn't want to hurt him, Syd," I fumed.

"Forgive me, Katherine, but that is incorrect. You only said that I was not to kill him."

I frowned. "No I didn't."

"I apologize for having to contradict you. But I believe in this instance, your memory is at fault, Katherine."

Now, a voice – *my* voice – issued forth from the robot. "Uh, we want to take him alive, Syd."

I blinked. "Was that a recording?"

"Affirmative."

"You mean, it records our conversations?" Corano wondered.

"Of course. I record all interactions for future analysis, in order to adjust my programming so that I may better fulfill my duties."

"That's creepy," the tactical officer said.

"You're not kidding," Frank agreed. "That's worse than arguing with a woman. At least when a woman tells you that you said something you don't remember saying, it's just her word against yours. This bastard has receipts."

"So do we," Maggie declared dryly.

All of this seemed off topic. "Alright," I agreed. "I did say that. But I didn't want him blinded or paralyzed either."

"I apologize, Katherine. I was unaware of your intentions. I will endeavor to do better in the future. However, I must point out that my primary mission is your protection, and you were in the direct line of fire."

"He's right," Maggie sighed. "Rex didn't leave us much choice. He's lucky he's alive, and hopefully he'll be alright – in a world of pain, but alright. Still, you did what needed to be done Sydney. Good work."

Concern for Rex's well-being quickly shifted to concern for the *Black Flag*'s. An errant shot had blown out one of the electrical relays in the hall. That had been the source of the abrupt loss of light.

But it hadn't stopped there. The hit had been a direct one,

and the surge of energy caused a cascade failure down the entire length of deck. Half the ship was running on critical and emergency systems only.

"Fuck," Maggie fumed. "We've got life support and gravity here, but that's about it."

"We're going to have to gut the wiring in this whole section, too," Drake sighed. He'd pulled off a panel of wall, and was poking around inside the conduit that ran behind it. "It's been cooked." He drew his hand back suddenly. "Shit. Melted, not cooked."

"We're lucky we didn't have an electrical fire," I observed.

"Damned lucky." Maggie sighed. "Do we have what we'll need?"

Drake shook his head. "No chance. I've got enough for minor repairs. We can get the brig operational again. For anything more than that, we're going to need to make a parts run."

"Well, I guess that's more to add to the list for Kraken's Drop."

"That means flying lame for days," Corano said. "I don't like that."

"No. But even if we divert to some place closer, that only buys us, what? A day? Day and a half at most?"

The Esselian nodded. "I still don't like it."

The matter was settled, though, when Fredricks found us. "I tried to page you, Captain," he declared, "but, well, the problem is – medbay's gone dark. No power, no paging."

"Gone dark?"

"I don't know what happened – whatever happened here, I

guess." Fredricks was the ship's medic. He was an older man, human and unreserved with his expressions. He was frowning at the moment, his dark eyes casting a bewildered look around him. "What the hell *did* happen here?"

"It's a long story. Short version, Henderson shot the place up, Sydney nearly beat his brains out."

If this elucidated matters for Fredricks, his face hadn't caught up to his brain. But he said only, "Oh. Right. Well, anyway, I can't do anything until I've got power."

"Drake, you think you can get the brig and medbay back online?"

"Not if it's cooked like everything here. I've got enough for one room or the other, but not both."

"We need the brig," Corano said. "Henderson's already proved himself adept at escape. Without the brig, who knows what he'd do."

Maggie nodded. "Yeah. That's got to be the priority."

"Copy," Drake said. "I'll get started right away."

"Hold on," Fredricks said, frowning again. "Captain, we can't fly without a medbay. If someone gets hurt-"

"We'll be at Kraken's Drop within two days," Maggie reminded him.

"Two days is an eternity when you're bleeding out," he countered.

"We could detour to Yukon Station," Corano offered. "That's only about a half day from our current position."

"I don't want that son-of-a-bitch on my ship any longer than necessary," Maggie sighed.

"Speaking of," I wondered, "Fredricks, can you take a look at him? Syd was saying…well, stuff about paralysis and whatnot."

"Can't we just let him die?" I frowned, but he laughed. "I'm just kidding. Mostly."

Henderson was still unconscious, and still bleeding. Fredricks glanced him over, prodding here and pressing there. Then, he said, "Well, your little robot there really worked him over good. He's got broken bones, I'm guessing a few fractures, and a lot of swelling. He needs medical attention. And sooner rather than later." He stood, shrugging. "Which I can't provide, until the power's back."

"What happens if he waits until we get to Kraken's Drop?"

"Well, I mean, I can't say for sure. But if I were treating him? With the kind of hit he took to the noggin', I'd put him in the freezer until the swelling went down. Better a popsicle now than a vegetable later."

"In English, please, Fredricks."

He stared down his nose at Mags and shook his head. Then, slowly and in pinched tones, he explained, "I mean, ma'am, I'd put him in a medically induced coma at low temperature while his body recovers, to avoid long term brain damage."

"Oh."

"Which," he said, in the same patronizing tone, as if he was addressing the most ignorant of Philistines, "is not going to be possible. Because, again: no electricity."

"You think that's really necessary?"

He shrugged. "Depends on how much you hate the guy, I

guess."

CHAPTER SEVENTEEN

Maggie tried, but couldn't rationalize taking the chance. "Son of a bitch," she decided. "We're going to have to detour."

Yukon Station was a settlement on the tiny planet of Yukon. Back in the day, it had been a prosperous mining planet. The ore had long been carted off, though, and these days it was a trading post and way stop. It was close enough to Kraken's Drop to be fertile ground for illegal trades – a drop off and pick up point for business that couldn't be conducted planet side, or by persons not welcome on the planet.

It was not, however, the sort of place to bring an injured man. "I want to refrigerate this bastard as soon as possible," Fredricks decided. "If we make a run to Terrence, I can pick up a portable regen bed. I've been saying we need one of them forever now anyway."

Maggie grimaced. "This isn't an excuse to beef up sickbay, Fredricks."

"I know. But we do need one – as this disaster proves."

"How often does something like this happen, Fredricks?"

"It only takes once," he declared sagely. "Thank God, this time, it was Henderson. But next time, it could be one of us. And if we get a portable unit, we can move it anywhere in the ship that has power."

Maggie sighed. "Alright, alright."

"And the new models are more versatile than that stationary dinosaur in medbay. They can do a lot more than put someone on ice. They can treat burn wounds and-"

"I've heard the spiel before," Maggie interrupted. "And I said alright. We'll go to Terrence too. But first, we stop at Yukon and get the parts Drake needs."

"That's another six hours of travel time. The longer we wait, the worse Henderson's prognosis."

"Flying lame is a danger to the entire crew," Corano observed. "Strategically, Yukon is the better first stop."

"We could do both," Frank offered. "Someone take a shuttle to Yukon – we won't be able to fit one of those units in a shuttle, but there'll be no problem getting Drake's gear. And take the ship to Terrence."

"Can't we get everything at Terrence?" I wondered. Terrence was a midsized planet, with a healthy economy. "Why split up at all?"

"Yes," Maggie nodded. "But they play by the rules on Terrence. You're not going to find someone who'll sell off the books there. Not with the time we have to spend, anyway."

"Does it matter?"

"After Henderson's call to Esser, I promise you we're on a watch list, Kay. We don't need to advertise that we're not running at a hundred percent. You bleed into the waters, the sharks circle."

"Oh."

"The portable bed is just an upgrade. A deck's worth of new

wiring is blood in the water."

It wasn't long before Henderson was sedated with painkillers, and the *Black Flag* turned toward Terrence. Maggie would take the shuttle, she decided. "Corano, you get the ship to Terrence and get the regen unit. Drake, you help Fredricks get it installed right away."

"Yes ma'am."

"Copy that."

"I'll take the shuttle and get the stuff. Unless we run into issues, we should be able to meet about half way between Yukon and Terrence." Now, she glanced up at me. "Kay, you want to come with me?"

"Me? I mean, yeah." I was surprised by the question. I was surprised that she thought to include me. But I'd followed her all over this damned ship yesterday, running so hard I could still feel the ache in my muscles today, just for a chance to spend time with her. My heart was doing backflips at the idea of hours alone in a shuttle with Maggie Landon. Of course I'd say yes to that.

She nodded. "Good. I know you're not familiar with the *Flag*'s systems yet, but it'll be good to have another set of eyes look over what we buy." She grinned. "The funny thing about working with dirtbags is, dirtbags don't tend to be very reliable."

I grinned too. "Of course. Happy to help."

We shipped out shortly thereafter, Sydney protesting all the while that I was interfering with his primary mission by leaving him behind. Even if Maggie would have considered it – and I doubted she would – the last thing I wanted was an eight-hundred-pound robot getting in the way of this opportunity. My nerves were already doing a fine job of that. I found myself tongue-tied. My palms were sweating, and my brain seemed to lose all ability to engage in small talk.

We sat for several minutes in awkward silence after leaving the *Black Flag*. "It's a pretty short flight, right?" I managed at last.

"A few hours from here."

"Ah."

Silence returned, oppressive and overpowering. If the cosmos was giving me an opportunity, it seemed it would be an opportunity to prove myself an ass rather than to get to know Maggie better.

"So, uh, you been to Yukon Station before?"

"Now and then. There's a few good traders there. Depending on what you're looking for, anyway."

"Ah." I searched my mind for something to add, some further question to ask. It remained blank.

"How about you?"

"Me? Oh, uh, no. Never been."

"You haven't missed much."

"Oh."

"It was probably never much of a planet to begin with, but after the mining, the atmosphere's mostly shot. There's dust storms and terrible winds, and that's about it."

"Sounds awful."

She nodded, and then silence settled again.

I licked my lips nervously. She'd been the one to really break it last time. It was my turn to keep the conversation going. "What about the miners? They still live there?"

"No. No one really lives there. A bunch of itinerant merchants, mostly. A few long-termers. But the miners moved off years ago."

"Ah." The topic seemed expended. I sucked in a breath. "Hey Maggie?"

She glanced back at me from her control panel. "Yeah?"

"Thanks. For asking me to come, I mean."

She held my gaze, and for a long second didn't speak. Then, she shrugged. "Of course. Drake was busy, and I'm not much of an engineer myself."

"Still, it's nice to get off the ship."

"We're still on a ship."

"But a different one. And we'll be on land soon. It'll be good to be on solid ground again."

"Don't thank me until you see it, Kay," she laughed. "This is no Santa Valentina. It really is a hellhole."

I grinned. "Beggars can't be choosers."

She hesitated a moment, then said, "You'll like Kraken's Drop better."

"Kraken's Drop? You mean, you think it'll be safe for me to disembark when we're there?"

She shrugged. "Well, they don't care much for the Conglomerate there, so it's not likely we're going to run into any agents. You've never been there, so no one'll recognize you. I don't see the harm."

I was grinning ear to ear now. I had just assumed it, like Santa Valentina, would be another layover spent onboard the *Black Flag*. "Awesome."

CHAPTER EIGHTEEN

Conversation had gotten easier as the day progressed. She'd asked me about Jake, and we'd talked about how close we'd been as kids, and how abrupt the end of that relationship had been.

"That's rough, Kay. I'm sorry."

I shrugged. "It was years ago. I'm over it."

She smiled, as if she didn't believe the words anymore than I did. "You never get over that kind of thing, Katherine. You just learn to live with the pain."

I swallowed the lump that rose in my throat. I didn't want to dwell on that too long, because, for all my outward indifference, she was right: it still hurt. Talking about it was picking at a scab I didn't want to touch. "What about you, Mags? You got any brothers or sisters?"

"I had one. A brother, Bill. He's dead, though."

"Oh, Mags. I'm so sorry."

She smiled, one of those sad, defensive smiles she'd put on when we delved into topics that were too painful. "Thanks. It was a long time ago."

"What happened?" I asked. "If you don't mind my asking?"

She shook her head. "He was a test pilot, flying experimental craft. In the army."

"You were in the army too, right?"

"Yeah." She nodded. "We signed up together." Her smile grew a little less sad, a little fonder. "He was the brains of the Landon family. I was the glory hound. He branched into design, I got my wings."

I smiled at the fondness in her tone. If Maggie's estimation of his intelligence was rooted in more than sisterly affection, I thought, he must have been a genius.

"I reached Captain a month before Bill did." She grinned. "He was pissed." She seemed, for a moment, to lose herself to memories. She grew silent, and when she spoke again, her tone was low. "They were working on a project. I don't know much about it, it was classified. Still, Bill was worried. He didn't think they were ready, but the brass was pushing them to meet deadlines.

"When the day for the test came, he didn't want to send someone else up there. So he did it himself. And…" She shook her head. "He was right. It was a suicide mission."

"Oh Mags," I said, reaching a hand out instinctively to hers. Her eyes met mine, and there was, I saw a mist in them. "I'm so, so sorry."

"He died so someone else would live, Kay." She smiled, blinking back the tears. "So that other test pilot wouldn't be sent up in a crate that wasn't going to make the trip back. It didn't get more 'Bill' than that."

"Is that why you got out?" I asked.

She surveyed me with startled eyes. "What?"

"Of the service, I mean. Is that why you didn't sign up for another tour?"

She glanced down at my hand and hers, still clasped together. "I couldn't stay in. Not after that. He told them – he told them it wasn't ready."

I squeezed her hand. "Oh Maggie."

She raised her eyes to mine. "You're the only person I've ever told that, Kay."

It was my turn to blink in surprise. "I am?"

"Yes. I don't know why. Just…I think, sometimes, you understand me."

I felt my heart quicken. "Maggie…"

But, abruptly, she laughed. "That sounded stupid, didn't it? What I mean is, it's been a long time since I've had someone my own age, another human, to talk to, someone who isn't one of the crew." She smiled, then pivoted in her seat, her hands slipping out of mine. "But I should doublecheck our heading."

The rest of the trip was spent on safer topics. Still, I couldn't quite lose the heady sense that, for half a second, Maggie had opened up to me; and I'd seen a tenderness, an interest, that made my heart flutter.

I felt a bit of an imbecile, as if I was reverting to a hormonal teenager, erratic with hormones and the thrill of a first crush.

In a sense, Maggie was a first crush. She was the first woman I'd ever been attracted to, and I found myself – not unlike the teenager of a decade and a half ago – introduced to a host of new sensations and realizations about myself.

It was as if I was seeing the world through new eyes, or rather with eyes that finally saw. I'd spent a whole lifetime surrounded by women, but I'd never seen the sensual beauty in the simplest aspects of the feminine before. But everything about Maggie revealed some new facet of it – from the strength in her muscular, confident form to the impish gracefulness of her high cheekbones and dancing eyes, she left me reeling. I'd spent our entire run the day before concentrating on my own breaths, on my own aching calves, to avoid looking at her, to avoid soaking up the sight of her curves and angles.

I'd felt my breath taken away before by the masculine. Now it was Maggie. It was her strength, her beauty, her confidence that stirred me.

And the idea that maybe I had stirred something similar in her damned near left me giddy.

It was only with effort that I was able to force myself to attend to the mission as we reached Yukon Station airspace. "Let me do the talking," she was saying. "I've worked with some of these characters before, so they trust me."

"Understood."

"But if you see any issues, speak up."

"Alright."

When Maggie had described Yukon Station as a hellhole, she hadn't been kidding. It was barely large enough to be classified a planet at all, orbiting a blue giant at the far end of its habitable zone. It was a vast red rock covered in dark, dirty clouds and sparse patches of inky water. Little vegetation remained, and most of the old settlements had been destroyed by harsh winds and vicious storms. The main port, behind its protective dome, stood undisturbed, but it was not much to write home about either.

Old buildings, cheaply constructed and limited infrastructure were the key takeaways as we jetted overhead to the docking port.

I was peering out the window, through the thick, particle-heavy air, when Maggie caught my eye. She was watching me, grinning. "I told you," she said.

I smiled back. "It still beats the interior of that ship. No offense to the *Black Flag*. But I'm sick of metal hallways and endless night outside the windows."

She laughed. "You're a landlubber, Kay."

We were cleared to land and docked in a rented space. "They charge by the hour," Maggie had said. "So let's make this quick."

We hired a cab to get us to the center of town. My earlier observation about Yukon Station's infrastructure stood the test of our first experience with it. The streets were narrow and full of hairpin turns. Patches of loose gravel and sporadic potholes in combination with a driver who prioritized speed over comfort meant we spent the entire trip tossed this way and that.

If the settlement had been busier, I thought, these roads would have been dangerous to traverse. As it was, I wouldn't have wanted to be a pedestrian on the streets of Yukon Station. Our driver did not seem to be an outlier in his habits. The cabs and transports that passed us were whipping by at the same breakneck speed, jostling their passengers and cargo as they went.

"Drop us off at Ace's," Maggie had told him when we got in. Now, we pulled up outside a sprawling set of interconnected buildings. To judge by the varying shapes and heights of their facades, they had probably been distinct businesses at one point in their history. Now, they were all *Ace's Goods and Gear.*

Or so the neon sign outside the central building declared, anyway. I shivered at the dilapidated fronts and unwashed windows, the quiet stretch of street around us. *Ace's Goods and Gear* was the type of place that showed up in horror movies, and left you wondering what in the hell was wrong with the protagonists who traipsed inside without a concern.

Just like we were doing. "Uh, Maggie, you sure this place is…well, safe?" Visions of corpses in basement freezers were filling my mind at the moment.

"Of course. Ace is a scalper and a bit of a creeper, but that's about it."

"Okay." I was still leery, but I followed her in anyway. The interior didn't do much to put my mind at ease. Rather, the dim lighting overhead, eons of dust underfoot, and voyeuristic paintings on the walls only heightened my unease. "Jesus," I murmured, glancing around. "It's like a pervert's art gallery." There were pinups – and images that left even less to the imagination – of men and women, human and alien, on just about every free surface.

Maggie laughed. "Don't let him see it makes you uncomfortable. He will try to throw you off your game. The pictures are one of his tactics."

"One?" I dreaded to think of what else might lay in store.

"Yeah. He's an emotional vampire. He'll hone right in on anything you're showing and try to use it to his advantage. Oh. And he's a hugger."

I grimaced, but there was no time to wonder what the hell we were doing in the lair of such a creep; because said creep emerged from a room in the back. "Well bless my bagpipes. It's Magdalene Landon, come to see old Ace."

Bagpipes? I wondered. He was an Esselian of moderately advanced years, his copper skin beginning its change to green.

"Good to see you again, Ace." As if this was an invitation, he moved in to hug Maggie. She stepped back, stretching out a hand and laughing. It was a forced laugh. "I'm more a handshake type, Ace. You know that."

He grinned, taking her hand in his long fingers. "That's right. Still, you can't blame a man for trying."

I could, and to judge by her forced smile, so could she. But she said, "So, how's business?"

He, though, moved in my direction. "Now this is a new face." He glanced me up and down with a smile that made me cringe. "And what a face. I'm Ace."

He stepped in to hug me, and I stepped back. "I'm Katherine. Also, not a hugger."

"My loss," he grinned. "So, Katherine, you a new member of the crew?"

"Something like that."

"Ah." He threw a significant look at Maggie, and his grin broadened. "So that's the way the wind blows, eh, Magdalene? Well, well. Always figured your flag didn't fly on a pole, if you get my drift."

She flushed, and despite the inanity of the phrase, so did I. "Kay's a business partner," she said.

"And I'm an honest merchant." He laughed. "But whaddaya need, Magdalene? Let's see if I've got it in stock."

CHAPTER NINETEEN

Ace had the hardware we needed. "Although," he'd added with a wink, "unfortunately not the hardware you want."

Maggie had the patience of a saint, because while I was grimacing, she just laughed. "When'll it be ready, Ace?"

"For you, Magdalene? Give me two hours. I'll have it delivered to the *Black Flag*."

She nodded and paid out the credits he'd asked for.

"Anything else I can do for either of you? Or both of you?"

"We're good," Maggie said.

"Alright. Well, keep me in mind in future, girls."

"No thanks," I muttered as we stepped into the afternoon.

Maggie laughed. "You survived," she teased.

"Yeah, but you could have warned me he was such a creep."

"I told you he was a creep."

"Yeah, but not *that* level of creep."

She laughed again. We were headed down a rough sidewalk, toward the center of town. "Well," she said in a moment, "how about

I buy you a drink to make it up?"

My heart skipped a beat, and I glanced at her. Her eyes were focused on some point in the distance. Was this a drink between friends? Or – did I dare to hope? – something more? "Oh," I said. "That, uh, sounds good."

She glanced sideways at me, a quick, hesitant glance. Catching my eye, she smiled. "Great. There's a little place up the road. Seedy as hell, but they make a mean Turelian Tempest."

A Turelian Tempest was a mixed drink with a potent fermented Turelian cocoa bean base and vodka. I couldn't stand the things. They were too sweet and too strong for me. But right now? Strong sounded perfect. I said, "Sounds great."

We walked in silence for a moment, then she sidled closer and nudged me. "You should have seen the look on your face, though, Kay."

My tongue seemed to have suddenly turned to parchment. I was trying to concentrate on her meaning, but my mind was humming with the unexpected sensation of Maggie's nearness. Finally I managed, "When?"

"When he tried to hug you."

I shivered. "What a creep."

"Yup. I almost knocked his lights out, first time he tried it with me."

I laughed. "Now that's something I would like to see."

She smiled at me, catching my eye for half a second. "He tries to touch you again, maybe you will." Then, she glanced away.

My heart hammered in my chest and impulsively I reached

out a hand. She glanced up, surprised, as my fingers intertwined with hers. Then she smiled again, and leaned into my arm.

We walked in silence after that. It was probably just as well. I wasn't sure I'd be able to hear anything over the thunder of my pulse in my ears anyway, and I was too nervous to talk. I was holding her hand, her body pressed into mine as we went. She was close enough that I could smell the faint fragrances of her shampoo, feel the warmth of her body next to mine. My head was full of nothing else. It was a miracle I didn't trip over my own feet at that point.

I was a tongue-tied fool, and that was for certain. But I was the happiest tongue-tied fool on the whole damned planet.

The place she had in mind was a hole-in-the-wall called *Shooters*. It was larger than I'd anticipated, but every bit as seedy as she'd promised. That, I was quickly coming to see, was a feature of the planet. Dirty windows and dim lights abounded, as if the residents feared what too much illumination might turn up. Or maybe, considering the state of the world, water was a scarcity and cleanliness the first sacrifice.

Either way, it didn't inspire confidence. Still, I was a little too wrapped up in the moment to care. Maggie opened the door, and I stepped in first. "You want a Turelian?" she asked as I stood blinking in the doorway, my eyes adjusting to the lighting.

"Sure."

"Get a table then." She flashed me a grin. "I'll be right back."

Goddammit. That woman's eyes could make my heart and stomach do backflips at a glance. "Alright."

I chose a booth in the rear of the bar, away from most of the other patrons. I wasn't sure of the time scale on Yukon Station, but I assumed the day must have been more advanced here than it was by our clocks. *Shooters* was already fairly full and the din intense. New faces matriculated in as I waited. The people, like the place, didn't inspire confidence. They were rough and coarse. That didn't bother me. I'd flown to job sites in the company of construction crews and freight hands. I was used to the kind of language that drifted across from distant tables. It had long since ceased to shock me.

But these men didn't strike me like the crews I'd worked with. Those workmen tended to have a better capacity for beer and more colorful vocabulary than I'd had, but other than that, we'd been much the same.

These men had a dangerous edge to their glance, a hard look in their eyes. It didn't take much imagination to figure out that these were crews not engaged in legal activities. These were pirates and smugglers, the hushed business they discussed over their plates and drinks illegal, the cargo in their holds probably stolen or contraband. I shivered. We were in a wolves' den, surrounded by wolves.

I glanced up, looking for Maggie, and my eyes found her. She was at the bar still, waiting on our drinks. She must have felt my gaze on her, because she turned and flashed me a smile. I smiled too.

The bartender returned, and her attention was drawn. I frowned absently in thought. I had called Maggie a pirate, hadn't I? I'd thought her no better, no different, than anyone else here. And yet…and yet, how different I felt now.

She was nothing like the crews around me. She was a thief, but who did she rob? Thieves and cutthroats. And even in her dealings with cutthroats like Henderson, she dealt honorably – more honorably than he deserved, in truth.

How many captains, privateer or otherwise, would have gone out of their way to save someone like Rex Henderson?

Even in her dealings with cutthroats like me, my mind put in. She'd given me no choice but to join up with her. She'd threatened to leave me to the Conglomerate's tender mercies if I refused. But what had Maggie known about me then? Nothing more than that I worked for the syndicate. And as she learned of the circumstances of my work with Henderson, her opinion had softened. And now, here we were, getting drinks.

I felt for the stone that hung at my wrist and smiled. Maybe my luck was finally changing after all.

CHAPTER TWENTY

Maggie sidled into the seat across from me, two Turelian Tempests in hand. She handed me one and took a sip from her own. "I hope you're hungry. I ordered a basket of sand snappers."

"A little," I admitted. "But what are sand snappers?"

She grinned. "You'll find out."

I pulled a face, and she laughed. Then, I took a sip of my martini. And shuddered. It was every bit as bad as I remembered.

She watched me for a moment, then glanced down at her drink. "What Ace said, by the way? About my flag?" I rolled my eyes at the memory, but she continued, "It's true. I…I've never been interested in guys."

She glanced up, studying my features as if trying to gauge my reaction. I took another sip then grinned at her, declaring saucily, "That's the best news I've had in a long time, Mags." I flushed as I said it, though. The Turelian Tempest was working its magic, but liquid courage could only do so much. I was still me, after all.

She smiled. "You too, then?'

"It's more complicated than that for me," I said mildly. How did you tell someone that she was the reason you'd discovered an entirely new facet of yourself? That meeting her was a jolt of electricity, a shock to your entire system? That she'd changed your world, in ways you'd never imagined?

She nodded, then bit her lip. "Kay?"

"What?"

"You and Frank…is that over? Or…well, he's a good guy, and I don't want to hurt him."

It took me a moment to comprehend what she was saying. "Me and Frank? No, Maggie, we're just friends. That's all we've ever been."

"You sure?" She was studying me again. "I don't think he thinks you are, Kay."

I laughed at just how wrong she'd gotten it. "Of course I'm sure, Mags. To be honest, I think he thinks I'm kind of an imbecile who is going to get myself killed." I grinned at her. "But me and Frank? That's what you've been thinking, eh?"

"Well, I'm glad to hear it." She flashed an impish smile. "In fact, that's the best news I've had in a long time, Kay Ellis."

The sand snappers arrived shortly thereafter. They appeared to be some manner of tiny, pincer-bearing crustacean. They'd been battered and deep fried, though, so any further identification was not possible. Maggie laughed at my skeptical expression, then picked one up and popped it in her mouth.

I cringed at the sound of crunching that ensued. Whatever these things were, apparently they still had their shells on them. But I forgot the sensation as quickly as it came as I watched her. There was a smirk on her lips and a twinkle in her eyes, as if she was still amused by my reaction to the sand snappers. But the light that caught in her hair, the arc of her jawline to her chin, the precise angle of her nose: it all struck me in the moment. It was stupid – probably the drink talking, though I'd only had a few sips – but I blurted out, "God you're gorgeous, Mags."

She seemed surprised by the comment, and I could feel my face flush. I glanced down, but felt her fingers on my hand the next instant. She'd reached across the table and taken one of my hands in her own. She was smiling at me. "You're not so bad yourself, Kay."

Then, she turned to the snappers. "But, damn it, eat some of these things so I don't eat the whole basket myself."

I glanced at the snappers too, and then back at her. This wasn't the first time I'd seen her shy away from the moment. I confess it touched my heart a little to see.

It had taken every ounce of courage, and an ounce or two of liquor, on my part to say what little I'd said. How could it have been otherwise? She was confident and beautiful and brilliant. And I – I was just me. Of course the idea of boring, bland, confused me showing interest in her was terrifying. I was way out of my league.

But the realization that it hadn't been entirely effortless on her part, that she felt some of the same anxiety I did, boosted my ego almost as much as the fact that she'd not laughed off my interest in the first place.

I forced my head into the moment, though. "I don't know, Mags. They look pretty creepy."

She shook her head. "At least try one, you goof." When I only pulled a face, she plucked one out of the basket. "Here."

She brought the snapper to my lips. That, of course, wasn't fair at all. She could have been spoon feeding me cyanide, but if it was coming from her hand, I probably would have taken it all the same.

It wasn't fair, but it worked. I cringed as I bit through the shell and heard it give way. Still, once that part was over, it was pretty good. The meat was rich and tender, and the flavor very good. "They're not bad," I admitted.

"See?"

"Yeah, yeah," I grinned, reaching for another.

The sound of Maggie's pager cut off anything further she might have had to say on the matter. She glanced down at it. "It's the *Black Flag*." I nodded, and she answered the call. "Landon here." She frowned after a moment. "Repeat please. Having a hard time hearing you, Frank."

She tried two or three more times, then said, "Hold on, Frank. I need to step outside." She turned to me. "Sorry, Kay. I can't hear a thing he's saying with this racket. I'll be right back."

I nodded. "Hurry. Or there won't be any more of these left by time you're back."

She grinned and headed to the exit. I kept picking at the snappers. I wasn't entirely joking. Once I'd gotten past the idea of crunching down a shell, I found I rather enjoyed them. Morbid? Sure. Delicious? Absolutely.

I was on my fifth or sixth snapper when a passing form stopped at our table, and slid into Maggie's chair. I froze, my hand hovering above the basket. "Uh, that's taken."

The newcomer was male and human, somewhere in his forties. He was wearing a jumper suit. *A freight hand*, I thought. *Probably from one of the ships in dock.*

He smirked at me. "Looks like you got stood up."

I frowned. "No, she's coming back."

"You sure?" another voice sounded, this time to my side. I

started. It was another man, this one wearing the patches of a tactical officer. I hadn't seen him approach, so I realized he must have come from behind me.

Alarm replaced surprise. I was boxed in between the pair of them, with a wall on one side of the booth and him on the other. "Quite." I tried to keep my voice calm. "So you should go."

I yelped as I felt a hand come to rest on my thigh. The man across from me grinned. It was, I saw, his hand, for his form leaned forward, his arm reaching under the table. I pulled at it, trying to pry it off. But his grip tightened until his fingers were squeezing into my leg.

"That hurts," I said. My voice was trembling and my hands shaking. "Let me go."

"We're not going to hurt you, honey," the tactical officer cajoled, brushing a hand across my chin.

I swatted it away. "Leave me alone."

"We got a place, just down the road," the freight hand said, tracing his fingers up my leg. "It's going to be a party."

I squirmed in my seat, pulling away from the pair of them. "I'm not interested. Now leave me the hell alone."

They exchanged glances, then shrugged. "Your loss."

I loosed a breath as the one stepped away from my seat and the other vacated Maggie's. I was, I realized, shaking. I glanced around. Maggie was still gone, and the few people who had been looking over turned away as soon as my eyes reached them.

I decided it was well past time that I was gone too. I pushed to my feet, and the same moment felt a pair of hands seize me from behind. My back thumped hard on the seatback as I was hauled over the booth. A hand clamped down over my mouth, and another set grabbed at my flailing legs.

For half an instant, sheer panic overtook my senses. But then adrenaline kicked in, and I started to struggle in earnest. I caught glimpses of the two men who had grabbed me – they were the same who approached me a minute ago. I saw, too, where they were headed: a backdoor a few strides away.

Whatever happened in here, I knew that I could not let them get me outside. Fear and rage competed in equal measures in me, and I reached hands for the nearest captor. That was the tactical officer, whose paw was clamped over my mouth. I clawed for his face, but he pulled back, out of reach.

We were another step closer to the door. A few faces turned our way, and then turned aside as quickly.

I yanked my legs toward my torso, and then back again with every ounce of strength in my body. I felt my second captor stumble. My first captor was still shielding his face from my wrath, so I reached now for his lower half. I grabbed a handful of his manhood, and twisted and squeezed like my life depended on it. Because, I felt instinctually, it did.

He screamed and dropped me. The freight hand had by now recovered his footing. I saw from the corner of my eye a blur of motion, and raised an arm seconds before a bottle shattered against it. Pain stung my senses, and I could feel the burn of fresh blood seeping from my forearm.

I pushed to my feet, fighting through the pain, and turned on him. He was grinning, a hungry look in his eyes.

Then, I felt a form collide from behind with mine. A rush of movement and fresh agony swept me. A hand clamped against my throat, and I gasped for air. A second later, my back impacted with the wall, and I was staring into the bloodshot eyes of the tactical officer.

"You're going to regret that, you bitch."

I pulled at his hand, desperate to breathe. Tears welled in my eyes. "Please," I croaked. "Please stop."

He grinned now, and behind him so did the freighter hand. "Get her in the car," the latter said.

Then, in a blast of light, his head exploded. I blinked, stunned; dazed; terrified; and still choking for air. A spray of blood hit the tactical officer, and a few droplets reached me too. He spun around, and I felt myself dropping to the floor.

My lungs heaved and my body shook as I sucked in great gasping mouthfuls of air. A second later, I started. The tactical officer hit the floor in front of me, a hole burned through his chest.

The immediate crisis – suffocation – averted, I tried now to get my bearings and understand what had happened. *Shooters* was in chaos. Bodies were cramming this way and that to get out. Fists were starting to fly, in no particular direction but everywhere at once.

But there, at the far end of the bar, standing tall and fearless, was Maggie, smoking gun in hand.

I understood now. She had saved me. Maggie Landon had returned in the nick of time and rescued me.

CHAPTER TWENTY-ONE

I fell into her arms, shaking. She clutched me to her with one hand for half a moment, and then drew me behind her. All the while, the gun was still trained on a handful of figures who pursued me. They were, I gathered, shipmates of the two dead men. "One more step and you can join them in hell," Maggie said.

"You murdering bitch," one snarled. "You killed them."

"You touch my crew, you die," she said, and her tone was ice cold. "Anyone else want to find out the hard way that I'm not joking?"

They hesitated. The bartender, meanwhile, was railing at all of us, decrying the damage to his establishment. He was, I assumed, the owner. "Who is going to pay for this?" he demanded. He turned on the crew Maggie had at gunpoint. "You? Is your captain going to reimburse me, Archer? Are you?"

One of the men scoffed. "It wasn't our fault."

"Biff's dead, and so's Wade. I can't make them pay, can I?"

"Fuck you, man," Archer said. "You're not pinning this on us. We got nothing to do with it. It was their idea, it was their stupid plan."

"Get the hell out of my bar, then. And take those rotting sacks of shit with you."

Maggie didn't put her gun away until they were gone; and they didn't leave without a barrage of threats.

Then, it was her turn to be chewed out. "That's hundreds of credits of damage," the barkeep fumed.

"Get 'em from Slater. Those pieces of shit attacked Kay. You know I didn't have a choice."

"Slater's never going to pay. You know that, Magdalene."

"You let trash like that into your bar, Rick, what do you expect?"

He stared daggers at her. "I've never had a problem with them before. Not until you and she walked in."

"I was eating snappers," I protested. "Sitting there in my seat, minding my own business. I didn't do anything."

"Maybe I'll file a grievance with the Union licensing board," he mused. "See what they think about one of their privateers coming into my bar and shooting the place up?"

Maggie looked like she was about two seconds away from putting a fist down Rick's throat. But, in the end, she decided against it. "How many credits, you son of a bitch?"

He gave her a figure, and she paid it. "A pleasure doing business with you, Maggie."

"Go to hell."

We left after that, and Maggie hailed the first cab we saw. She was quiet and alert, her gun at her side the entire time. I was still shaking, and she wrapped an arm around me wordlessly.

We reached the shuttle just as Ace was wrapping up his delivery.

She touched my arm gently, and said, "You go in, Kay. I'll deal with him."

I did, and I heard his laugh, loud and annoying as ever outside. I was grateful to be spared that.

I headed to the bathroom. I'd stopped trembling, but my nerves were still shot. I'd been in tough situations before, but nothing that rough. I had no illusions about how near I'd come to being raped or worse.

I was covered in blood, too – my own, from the gash on my arm, and the freight hand's. Numbly, I washed it off. I pressed a bandage onto the wound, and then washed my face again.

When I heard Maggie bidding Ace a goodbye, I raced out to see her. As my nerves settled and my senses returned, I was keenly aware of one thing: Maggie was the reason I got away unscathed.

Two things. I was nuts about her. The sight of Maggie standing there when all hope seemed lost, the feel of her arm around me as we'd driven back; if I hadn't been sure before, that would have done it.

She, though, was all business when she stepped into the shuttle. She glanced me over, and said, "That cut looked bad. Did you sterilize it?"

"I cleaned it," I said.

"We need to disinfect it. I'll get this crate in the air, check in with *Black Flag*, and then we'll take a look at it."

"Maggie," I said. "I didn't thank you."

Her gaze softened. "Of course, Kay. Anytime." Then, though, she turned to the control panel. I took a seat as she ran through pre-flight and radioed in our situation.

She didn't get into details about what happened to me. "Ran into trouble with Slater's crew. Had to put a few of them down," was all she said.

"You two okay?" Frank wondered.

"Of course."

"Roger that. We'll be leaving Terrence in about an hour."

"Meet you en route."

Once we were out of the atmosphere and auto pilot took over, she turned her attention to me. Her manner was still distant, professional but lacking the warmth of earlier. I was simultaneously confused and pained. Did she blame me for the fight? Did she think I'd done something to provoke it?

She pulled off the bandage I'd applied and scrutinized my injury. "It is deep. Let me get the medkit." She vanished for a minute, and then returned with supplies in hand. "This is going to hurt."

I was already hurting, though less because of the physical injury. "Okay," I said quietly.

She got to work. I winced as she disinfected the cut, then wrapped it. I was, I realized, shaking again.

"You alright?" she asked, and her tone was brusque.

"I'm fine."

She tied the bandage off, and I cringed. I didn't have much experience with field dressings, but this one was tight. "Ouch."

She was focusing on the bandage wrappers littering the deck, refusing to look at me. "Don't be a baby." Her tone was still hard, and I flinched at it.

I could feel the sting of tears in my eyes, and I blinked them away. "I'm sorry, Maggie," I said. "I didn't mean for…well, things to go to hell like that."

She glanced up at me now. "Dammit, Kay, don't cry."

The tears burned hotter at her words, but I choked them back, lowering my head. "I'm sorry," I said again.

"Don't be sorry." Her tone was gentler now, and she lifted my chin so that our eyes met. "I'm not mad, Kay. I'm just…" She shook her head. I tried to understand the expression in her gaze, but it was too harried, too confused to be made out.

"I'm sorry about the credits," I said. "I'll reimburse you."

"You think that's what this is about?"

"I don't know," I answered honestly, searching her eyes. "What is it about?"

We stood there for a moment, face to face, her fingers still on my chin. Then she spoke again. "I can't stop thinking of – well, earlier. You can't ever let them see you like that, Kay. You can't let them see you afraid. You can't let them see you cry. Men like that, they're hyenas. They're drawn to your fear. They're drawn to your pain."

I felt tears returning to my eyes. "I'm sorry," I said again. "I'm not brave like you, Magdalene." I thought of her standing before that pack of ravening wolves, courageous and unintimidated. "I'm not fearless like you."

"God, Kay, I was so fucking terrified." Her tone was low and raw; so raw it surprised me.

"You were?"

"When I saw them on you…" She shook her head, moving closer, so that I could feel the press of her body against mine. Her fingers traced up from my chin, along my jawline.

I felt my breath catch, my throat go dry, as she brought her lips to mine. She hesitated as our mouths met, and I reached a hand to her waist.

Slowly, with trembling fingers, I traced up the small of her back, feeling the shape of her body under the fabric. I pressed closer to her. She didn't hesitate now. She pulled me to her, kissing me with a fire and a need that mirrored my own for her.

She reached a hand under my shirt, and my skin danced at her touch. She moved her lips down from mine to the skin of my neck, gently, so gently, kissing where earlier I'd been mauled. My breath caught in my throat. "Magdalene," I whispered.

"Call me Maggie," she said, her voice low and husky as she kissed at my chin and throat.

"Maggie," I said, "I've never…well, been with a woman before."

She met my gaze again, and the desire in her eyes made me quiver. "Well then," she said, an impish grin on her lips, "good thing we've got a long trip back and a cabin all to ourselves, isn't it, Katherine?"

She lifted my shirt over my head, and then took her time, exploring my skin with her hands, with her lips, with her tongue. My heart was racing and my body trembling. "Oh Maggie," I whispered again. Her pace was so slow, so amazingly, frustratingly slow that I wasn't sure if she was intent on torturing me or making love. Every sensation was a pleasure, and yet I wanted more, so much more.

Hesitantly, I reached under the fabric of her shirt, and let my hands explore her back, her sides, her stomach. I moved with less precision and more clumsiness than she caressed me, but the feel of her skin under my fingers thrilled me. She seemed to like it too, because now she pressed me against the bulkhead. Her breath was coming quickly, and her eyes burned with desire.

She was in the process of unfastening my bra when a *ding* sounded from the console.

"Oh God," I said, and not in the way we'd been leading up to. As timing went, I couldn't think of anything worse.

"Shit," Maggie broke off from kissing me, panting. "I'll be right back." She put a final kiss on my lips and grinned. "Don't you go anywhere, beautiful."

When she reached the console, though, she frowned. "Dammit. It's *Black Flag*. I got to take it, Kay."

I nodded, then realized she was waiting for me. I glanced down. "Oh." I was standing there, one bra strap off my shoulder and midriff bared, in the direct line of view of the camera. "Sorry." I slipped the top back on, and she grinned at me.

Then, pulling a business-only expression onto her features, she answered the call. "Landon here."

"Dammit, Captain. You sleeping on the job or something?" It was Frank's voice. "You scared us."

"Get to the point, Frank…"

"I think you might have some bogies on your tail."

"Bogies?"

"We're about three hours out, but it looks like someone left Yukon Station right after you took off."

"Shit."

"Yeah. Keep your eyes open. That shuttle should be able to outrun most raider rigs. But you don't want to be taken by surprise."

"Copy that."

"Alright, *Black Flag* out."

She sat in silence for a moment after the transmission ended. I sidled up beside her, wrapping an arm around her shoulder. "You think we're in trouble, Maggie?"

She started at my touch. "No. No, I don't think so Kay." Her brow, though, was creased. "But I am going to have to keep an eye on this." She gestured at the panels and the various sensor readouts.

"Oh."

"I'm sorry."

"Don't apologize, Maggie." My disappointment was palpable. My body still ached with anticipation, my head still reeled from her touch. But there were raiders after us. That came first. I leaned over and kissed her on the cheek. "Business before pleasure."

She wrapped an arm around me, but her attention stayed focused on the controls. "Yeah. You should probably try to get some rest, Kay."

"Oh." I hadn't anticipated that. "I can wait by you. I don't mind."

"It's going to be a few hours yet." She slipped her arm off of me and turned to a different panel, so that mine fell away from her. "You'd be better off trying to get some sleep."

"Oh." I blinked, too surprised to know what to say except repeat, "Oh." Then, "Uh. Alright then."

They were a long few hours, some of the longest I've ever waited. I lay in the cot, sleep far from my mind. My thoughts were with Maggie and how she'd felt in my arms, with the desire I'd seen in her eyes and the way my body responded to her touch. And, now and again, like cold water on the fire of my passions, with the way she'd turned her shoulder to me, the way she'd practically dismissed me. One minute she'd been all heat, and the next cool as ice.

Had I read her wrong the first time? Or had I just misinterpreted her distance the second? Was it just the job, and getting us out in one piece, that made her seem so far away now?

I didn't know, and that, more even than the feeling of being so close to Maggie and yet so far away, was an acute torture.

CHAPTER TWENTY-TWO

The trip back to the *Black Flag* was uneventful. We saw no sign of Captain Slater or his ship. When we reached the rendezvous and disembarked, we were swamped by crewmates. Frank turned concerned eyes to the blood-stained dressing on my arm. "I thought you said everything was okay?" he wondered of Maggie. "What happened, Kay?"

"Nothing," I mumbled.

He studied me with a worried expression, then said, "Well, let's get you to Fredricks, anyway, for a proper look at it."

I started to protest that it wasn't necessary, but Maggie interjected, "That's a good idea. I just put a field dressing on it, Kay. Fredricks can stitch you up."

Frank walked back with me. "You're about to see a rare thing, Katherine," he told me. "Fredricks is walking on air now that he got that regen unit. So savor the sight. Who knows if we'll ever see it again."

I smiled, but wanly.

"What's wrong? What happened down there?"

"Nothing much," I said, studying my shoes.

He stopped walking and turned to face me. We were alone in

a stretch of hall. "Don't lie to me, Kay. What went down on Yukon Station that's got you and the captain so damned spooked?"

It was his mention of Maggie, and her nerves that had been so on edge since we escaped, that did it. Before I knew what was happening, I was blubbering like a fool, a torrent of tears pouring from my eyes. The story came out in broken bits and pieces, but it was enough for him to get the gist.

He held me as I sobbed. "You're okay now, Kay. But if I ever see one of Slater's crew, I swear, they're dead."

When I'd finished, we completed the journey to our makeshift medbay. It was in one of the cargo bays that still had power. The portable regen unit had been set up, and what could be carried from sickbay had been. Fredricks called, "Captain told me you'd be heading down, Kay. Take a –" He broke off at the sight of me. "Jesus. What happened?"

My face, I was sure, looked monstrous. My cheeks felt swollen, my eyes stung from shedding so many tears. "Nothing," I said.

"Are you in pain?"

"It's not that kind of pain, doc," Frank said shortly. "She's had a shit day."

"Oh." He glanced between us. "Okay. Well, umm, take a seat."

I did as I was bid.

Frank, meanwhile, said, "Kay, I'll wait outside. Give you some privacy with the doc." He smiled. "I'll see if I can get Dave to cook up something worth eating, too."

"Well," Fredricks said after he left, "tell me what happened."

"I got hit. With a bottle."

He fixed me with a quizzical look. "I know Kudarians are protective of their mates, but that was more than 'someone hit her' protectiveness. If I'm going to treat you, I need to know what I'm dealing with."

I felt my face flush. "We're not…mates."

"I'm your doctor, Katherine," he said with a sigh. "And I've been an adult for a long time. I know all about the birds and the bees. I promise you, nothing you say will shock me."

"But it's true," I protested. "We're not mates, or lovers – or boyfriend and girlfriend."

He frowned. "Alright, I lied. That does shock me." His frown deepened. "You're sure?"

"Very," I said, exasperated.

He shook his head. "Alright. Well, that's a first."

"What?"

"I was wrong." I frowned at him, and he shrugged. "Anyway, what happened to you back on Yukon Station?"

"I told you. I was attacked, and one of the guys hit me with a bottle."

"Attacked how?"

I felt irrationally embarrassed by the question and stammered out an answer. "Roughed up. Mostly. Hit. Dragged over a booth."

Fredricks' gaze was concerned now. "Tell me what happened, Kay. From the beginning."

I did, and he listened with a frown that only deepened as I went on. This time, I made it through the story without tears. I think I'd expended all of them on Frank.

"Well," he said when he spoke again, "always knew Slater was a coward. Never knew just how big a piece of shit he was though."

"Who is he, this Slater?"

"Used to be a privateer. He was busted breaking too many rules, so he lost his license. Now – officially – he's back to 'independent operator.'" He shook his head. "He's a raider, or so scuttlebutt has it. Hitting settlements, extorting protection money, stealing supplies: that kind of thing."

I nodded. I'd spent years crossing the universe for jobs. Pirates and privateers had been a concern now and then, but I had never realized just how many different shades of gray, how many different types of legal and illegal vultures there were in these skies. I'd never realized, either, that some of them weren't vultures at all.

"I'm just glad the captain was there," Fredricks was continuing.

"Me too."

"Slater's boys don't give up easily."

I remembered Biff – or had it been Wade? I never learned who of the two was whom – and how his head evaporated in front of my eyes before he stopped coming after me. "No. They don't."

Fredricks smiled kindly at me. "But, you're safe now, Kay. That's what counts. Let me take a look at that arm, and we'll get you all patched up."

Frank was waiting as he promised, and he smiled at me as I came out. "Well?" he prompted.

I was grateful for his presence. I didn't want to be alone. But the light in his eyes as I stepped out worried me too. I couldn't forget Maggie's words of earlier. I'd laughed them off at the time, but now I wondered if the joke had been on me all long. I remembered Fredricks' comment, too, about Kudarians and their mates.

I liked Frank. I liked him a lot. He'd been the first member of the crew to warm to me and had been a good friend to me. In another set of circumstances – if I'd never met Maggie Landon – I probably would have been falling for him now.

But I had met Maggie, and as much as I liked Frank, it wasn't *that* much. Now, his smile troubled me. I didn't want to hurt him. Maggie had been right when she said he was a good guy. He was; and the last thing I wanted was to make him think I felt more than I did.

I considered how our friendship might be seen through his eyes. I knew already how it had been perceived by Fredricks and Maggie. We'd given them the impression that we were a couple. Had I given him the impression, somewhere along the way, that he had a reason to expect we might be a couple?

If I had, it hadn't been intentional. But as he examined my arm, turning it in his great hands with a tenderness that his usual boisterous manner did not hint was possible, I felt a pang of worry.

I swallowed. "Frank?" I said.

He caught my gaze. "Yes, Kay?"

"I…" I took a breath, and then went for it. "You know the worst part of the whole damned ordeal?"

His brow creased, and he shook his head.

"Mags and I were on a date. Our first date."

"Oh." His expression fell, and it knocked the wind out of my lungs.

He does care for me.

But then he smiled. "I was wondering when that'd happen."

"You were?"

He shrugged. "I kind of guessed it was in the works."

"You did?" The declaration stunned me a little. Did everyone and their mother have an insight into my love life that I myself was lacking? "How?"

He smiled. There was a color of disappointment in the smile, but not surprise. "I don't know. The lovesick simpers between you two were the first giveaway."

I flushed, then laughed. "I guess that would do it."

He laughed too, and wrapped an arm over my shoulder and squeezed me. "Come on, Kay. Let's head to the mess hall. I called in to David. Told him you were recovering and needed to keep your strength up – so he needed to make something edible."

"Recovering? Jesus. He's going to have a fit when he sees what I'm 'recovering' from."

"Well, if that's what it takes to get good food around this place," Frank grinned, "I regret nothing. In fact, you're about to be the hero of the crew." We turned, and his arm slipped off me. "Come on."

CHAPTER TWENTY-THREE

I felt better after my conversation with Frank. There was no mistaking his disappointment, but he'd maintained the same jovial, attentive friendliness throughout our time together. Here, his perceptiveness seemed to have done him a good turn, in that he was less surprised by Maggie's interest in me than I was.

He'd been right about a good meal, too. David had thrown together a bucket of vegetables, chicken and gravy, which he then littered in biscuits. "Pot pie," he called it. It looked nothing like any pot pie I'd ever seen, but it tasted damned good all the same.

He had scowled at Frank. "I thought you said she'd been wounded?"

"She was," the Kudarian answered, tapping my arm a few inches above the bandage.

David's scowl deepened. "That's not the way you made it sound."

Frank shrugged. "Well," he said, "if you made decent food more often, we wouldn't be reduced to subterfuge, would we?"

"You know I just used my pre-cooked chicken for this? That was my emergency supply. Now I'm going to have to prep more."

"You *are* the ship's cook," he reminded him with a grin. "That seems to fall within the parameters of your job."

"Only a dumbass pisses off the man who cooks his food," David warned ominously.

Frank laughed. "Only a dumbass threatens the man who pilots his ship."

After we finished eating, the Kudarian said, "Well, I better get back to the bridge before the captain sends a squad to track me down."

I grinned. "Alright. And Frank?"

"Yeah?"

"Thanks. For – well, being here for me."

"Anytime, Kay. Anytime."

I sat for a minute longer in the empty mess hall after he'd gone, then sighed and got to my feet.

"Did you like it?" David asked as I passed.

"It was great. Thank you."

He nodded. "I'm glad you're okay, Katherine. We all are." Then, he shuffled back into the kitchen.

The comment left me unusually affected. I felt positively weepy, and I took a moment to compose myself in the hall before seeking out the rest of the crew.

But it wasn't the rest of the crew I was really seeking. It was Maggie.

She wasn't on the bridge. Kereli glanced up at me when I asked where she was. "She's working with Drake, last I heard." The Esselian flashed me a smile, and wan though it was, it might have been the first time I'd seen the expression on her face. "Somewhere down by medbay."

I thanked her and headed in the direction of medbay. Sure enough, Maggie was there. Half of her was, anyway. The rest seemed to have been stuck behind the wall paneling. "Mags?" I asked.

I saw her start, and then, grunting, she pulled herself free of the wall. Her hair was tousled, and she was smeared with soot. Somehow, through all of that, she managed to be insanely sexy. The greens of her eyes seemed brighter, the red of her hair fierier, under that grime.

"Kay." She was on her feet now. "How'd it go?"

"Oh, fine. He stitched me up and says I'll be good as new."

She put her hands on my shoulders, then, as soot smeared on me at her touch, retracted them as quickly. "Sorry."

I grinned. "Don't be, Mags." I stepped closer, lacing my fingers through hers. "How long do you think this is going to take?"

"All day," she said with a grimace. "If not longer."

"Oh." I tried not to sound too disappointed. I smiled. "Well, I'm reporting for duty, Captain. Put me to work."

She smiled too. "No, Kay. You need to give those stitches time to set. We got it covered."

"You sure?"

She squeezed my hand. "Quite sure. You rest, Katherine." She leaned in, kissing me tenderly. "If we get this done early enough, we'll have time before we reach Kraken's Drop."

"Time for what?" I murmured mischievously.

She grinned. "Well, we'll have to wait and see, won't we?

Now get out of here so I can concentrate on my work." She kissed me again. "And not you."

"Aye aye, Captain," I grinned.

My heart was a little lighter after that. Maggie's reception just now set my mind at ease regarding her distance of earlier, and dancing with the thoughts of what the new day held in store.

The current day, though, was far from over. On the contrary, it dragged and dragged on. The repairs went long. I offered to assist again, but was again turned away. The crew seemed to be of the impression that, after my ordeal on Yukon Station, the best course of action was to 'rest.'

But rest was far from my mind. On the contrary, those periods of solitude and silence that followed while the rest of the crew was occupied were painful to endure. My mind would return, unbidden, to *Shooters*. I'd remember with a shudder the feel of an uninvited hand. Blind terror would spring into my chest, welling around my heart, at a shadow or an unexpected sound.

It was a long wait. And still the work dragged on. I knew it had to be done, and I had no intention of being a burden to the crew. They were busy; Maggie was busy. I knew that.

As night rolled around and they were still hard at work, I turned in. But sleep didn't come. Every time my mind relaxed and my breathing slowed, those same images would return. I'd start back to consciousness, gasping and trembling, half expecting to see Biff or Wade leering at me from the shadows of my room.

After the fourth or fifth time of this, I got up and dressed. It was clear that I wasn't going to sleep anytime soon. So I wandered the halls of the ship for a while, coming finally to rest at the nook I'd discovered early on. I sat there for a time, watching the great expanse of empty space, dark and cold. There was something oddly comforting in that ambivalent nothingness.

I sat there a long while, thinking of nothing in particular, studying nothing in particular, until my mind was as empty as the void beyond the porthole.

"Kay?" I stirred. Maggie's voice seemed far away. "Kay?"

I blinked. I had, I realized, fallen asleep in that little alcove. Maggie was sitting beside now, shaking me gently.

"Mags," I said sleepily.

"What are you doing out here? Shouldn't you be in bed?"

"I couldn't sleep."

"You were asleep."

"I know…I mean, I couldn't sleep earlier, when I was trying to. I kept thinking…about earlier."

Her forehead creased. "Oh Kay."

I yawned, trying to force the sleepiness out of my eyes. I'd waited so long to see her, I didn't want anything to interfere. "What time is it? It's not morning already?"

"No. It's almost midnight."

"What are you still doing up?"

She shook her head. "Re-wiring. It's endless. Drake's pressed us all into service."

"I can help," I reminded her.

She put a hand on my shoulder. "You can tomorrow, if you

want; but you don't have to. Right now, though, we just wrapped up."

"Oh."

She rubbed my shoulder. "Come on, Kay. Let's get you to bed. And then me. I'm exhausted. And you're falling asleep in the window."

I nodded, and we got to our feet. I wrapped an arm around her as we walked, and leaned into her. "How'd you know where to look for me, Mags?" I wondered.

"I thought you'd be asleep already, actually," she said. "I go there to think sometimes."

"Me too."

She wrapped an arm around me now, rubbing her hand up and down my back. "I'm glad I found you, though."

"Me too."

We reached my quarters, and she brushed my hair back. "Get some sleep, beautiful. I'll see you tomorrow."

"Maggie," I said, "don't go."

"I'm tired, Kay. Drake's expecting me to be up at oh-five-hundred and-"

"I know. I don't mean that." I'd long since abandoned thoughts of resuming our amorous tryst any time soon. I knew the ship had to take precedence now that we were back onboard. "I just…I don't want to be alone, Mags. That's why I couldn't sleep earlier. I kept thinking…"

She nodded. "Of course, Kay. I…I hadn't thought of that."

She followed me inside, and I led her to the bed. Another time, and I would have been overwhelmed with the thought of Maggie at my side, in my bed. But I was too tired to be nervous. The day had, finally, hit me, and I wanted nothing more than to surrender to sleep.

"I need to shower. I'm disgusting. You don't want me in your bed like this."

"You're never disgusting," I told her. "But go ahead. I've got pajamas. Give me a second." I headed to my dresser and pulled out a freshly washed pair. "There you go."

"Thanks. I won't be long."

She headed to the bathroom, and I changed and slipped between the sheets. I yawned, listening to the water running in the room beyond. It was a comforting sound, like rain falling outside a window. I was half asleep by time her shower ended.

She came out a few minutes later, dressed in the pajamas I'd given her. We were about the same size, but she looked a lot better in them than I did. It was a cotton pants and button-down shirt set. They were functional and comfortable, but there was nothing sexy or sultry about them.

Until, that is, they were on her. I had to remind myself that I was tired and so was she, as Maggie slipped into bed beside me.

"Thanks for staying," I said.

"Of course." There was an edge to her voice I didn't expect. She was I realized nervous. There was a tension in her muscles, a quickness to her pulse as she rested against me.

I put my arm around her. "Don't worry, Mags," I said. "I don't snore."

She laughed a little, wrapping an arm around me, and seemed to relax. "Good night, Kay."

"Night Mags." And this time, safe in her embrace, I slept, and no memories of Biff or Wade or the Slater crew invaded my dreams.

CHAPTER TWENTY-FOUR

I woke to Maggie shifting quietly out of bed. "Mags?" I wondered.

"Shh, Kay," she whispered. "Sleep."

"What are you doing?"

"I have to go. Drake's expecting me, remember?"

"Hell. Is it five already?"

"Almost. And I have to get fresh clothes from my quarters."

I yawned, moving to rise. But she put a hand on my shoulders. "Sleep," she said. "You need sleep, Kay." I would have protested, except that she planted a kiss on my brow.

I smiled sleepily. "Night, Maggie."

"Night, Katherine."

And I did sleep, waking some hours later. The crew was back at work replacing the burned-out conduit and wiring. This time, I insisted that I was more than ready to do my share, and Drake let me join.

It was painstaking, sweaty work, squeezing into tight places and fighting uncooperative gear all the way. The *Black Flag* wasn't an ancient ship, but she wasn't the newest model either. Most of the wiring seemed as if it hadn't been disturbed since the ship was constructed – and it didn't care to be disturbed now.

Still, it passed the time.

We finished about an hour before we reached Kraken's Drop. There were still a few rooms without power, but all the halls and primary areas had been restored.

I headed back to my room for a shower. I was twice as grimy as Maggie had been the night before, and I'd worked for about the same time.

I'd just gotten out of the shower and dressed when my doorbell rang. I was still towel drying my hair, but I glanced up. "Come in."

It was Maggie. "Hey," she said. "I'm heading up to the bridge. We're approaching Kraken's Drop. You should see this. It's gorgeous."

She stretched out a hand for mine, and I didn't need a second urging. "Listen," she said, "I know, as first dates go, that one pretty much topped the charts of hell. But would you give me a second chance, Kay?"

"You know I will," I said.

Her grin lost some of its nervous edge. "Good. Then – there's a place on Kraken's Drop. A nice place, this time: *Dark Water.*"

I nudged her gently. "Don't beat yourself up, Mags. That wasn't your fault."

She stopped and turned to face me. "I should have been smarter, Kay. I should have."

I squeezed her hand. I understood, now, her moments of

distance. She blamed herself. "No one can predict everything. Not even you, Maggie Landon. Sometimes, life just smacks you. And you've got to roll with the punches. Remember?"

She smiled as I quoted back her words to me. "You shouldn't get your advice from idiots, Kay."

"Don't say things like that, Mags."

She held my gaze for a minute, and then nodded. "Alright. Roll with the punches."

"Good."

"But maybe after we scope out my contact, I can take you to *Dark Water* for dinner?"

"How nice did you say it was?"

"Semi-formal."

"I don't have anything like that, Mags. All I have with me was what I took to the job site on Deltaseal."

She shrugged. "Me either. But the markets here are huge. We could do some personal shopping first."

I hesitated. The last planet I'd been to that catered to smugglers was Yukon Station, and that was an experience I was not keen to repeat. "Is it…safe?"

"The Sciline do not allow the Conglomerate on their shores."

"I didn't mean Henderson's people. Just…they get a lot of pirates and raiders here, right?"

A light of understanding lit her eyes. "Oh, it's nothing like Yukon, Kay. There's a lot that happens here that the Union wouldn't approve of, but it's commerce. Rules are broken, transactions happen off the records, taxes aren't paid: but no one gets hurt."

I nodded. "Okay."

She pulled me close. "Nobody's going to hurt you, babe."

I squeezed her hand. "Alright," I said. "Then it's a date."

Frank glanced up as we entered. Maggie had slipped her hand out of mine and adopted the familiar all-business attitude, but he wasn't fooled. He flashed me a grin, and I flushed.

"Status, Frank?"

"Waiting on clearance from air control to approach."

She nodded, then turned back to me. I sidled up beside her, leaning on her seat back. "Beautiful, isn't it?"

It was. Kraken's Drop was a great blue globe, dotted here and there with little patches of greenery. Broad swaths of cottony cloud veiled sections of this orb, but what was visible was stunning. "Wow."

"She's a looker, isn't she?" Drake asked. I realized he was talking to me.

"Yes. Never seen anything like it before."

"You ever meet a Sciline?"

I shook my head. "No."

"Well, they're nature's way of balancing things. Fill the most beautiful planet in creation with the ugliest devils you'll ever see."

A few of the bridge staff laughed. "They do take some getting used to," Maggie agreed. "Although in fairness, they probably think we're repulsive too."

"That's just because they can't see clearly through those bug-ugly fish eyes."

I laughed too. "That's harsh, Drake."

"You'll never look at seafood again the same way," Frank offered. Half the room groaned, and the other half laughed. I was among the former. He smirked to himself, seemingly pleased with both sets of reactions.

"They do *have* great seafood," Maggie said. "The biodiversity on this planet is incredible – and most of it is underwater."

"So all their food is basically seafood," Frank said. "Which is definitely cheating."

She shook her head. "How much coffee have you had today, Frank?"

"Not enough, ma'am."

"You sure about that?"

"I'm just excited about shore leave, Captain."

"Especially after getting that big ass of yours stuck in the walls," Drake snorted.

Maggie and I exchanged glances – this was a story I had not heard before, and I gathered, neither had she – and the Kudarian grimaced. "If they'd designed ships for real men," he declared, "and not children and humans, it wouldn't be a problem."

This time, he got only groans. "Maybe," Drake needled, "if you laid off the carbs, it would be less of a problem."

He shook his head and sighed. "Some men are just bigger,

Sage. You're going to have to come to terms with that. Insecurity's an ugly thing."

"Like your face."

I laughed at about the same time Maggie did. "Boys, boys, wait until we land – so you can take it off ship."

To judge by the smugness of their expressions, both men seemed pleased with the outcome of the conversation, as if they'd got the better of it. Frank was smiling to himself, and Drake was smirking into his console. Maggie, meanwhile, caught my eye, and we shook our heads at one another.

"Ah," the Kudarian said in a moment. "Just got the go-ahead. We're cleared to land."

"Thank God," Maggie murmured, low enough for my ears only. "Before they whipped out the measuring tapes."

CHAPTER TWENTY-FIVE

The docking ports on Kraken's Drop were built off the islands dotting the planet. Some were natural, but most were artificially constructed. We touched down on a massive floating base. There were a smattering of buildings on the platform, but it was largely divided into ports for space craft. At the edges, there were a few water vessels docked as well.

"Fishing ships," Maggie said, catching the direction of my eyes. "The pleasure boats usually hang out on the natural islands. You need a lot of credits to get a yachting license on Kraken's. And if you've got that kind of money, you can usually afford to dock there."

"Doesn't matter where you go," I laughed. "It's always the same."

"Yup."

We'd agreed to spend two days on planet, giving everyone a chance to stretch their legs, and Drake an opportunity to finish his repairs. "Unmitigated, straight up bullshit," is what he called it. "You know the last time I've been here?"

"You've got leave too," Maggie sighed. "Just make sure you assign shifts before you go."

"Still bullshit. It means extra work for me, and less shore leave."

"That's what you get for being indispensable," she told him with a grin. "But how does time and a half sound?"

That gave him pause. "Double sounds better."

"Fine. But no more bellyaching."

"You got yourself a deal, Captain," he smirked.

Right now, the first party of leave goers was on their way down. That included me, the doctor, Maggie, Frank and Ginny, whose concussion was not going to stop her from having a good time. "Make sure it's not too good a time," Fredricks had warned her dryly. "You mix alcohol with what you're on, and you don't have to worry about long term damage. Because you don't have long term."

We were in a kind of elevator – a glass tube that met us at the surface. Once we'd stepped inside, the doors had sealed and we'd begun our descent. It was a slow journey down. "These chambers are pressured," Maggie said, "but some species require longer to adjust as we get deeper. So it's a slow ride."

I didn't mind for two reasons. The first was, it was a beautiful journey. We were suspended in a glass tube in the waters of an endless ocean. Creatures and ships passed by in an array of colors and shapes and sizes. Fishlike forms and mammalian figures flitted past. Now and again, a deep-sea aquatic bird would dart down in pursuit of something.

The other reason was that, as soon as we'd stepped off the ship, Maggie's posture and attitude had relaxed. We were standing together near the rear of the carriage, and she slipped an arm around my back and waist. It was done softly, as if she didn't want to draw attention to us. But it sent jolts of electricity through my body all the same, and I leaned into her embrace, in the same inconspicuous way.

We watched the light from the surface grow dimmer and

further away together. We watched the depths expand and deepen. When I heard her sigh, a quiet, contented sigh, I rested my head against her shoulder. We might have been the only two people on the planet, as wrapped up in the moment as I was with her.

I heard Frank cracking jokes behind us, and Ginny and Fredricks groaning at them. I heard David threaten to poison him next mealtime if he didn't shut his mouth. But their banter seemed a thousand lightyears away from me and Maggie.

But, like the saying goes, all good things come to an end, and eventually we reached our destination. A glowing dome filled the blackness below us, growing larger and larger as we neared.

"There it is," Maggie said. "Alien's Landing." I smiled at the use of the word alien to describe humans. From the perspective of the Sciline, of course, that's what we were. And this was their world. They did not need domed cities to keep out the water. They had evolved with lungs that could filter oxygen from water or air, and so such structures were superfluous. Their cities traditionally were built underwater.

But to the aliens around them – humans and Kudarians like us, and most of the rest of the known races – that was not possible. So Alien's Landing was, as strange as it sounded to my human ears, aptly named.

Our carriage locked into place, and we stepped into a well-lit visitor's center. It was designed similarly to one of the larger space stations, except, of course, that it was under water as opposed to in the void. But the layout was instantly recognizable. Information kiosks and maps of the structure were arrayed to greet visitors.

Once newcomers had gotten their bearings, long hall, with lanes for motorized carts, stretched out. It was practically a city. "Alright," Maggie said. "Let's get to the hotel first and check in. I already reserved the rooms, so all we need to do is grab our keys and leave anything we don't want to take with us."

"Then I'm hitting the all-you-can-eat sushi bar," Frank decided.

"You're going to trust fish you get at an all-you-can-eat place?" David scoffed. "Are you suicidal?"

"I eat your cooking, don't I?"

The cook shook his head. "You deserve what you get."

"Forget him," Fredricks declared. "It's the sushi bar owners I'm worried about. He'll put them out of business."

"I know what I'm doing," Ginny said. "I'm checking out the shops."

The three men rolled their eyes, and the doctor ventured, "I can't think of anything less appealing."

"Oh yeah? What are you going to do, Mr. Exciting?"

"I'm going to the salt water spa," he said. "And getting a good massage and then a long soak in one of the Scilinian brine baths."

"That actually does sound nice," Ginny conceded.

"You should try it. You'll be rejuvenated for a year."

"Oh God," Frank groaned. "I'd rather have my tonsils removed. Without anesthesia."

"It can be arranged," Fredricks offered.

David laughed. "What about you, Captain? And you Kay?"

"Shopping," I said.

"Women," Frank sighed.

Maggie said, "Meeting my contact, but then I've got some stuff to pick up too. And I got a table at *Dark Water*."

"Ohh, nice," Ginny nodded. "Those reservations are hard to come by."

She grinned. "Yeah. Lucky for me, the maître d' is kind of an acquaintance."

"You served together, right?" Frank nodded.

"With his brother."

"Ah."

Our hotel was not far from the landing site. Here was where I got my first good look at one of the Sciline. The hotelier who checked us in was a young Scilinian woman, obliging and welcoming.

She spoke good English, but in tones that sounded – for lack of a better word – aquatic. If a river running over stones could speak, it would be the nearest thing I could imagine to Scilinian speech.

Her appearance was every bit as startling as the crew had led me to believe it might be. She was tall and humanoid in form, with webbed appendages that seemed a cross between fins and arms. The eyes Drake had alluded to were not quite as fishlike as I'd imagined, but rather than sitting in sockets like a human's, they seemed to bulge from her face. She wore no clothes, for she had no need of them: her skin was a layer of fine scales, from the tip of her hairless head to her webbed feet.

In all my travels, I had yet to meet a humanoid who looked so distinctly inhuman. Her manners, though, were as suave as the best I'd witnessed in my own species, and I made an effort not to stare. She was strange to me, but, as Maggie had said, I – with my smooth skin and comparatively tiny eyes, my finless form and vulnerable skin – was probably a monstrosity in her eyes.

And if she'd had the good taste to hide any misgivings she might have at the sight of us, well, I could manage my own surprise.

CHAPTER TWENTY-SIX

We'd split up after getting our keys. Maggie headed to her rendezvous, and I headed to the marketplace. We'd agreed to meet in a half hour to go dress shopping, but I had the idea of picking up a few articles of makeup first. I didn't usually wear it. I'd taken none with me to Deltaseal, so I hadn't worn any in eons.

But listening to the crew discuss *Dark Water*, I had the sense that Maggie had gone out of her way to make this a night to remember. I didn't want to put in anything less than my best. I wanted to look my best for her.

It was surprising to me to see just how many of the shops here catered to humans. I found a store that carried what I needed, at more than I'd usually have paid. Still, I snagged a tube of mascara, some blush and lip color, and foundation. I picked up a bottle of perfume, too: something light and, fittingly, reminiscent of the ocean.

By time I meandered over to our meeting point, the half hour was almost up. A few minutes later, Maggie appeared. She spotted me before I spotted her, and she waved a greeting. "You ready?" she asked.

"Yeah. You get the codes?"

She nodded. "Oh yeah." Then she wrapped an arm around me and said, "Come on. There's some good shops just down this way."

"Why's there so much for us? People, I mean? Don't they have other visitors too?"

"Yeah, but we're at the human end of Alien's Landing. There's about twelve other sectors, geared toward visitors from other planets."

"Oh." That made a lot more sense. "I see. Still, they must get a lot of human visitors."

"Oh yeah. Between the Union's push to bring the Sciline government more 'into the fold' – which is politician speech for getting them to crack down on the illegal trade – and, well, the illegal traders, there's probably more aliens on their planet at any given time than Scilinians."

We reached the shop Mags had in mind. It was a swanky, two story space, with a wide range of women's fashions adorning window-bound mannequins. There was everything from beach wear to formal.

"So how formal is semi-formal here?" I asked. Depending on the planet, that could range from multiple mandatory layers of outerwear to "please keep your pants on while dining." Like everything else, formality was open to a wide range of interpretations.

She shrugged. "Jackets for men, dresses for women."

"What kind of dresses? Are we talking evening gowns? Cocktail dresses?"

Maggie grinned at me. "They serve food to dozens of races, Kay, who all have their own ideas about what constitutes semi-formal. I promise you, they're not going to care."

"Well, what are you going to get?"

"A dress."

I sighed. "Mags, that's not helpful."

"You're overthinking it."

I frowned at her, until I caught the twinkle in her eyes. Then, I laughed. "Maybe a little."

"A lot." She wrapped an arm around me. "What kind of dress do you want?"

I considered. "Nothing too long. I don't want to trip."

She laughed. "Okay."

"Laugh all you want, but I am uniquely talented, Maggie Landon. I'm able to trip over my own feet on a flat surface. When you've got gifts like that, you don't tempt fate."

I settled on a shimmering, ocean blue number. It hugged my form in all the right places, but didn't try too hard, either. With a hint of cleavage and a hem that reached the knees, it was just sexy enough to give me the boost of confidence I'd need to be seen on Maggie's arm.

She'd already picked a classic black, and while I searched for a pair of heels to match the dress, she vanished. I found what I was looking for – elegant sandals with a heel that, for me, was daring at three inches.

Then I went in search of her. She was cashing out, and she flashed me an impish smile as I approached.

"What's that?" I gestured to a second bag, beside her dress.

She opened it so I could peer inside, but only long enough to get a glimpse of a crimson lace bra. "That's for later."

Holy shit. I felt my face flush, and she laughed.

"Come on. You need to check out – we're going to have to get back and change, or we'll be late."

The truth was, I could have skipped dinner altogether. I wouldn't have argued earlier, but now, the thought of Maggie and that bag dancing in my mind, it took an effort to muster enthusiasm to go out at all.

Still, she was excited about it, so I tried to remember that I was, too. "We'd have been back already, if not for your indecision, Magdalene," I teased her.

She snorted. "I was starting to think we'd spend our whole shore leave here, with how long it was taking you."

"And miss *Dark Water*? I don't think so."

I put on my makeup and the dress. It struck me now – too late – that I should have looked for earrings or a necklace to pair with the ensemble. And no sooner than had I slipped them on did I reconsider the wisdom of those heels. *I'm going to trip and land on my face*, I thought with a sigh.

Still, Maggie was waiting, and there was nothing for it but to wear what I'd got; so I left my room. She was waiting outside my door, and she whistled as I stepped out. "Woah."

I flushed with pleasure, until I saw her. I'd seen her dress on the rack, but then it had just been a piece of fabric. I could scarcely believe this was the same thing. Now that it was on her, it seemed to have taken on a life of its own, becoming a long, elegant, shimmering silhouette of her figure. She'd pinned her hair up in a voluminous bun, and added, as near as I could tell, just a little color to her lips and cheeks. She was gorgeous. She was stunning. And me?

I was a plain jane going to the ball with Cinderella.

How the hell did that happen? I didn't know. Hell, I didn't even care. The fact was, for whatever wonderful, inexplicable reason, she'd asked me and I was going with her. "Holy shit, Mags," I said. It was far from eloquent, but it more or less summed up my reaction.

Her cheeks grew a little pinker. "Come on," she said. "I hired a cab. He's waiting."

CHAPTER TWENTY-SEVEN

Maggie had been right: my dress fit squarely into the blend of ensembles around us. I'd thrown a nervous glance around as soon as we'd entered. People were wearing everything from gorgeous, full length evening gowns like hers to glamorous, thigh high dresses. They were all elegant, and no one paid anyone a second look. The only thing approaching conformity was the attire of the gentlemen, and even this varied some from species to species and man to man. My nerves settled at the sight.

We were now two courses and a glass of wine into dinner. I was pacing myself. I didn't as a rule drink much, and I didn't want alcohol to dull any of my senses tonight.

The food was good – every bit as good as Maggie had said. But the truth was, it was largely wasted on me. My eyes and attention were focused on her. Anything else, no matter how good, was just extraneous to that.

"Have you thought any more about what you'll do, Kay? When we're done with this run?"

"I don't know," I said. "It might depend."

"On what?"

"On what you're doing."

She smiled. "You know, the *Black Flag* could always use

another hand."

"Could it? I thought you prided yourself on your lean crew?" I teased.

"I've been rethinking my stance."

I trailed my fingers across the back of her hand. "That sounds good to me, Mags."

"Good."

It was now that a youngish man in a waitstaff jacket approached our table. "Maggie?"

She glanced up, and then beamed. "Kev." She was on her feet the next instant, wrapping him in a hug. "I was wondering where you were."

"My shift just started," he said.

She turned to me. "Kay, this is Kev – Kevin Lang. I served with his brother Richard." Then, she turned back to him. "Kev, this is Kay Ellis, my – my girlfriend."

She'd hesitated to say the word, glancing back at me as if to make certain she wasn't overstepping. Far from eliciting any negative reaction on my part, though, my heart soared at the word. I smiled at her and offered him a hand. "Pleasure to meet you, Kevin."

"Likewise, Kay. Any friend of Maggie's is a friend of mine."

"How are you doing these days, Kev? How's the missus?"

He grinned. "Six months pregnant, so it varies from minute to minute. But we're hanging in. Surviving on chocolate and – believe it or not – pickles."

Maggie laughed. "Another one? Jesus. Poor Stacie. She was

pregnant last time I saw you guys too."

"That was two years ago," he laughed.

"Fair enough. So this'll be your second, right?"

"That's right."

"Congrats."

"Thanks. Oh, and I told Richard you were heading here. He said to say 'hi.'"

"How's he hanging in?" she asked, and this time her tone was less jovial.

Kevin's expression, too, lost some of the beaming qualities it'd had a moment ago. "You know: it's tough. But he'll make it. He's a fighter."

Maggie's jaw tightened, and she nodded. "That he is."

For a moment, they were silent. I had no idea what they were talking about, beyond the general impression that some calamity had befallen this man I didn't know. But what, I couldn't guess. So I was quiet too.

"Tell him I said 'hi' too," she said.

"I will."

"And tell him I'm sorry about Bert."

"I will."

"Thanks." She smiled. "I know I'm usually galaxies away, but if he ever needs anything, I'll do what I can."

Kevin smiled. "Thanks Mags. That'll mean a lot to him." Then, he glanced at me. "Sorry, Kay. Didn't mean to interrupt your date."

"No," I protested, "it's fine."

"I need to get back to work anyway, before I hear it from the old fish in back. But it was great seeing you again Mags. And great meeting you, Kay."

"Thanks, Kevin. Good to meet you too."

"Hey, I'm here for two days. Maybe I can take you and Stacie out? We can catch up?"

"Sounds good – but it'll be our treat. No, I insist."

And with that, he took his leave.

"Who is Bert?" I asked, once he'd gone.

"Richard's husband."

"Ah. What happened to him?"

"He died."

Despite the brevity of her answer, her tone conveyed a depth of emotion. "Did you know him?" I asked gently. "Were you friends?"

"Not well. We got along, but he and Dick met after I got out of the service. But…" She shook her head. "I never saw Richard so crazy about a person. Or so happy."

"Ah." I nodded. "How'd he die?"

"Belarian flu. He woke up with a slight fever, and twenty-four hours later…" She spread her hands. "He was dead."

"God," I said. "That's awful."

"Yeah. To be honest, I don't know what Dick's going to do." She glanced up at me. "It was so unexpected. He's been in shock, but…" She reached for her glass of wine, toying with the stem. "The truth is, Kay, my heart has stopped every time I get a communique from one of our old squad since. I keep thinking, what if…" She broke off, draining her wine glass.

"You think he'd hurt himself?" I asked.

"I think the only reason he hasn't yet is because he feels he'd be letting Bert down. And I don't know what I can do to help. I don't know if there's anything anyone can do to help."

I took her hand. "Oh Mags. Maybe you should visit him."

She shook her head. "I did. Right after. He didn't want to see people."

"How long ago was that?"

"About five months."

"Five months is a long time."

"Not when you're talking about…well, this kind of thing, Kay."

"Still," I said. "It wouldn't hurt to try, would it? Let him know he's got a friend thinking about him?"

She considered. "Maybe not."

We sat there for a moment, her hand in mine on the table, a pensive look on her face. Then, she sighed. "Sorry, babe. I don't mean to be such a downer."

I squeezed her hand. "You're not."

"I'm sitting in one of the best restaurants on the planet, with the most beautiful woman on the planet holding my hand." She smiled at me. "What the hell do I have to be moping about?"

She picked up the thread of a previous topic that we'd somehow dropped to chase some tangent earlier in the night. It was done at first with an effort but grew more natural as she kept at it. She was telling me how she'd acquired the *Black Flag*. "So, obviously, that didn't work out. The thing was a piece of crap. I was just about ready to hang it up when I see a posting for a freighter. The price seemed too good. I figured it was another hunk of scrap."

From the periphery of my view, I saw a figure approaching our table. It was Kevin again, and he wasn't coming empty-handed. "Hey, not to interrupt. Just wanted to give you this." He smiled. "West Corthian Red. On the house."

She grinned. "You know me well, Kev."

He nodded, dispensing a glass for each of us.

"Thanks," I said.

"You bet." Then, to Maggie, he added, "Oh, and Mags? I heard about Irene. I wanted to say – I'm really sorry."

Her face fell, but she said, "Thanks, Kev."

He nodded. "Of course. Well, I should go."

She was silent after he left, but her eyes spoke volumes. I knew, instinctively, that Irene had been someone dear to her; had been, or was. The fact was – as I was quickly learning – for all I felt *for* Maggie, I didn't know much *about* her. I knew enough to have a picture of her character. I was pretty confident in it. But beyond that?

I didn't know her story. I knew very little about her past or her family, and next to nothing about her friends and lovers.

"Who is Irene?" I asked.

She glanced up at my voice. "Irene?"

I nodded.

"She is – was – my wife."

CHAPTER TWENTY-EIGHT

"Your wife?" She could have, as the saying goes, knocked me over with a feather at that. We hadn't got to the point of sharing past mistakes, but I'd guessed, of course, that she'd had serious girlfriends before me. But a wife? That seemed like something she could have told me. "You were married?"

"For about two months."

"Oh."

She shook her head. "I was in love, she was…not as in love as she thought." She smiled. "Honeymoon to divorce court inside three months: that's got to be a record, right?"

That, I guess, explained why she didn't have any pictures around, and had never mentioned her. "Is that what he was talking about? The divorce?"

"Oh, no. That happened a long time ago. Before I got the *Black Flag*."

"Then what?"

Maggie's brow creased, and she lifted the wine to her lips. After a sip, she said, "Her ship got hit, about a year and a half ago. By pirates." She glanced up at me, and added, "Real pirates, I mean. Not privateers."

"Oh Maggie," I said. "I'm so sorry." I remembered, now, all the times I'd called her a pirate, and how adamant she'd been that she was no such thing. My words must have been salt to her wounds.

She shrugged. "It's the life, Kay. It's the risk we all take." She took another long sip of her drink. "It happens to us all, sooner or later."

"Oh Mags," I said, stretching out my hand to take hers again. I might not know her history, but I knew her well enough to tell when she was lying. She was lying when she pretended it didn't bother her. I'd seen it in her face the moment the name *Irene* had been dropped.

She forced a smile and sat up straight, pulling her hand out of mine to return to her fork. "Well, we shouldn't let this get cold."

For a space, we ate in silence. "You were telling me about the *Black Flag*," I said after a while. "How you got it."

"Oh, yes." She finished the story, but briefly and without much interest. Now and again, she'd comment on the food or the drink. "Nothing like the Corthian Reds."

"Now that's a texture."

"What do you think of that, eh, Kay?"

But she'd lost her spark. She was going through the motions, but her mind was elsewhere – far, far away from me.

When dinner wrapped up, she paid absently, and we stepped onto the station street. "Mags," I said, "are you okay?"

"Huh? Oh, yes."

I put an arm around her, and she stiffened. "You sure?"

She nodded. "Kay, I was thinking, I don't want to head back

just yet."

I couldn't say I was surprised by the statement. Still, it took the wind out of my sails a bit. "Okay."

"I want to get a drink first. I think I need something stronger than wine."

I nodded. "Alright."

"There's a club, not far from here. We could stop for a sunrise or two before heading back."

We did. It was a nice enough place, with a large dance floor, a king-sized bar, and plenty of tables. Even so, we still had trouble finding a table. Maggie ordered Keldian sunrises for both of us, and stared absently at the dance floor.

"You want to dance?" I asked.

She shook her head. "No."

I sighed, taking a sip of my drink. "Dammit it, Mags. Aren't you at least going to tell me about her?"

She blinked. "What? Who?"

"Irene." Ever since the mention of her ex-wife, Maggie had been distant. It didn't take much to figure out where her thoughts were now.

"Irene?" She laughed hollowly, glancing down at her glass. "She's dead. What's there to tell?"

"I don't know, Mags. Do you still love her?"

Her eyes darted up to mine. "What?"

I felt my heart sink. "Oh. You do."

She shook her head. “No, Kay. It’s not that.” She took a long drink. “I did love her. For a long time. I don’t anymore. Haven’t for a while. It’s not even Irene; not directly, anyway.”

“Then what is it, Maggie? And don’t tell me it’s nothing, because I know that’s bullshit.”

She held my gaze and then smiled again, a bittersweet kind of smile. “I was just thinking of the life, Kay. You know?”

“I don’t,” I said. “Tell me.”

“Irene was one of the toughest people I know. Damned fine captain, good ship, good crew under her command. Never thought I’d get the call that she was dead.” She shook her head. “But I did. I was still listed as her next of kin, from back when we were married.”

“That must have been awful.”

There was a mist forming in her eyes, but she blinked it back aggressively. “It’s the life, Kay. There are no guarantees.”

“That doesn’t mean it doesn’t suck when something like that happens.”

She reached across the table, brushing my cheek with her fingers. “Oh Kay.”

“Maggie,” I said, turning my lips to her hand.

She leaned over now, pulling my face to hers and kissing me with a fire that made me glad we were in the back, and the room was as dark as it was. Not that I minded, of course. I kissed her back, tasting the Keldian sunrise on her lips, savoring the urgency in her hands as they drew me to her, wishing not for the first time that we were back in our rooms.

She sat back a moment later, and drained her sunrise. She

flagged a waiter. "Another Keldian sunrise. How about you, you need anything?"

I shook my head. I'd barely touched mine so far.

"Very good," the waiter said, "Coming right up."

"You sure you don't want to dance?" I wondered.

She smiled but said nothing, turning to watch the crowd. I watched her. She was beautiful, so beautiful; and sad.

Her drink came, and she drained it in two mouthfuls. "Careful, Mags," I cautioned. "You're going to be sick."

She turned to me suddenly. "This was a mistake, Kay."

I blinked. "What was?"

"Tonight. Me and you. I'm sorry."

"Maggie…what are you saying?" I was stunned.

"This life, Kay, it's not your life. It's dangerous, it's deadly. It almost got you once already." She shook her head. "And I'm done burying people. I promised myself that."

"That…that was a fluke, Mags."

She stood. "I'm sorry, Kay. But – once this mission's over – I think it'd be best for both of us if we went our separate ways."

CHAPTER TWENTY-NINE

Maggie had paid our tab and called me a cab. "I'm not heading back anytime soon," she told me. She disappeared into the crowded bar as I sat, stunned, at our table.

I drained my Keldian sunrise and then studied the glass. My mind was a whirl of competing emotions. I was angry and humiliated. But mostly, I was hurt and shocked.

The waiter stopped by again. "Is your friend gone?"

"Apparently so."

"Ah. Would you like anything else?"

"Another sunrise. Double shot." The cab driver would have to find his fare elsewhere. I was way too sober to deal with how quickly my life had just crashed and burned.

"Coming right up."

I drank my way through the sunrise, and then another. Now and again, I'd catch sight of Maggie. She was mingling with the other clubgoers, laughing and drinking as if she hadn't a care in the world.

As if she hadn't just dumped me half an hour ago.

By time I'd finished my fourth sunrise, she was on the dance floor, wrapping herself around a pretty blonde. Kissing her with the same energy she'd kissed me.

I thought I was going to be sick. I felt it prudent to self-medicate with another double shot Keldian.

I called a cab soon after. I had put enough liquor in me to quiet most of my thoughts. My mind was more compliant than my body, though. It would not be so easily quieted.

I'd had been craving Maggie since she'd first held my hand, since she'd first kissed me on the shuttle. It didn't matter that she'd dumped me. I still yearned to be touched, to be loved.

It had occurred to me, my mind slowly succumbing to the drinks, that Frank would be back by now. Even his appetite for food would be sated by now.

He'd given up on it since I was dating Maggie, but I had, I knew, awoken a different kind of appetite in him. I wondered if it was too late to rekindle it.

Consequently, when I reached the hotel, I set my steps for his room, not mine, and knocked.

Frank opened the door, and his eyes widened to see me. "Kay? What are you doing here?"

"Can I come in?"

"Uh…sure." He stood aside to let me enter.

I waited only until he'd turned, and then pressed into his arms. He'd been surprised to see me before, but this stunned him. "Kay, what are you doing?"

I wrapped my arms around his neck, whispering, "What does it look like?" I stood on tiptoes, pressing my body into his. I could feel him tense with desire, and I smiled. "Kiss me, Frank."

"Kiss you?" He frowned. "What about Maggie?"

"What about Maggie?" I took one of my hands from his neck to run it down his torso. He felt, under the fabric, every bit as good as I'd imagined he would. I wanted to know how he felt without that barrier between us. I wanted him to want me to explore without that barrier.

"Kay," he repeated, and his tone was low, "what are you doing?"

"That depends." I pressed harder into him. "What do you want me to do?"

He groaned. "God, Kay, don't do this."

"Why?" I pulled his arms to me, and he didn't protest. I felt his fingers press into my back, and he leaned toward me.

I squeezed my arms around him. His lips moved for me, bypassing my mouth and heading for my neck. He started below my ear, kissing lower as he went. "Oh Frank."

He reached the nape of my neck, and I gasped as he traced the tips of his teeth over my skin. I wanted him almost as much as I'd wanted Maggie the day before; almost as much as I'd wanted her tonight. Only he was here, and she was…wherever she was, with whoever she was with.

"Take me, Frank."

He brought his lips back to my ear, kissing me as he went. And when he spoke, I shivered at the feel of his breath against me. "You know I can't do that, Kay."

"What?"

"You're drunk."

"I'm not."

He nuzzled against me. "You are. And however much I want you, I can't have you."

"Frank," I begged. "Please. I need you."

He kissed me once again, this time on the cheek, and then he pulled away and held me at arm's length. "Then tell me when you're sober, and I'm yours." He smiled and shook his head. "But we both know that's not true, Kay. It's not me you want. It's Maggie."

"She doesn't want me," I said, and the words stung to hear out loud.

He seemed confused. "Doesn't want you? Kay, she's nuts about you."

I shook my head. "She's not, Frank."

"Did you guys fight?"

"No. I – I don't know what happened. One minute we were fine – great – and the next…"

I felt suddenly less amorous than a moment ago. I felt more like crying than loving. It didn't help that my head was swimming.

"I need to sit down, Frank."

"Of course." He guided me to the sofa, glancing me over. "How much did you have to drink?"

I shrugged. "Just a Keldian sunrise." Then, I giggled at the skeptical rising of his eyebrows. "Or five."

Frank whistled. "I'm surprised you can stand."

"Me too," I acknowledged. "Especially in these heels." Then,

I smiled at him. "You're a hell of a friend, Frank. You know that?" My emotions were traveling the spectrum at breakneck speed.

He rolled his eyes. "Drunk compliments are almost as bad as drunk come-ons, Kay. I trust neither."

"I mean it."

He shook his head, but he was smiling. "You need to get to bed."

I grinned at him. "Alright."

"Your *own* bed," he said.

"Oh." I snuggled closer to him. "You sure?"

"Come on. Let's get you to your room."

It struck me that I was two-for-two with strikeouts – in two days, no less. *God, I'm pathetic.* I laughed at that, at myself and what a loser I was, then stood.

My head swam. Then, the entire room started to swim around me. If not for Frank's arm, I would have ended my already spectacular showing by faceplanting on the floor.

As it was, though, he caught me. "Steady, steady Kay."

I blinked. I wasn't sure I was going to make it to my room. "I think…I think…"

I didn't finish the sentence. The world went black, and when I next awoke, I was alone in an unfamiliar bed in an unfamiliar room.

I glanced with aching eyes around the room. I'd read somewhere that medieval humans believed migraines were the work of tiny devils, hammering away on the inside of a victim's skull.

Which was absurd, of course. That's how hangovers were made, not migraines. At least, that's how it felt at the moment.

Still, I was disoriented enough by finding myself in strange surroundings to push through the pain. *Where the hell am I*? It was a bland bedroom, one of the generic ones from the hotel. But none of my stuff was there – so I was clearly not in my own room.

I pushed out of the bed, and saw with a measure of relief that I was fully clothed. I was wearing the same dress I'd put on the night before. It was rumpled and wrinkled from being slept in – but on. That was a good sign. *Right*?

I was barefoot, but, glancing around the room, I saw my heels at the foot of the bed.

What the hell happened? The last thing I could remember was being turned out of Frank's rooms.

Good God. What a fool I'd made of myself. But, grabbing for my shoes, I decided I'd worry about that later. For the time being, I was more concerned with what I'd done after I left his room.

I stumbled out of the bedroom into the living room beyond, and froze. "Frank?"

The Kudarian's back was to me, but he turned at my voice. "Kay. You survived your Keldian sunrises." He grinned at the sight of me. "But just barely, I think."

"Frank, am I in your rooms?"

He nodded.

I gulped. Clearly, something had happened in the interval between when my memory cut out and now, because the last thing I could recall was him walking me out. "What happened?"

"You passed out. And I couldn't find the card to your room, and I figured I'd better not be seen carrying an unconscious woman through the hotel anyway…so I tucked you in and slept on the couch."

"So we didn't…?"

"Of course not. You were drunk."

"Thanks, Frank."

He pulled a face at me now. "You know, Kay, I didn't mind the idea of being your consolation prize. I mean, I'm no Maggie, but I think I could take your mind off her for a little while anyway." He grinned at me. "But thanking me because I didn't rape you? A guy could get hurt feelings really fast."

He was teasing, but I felt my face flush. "I'm sorry, Frank. For last night. For being such an idiot."

"It's okay."

"It's not. I…I shouldn't have done that."

"You were drunk." I was about to protest that it didn't matter, but he held up a hand. "No more beating yourself up, Kay. I think you've been through enough shit this week without adding self-flagellation to the list.

"Why don't you take a shower, and I'll order room service, and we'll pretend none of this happened. Okay?"

CHAPTER THIRTY

I felt better after a shower. I still *looked* ridiculous in my wrinkled, day old dress, but at least I didn't have smudged mascara and lipstick smearing my face anymore.

"Here," Frank said when I emerged, "coffee." He had a steaming cup ready for me, and I took it.

"Thanks, Frank. I owe you."

"Come on. Breakfast's waiting."

"I don't know if I can eat."

"You will eat," he declared firmly. "Nothing like food to get the mind straightened out."

"Is that a Kudarian home remedy?"

He grinned. "No sarcasm until you drink your coffee and eat your food, either."

I sat down across from him and his three plates of breakfast. "Frank?"

"You're not eating," he observed.

"I really am sorry."

He glanced up at me. "I already told you not to worry about

it, Katherine."

"I know. But – you're a damned good friend, Frank. And I appreciate it."

"Eat your eggs, Kay. And then…well, why don't you tell me what happened?"

I did, and he listened, shaking his head now and again.

"So," I concluded, "that's that. I am an imbecile."

"You're not."

"I am. I should have been able to tell she still loved someone else. God knows there were plenty of signs." I thought of all the times she'd stiffened when I'd touched her, or pulled from an embrace.

"Are you sure that's it?"

"What else could it be?"

"I've been on this ship since Landon took it over. I've never seen her take a shine to someone like she's taken to you. I don't think it's that she's got unresolved feelings for Irene, Kay. I think it's that she likes you, and that terrifies her a little."

I considered his words. Then I remembered the blonde she'd been dancing with the night before. "Well, she seemed to get over it quick enough, anyway."

"Maybe." He shrugged. "Or maybe she just needs time."

"She asked me out, Frank. Then she dumped me. Hours apart."

He nodded. "I know her pretty well, Kay. And if there's one thing she doesn't like, it's thinking she's vulnerable."

"So liking me makes her vulnerable?" I scoffed.

"Any relationship makes you vulnerable. It means opening yourself up to the risk of hurt, of rejection."

"Of getting dumped…"

"But it can also mean making you strong, if you like the right person. I think that's the part she's been missing."

I sat back in my seat, considering his words. For all his easy manners and terrible jokes, it struck me that Frank was perhaps one of the most insightful people I'd ever met. "Dammit, Frank, I never realized what a romantic you were. So what do you think I should do?"

"Give it time. They're her problems, not yours, and she's got to figure them out."

I sighed. "I don't know if I can take another stunt like that one."

"Certainly not if you cope with that many Keldian sunrises," he grinned.

I left Frank's room shortly after, with a hug and another thanks. My headache had mostly cleared, but I didn't dare put the heels on yet. I was still a little too under the weather for that.

I was fishing through my purse for my keycard when I heard my name. "Kay, there you are. I wanted-"

I glanced up. "Maggie."

She stared at me, at the heels I held in one hand, at the rumpled dress I was wearing; and then back at Frank's door. She, by contrast, was in a fresh set of her customary casual wear.

"Oh," she said, her voice flat.

I could feel my face flush. "Mags, it's not what it looks like."

"You don't have to explain, Kay." There was pain in her voice. "It's fine. You can do whatever you like. Or whoever."

I felt a surge of anger at that. *Who the hell is she*, I thought, *to judge me*? I'd spent these last days crazy with desire for her, and she'd dumped me without a second thought. "That's right," I said defiantly. Then, recalling the blonde in whose arms I'd last seen her, I added, "Just like you."

She flushed, then nodded. "I guess so. Well, I'll see you around, Kay."

"Maggie."

I returned to my room, tears stinging at the back of my eyes as I searched my bag for the key. Finding it at last, I let myself in, and sagged against the door. *Goddammit.* There'd been no mistaking the pain in Maggie's eyes, or what she'd thought seeing me leave Frank's room in yesterday's clothes.

And yet she'd been the one to dump me. She'd been the one to leave me there, feeling a fool. How could she fault me for moving on, if I'd moved on, when she'd been the one to tell me to do it?

"Goddammit," I said, aloud this time.

CHAPTER THIRTY-ONE

"I do not understand," Sydney said. "It is my mission to protect you."

"Yes," I agreed, "but I'm not in danger."

"You continue to exhibit indicators of heightened distress, Katherine. I have observed them for the past fourteen days, ranging in severity from mild to intense. I believe you are suffering from some manner of illness."

I sighed. We'd been underway for the past two weeks, and while Sydney's observations were not entirely without merit, his diagnosis was. "I'm fine, Syd."

"You know I do not like to contradict you," the robot answered in his politest metallic accents. "But my scans document otherwise. Using your prior stats as a baseline, the past two weeks of readings of your heart rate, communicativeness, respiration rates and other factors show a clear divergence. Something is clearly not right."

"Everything is fine."

"Are you suggesting, Katherine, that my sensors are at fault?"

He seemed almost offended by the question. Was it possible, I wondered, for a battle bot to feel offense, or was I anthropomorphizing him? "I'm not saying that, Sydney."

"Then I repeat, I do not understand: I fail to see an alternative. Either my observations are correct, or my sensors are malfunctioning. And I do assure you, I did test that hypothesis before approaching you. I've run full diagnostics, and found nothing to indicate that the issue lies with my hardware."

"All I'm saying is, I'm not sick."

"Pardon me, Katherine, but on what basis do you form such a conclusion? Have you consulted with Doctor Fredricks?"

"No. I've just been – sad."

"Sad?"

"Yes. You know, down. Depressed."

"Depression is a treatable mood disorder. Doctor Fredricks would be able to prescribe therapeutic or chemical-"

"I don't need drugs or therapy, Syd. I just need time."

"Ah yes. The human adage of 'time healing all wounds.' From a medical perspective, Katherine, that is very unsound advice."

I sighed. "Look, Sydney, I appreciate your concern. But there are some things about being human that are beyond your comprehension."

"I find that unlikely. My computing speeds are-"

"I'm not talking about computing speeds. I'm talking about human emotion."

"That is true," he agreed. "I do not understand human emotions. They seem an unfortunate burden."

"Lately, I'd have to agree," I laughed.

"Then I'm afraid we are at impasse, Katherine. There is nothing more I can do to assist."

"That's alright, Syd. I appreciate you trying."

"Trying and failing is no better than not trying at all: either way, I have failed."

"You haven't failed," I said. "You've made me feel better."

"Have I?"

"You have."

"Oh. Then, I suppose, I have not failed."

"No," I agreed. "However, if you don't get out of my way, I'm going to be late to the briefing. And that'll get me in trouble, and make me sad again."

He was standing in front of my bedroom door, where he'd ambushed me to present his findings and argue that I should schedule an emergency session with Fredricks. "That would be unfortunate."

"Very."

He trundled to the side. "Have a good day, Katherine."

"You too, Sydney."

I sighed as I left the robot outside my room. I'd already insisted that he stop following me around the *Black Flag* unless I requested his presence. The crew hated trying to squeeze past him in the narrower halls, and I was always afraid he'd roll over my toes one of these days. He'd protested that this made him less effective at his job, but complied.

Playing doctor was, apparently, his way of compensating. He

wasn't entirely off base, of course. I'd been in something of slump since getting dumped on Kraken's Drop. Maggie and I had barely talked since, and when we had, it had been with cool professionalism. Frank had been a damned good friend, but I was trying to be careful there too. I knew he had feelings for me, and especially after the ridiculous stunt I'd pulled at the hotel, I didn't want to hurt him.

We were about a week away from Deltaseal, and the truth was, I couldn't wait until the mission was over. My feelings for Maggie hadn't changed, but she showed no sign of relenting on her decision that we must part.

And while I appreciated his belief in the power of my elusive charms, Frank's predictions had fallen through. Magdalene Landon had no interest in me.

So the best thing for all of us was to go our separate ways. Like she'd said.

Today, we had a briefing in her ready room. We were nearing the borders of Union space, and we'd start work on the ID modules today if skies were clear. We couldn't work as long as there were other ships in sensor range. It wouldn't do to have the *Black Flag* morph into the *Lady's Reign* in front of some observant crewman's eyes. And for the same reason, we needed to be able to complete the change as quickly as possible, so that no ship would stumble across us in the middle of the change.

I arrived after most of the rest of the crew, shuffling in with the last few stragglers. Frank had already picked out a pair of seats and waved me over. He had a steaming mug of coffee waiting for me, next to a Kudarian-sized thermos for himself. "Thanks," I said.

"Of course. I was starting to think you might have forgotten the briefing."

I snorted. "That was all Sydney's doing."

"The robot?"

I nodded.

"What's he up to?"

"It's a long story. Suffice it to say, he's no doctor."

Frank laughed. "But he has the most updated Via Robotics medical library available."

I smiled. "Medical library notwithstanding, he still sucks at it."

"Well," he reminded me, "'Via Robotics makes no guarantees for the accuracy of any diagnosis made by a unit without proper licensing.'"

This time, I laughed. Frank's impression was spot on, down to the metallic edge in his voice. He fixed me with an affectionate look and grinned, but said no more as Drake plopped down in the seat next to me.

"Morning," the engineer greeted. "Another one of these damned early morning meetings."

"Morning."

Maggie, meanwhile, glanced up from her notes. We were all present, so she began. "Good morning, everyone." She ignored the grumble of discontent that met her greeting. "So we're about six days from Deltaseal airspace. That means it's time to lower the black flag, and raise new colors.

"It's time for the *Lady's Reign* to make her debut." She glanced at me and Drake. It was a quick glance; cold. "Drake and Kay will be leading. They'll be working closely with the bridge to pick a time when we've got the skies to ourselves.

"All I know for sure is, it'll be after we're out of range of Station Brag's sensors. So, sometime after ten."

"So we could have slept in after all," Frank murmured.

Drake nodded, but Maggie frowned. "I'm sorry, did you have something to add, Frank?"

He glanced up. I think we all did. Her tone was sharp and aggravated. Frank's eyebrows rose. "No ma'am."

She nodded. "Good. Anyone have anything to add? Anything useful, anyway?"

I blinked. Again, there was an edge to her voice, matched by an acidy gaze in the Kuridian's direction. I wasn't the only one to catch it, either. There were a few exchanged glances, but no one spoke. Frank's humor, for better or worse, was a staple of these meetings. It was surprising to see her react so negatively.

"Alright," she said, "in that case, we'll start preparations after breakfast. Dismissed."

I walked with Frank to the mess hall. He was quiet for a ways, then stopped. "Kay?"

"Yes?"

"You didn't…well, that stuff I told you about the captain? You didn't mention any of it to her, did you?"

"No. Of course not, Frank. Hell, I've barely spoken to her since – well, since Kraken's Drop."

He nodded, as if satisfied with my answer. "Hm."

"What?"

He shrugged. "I don't know. She just seems…well, pissy

lately. In general, I know, but like she's mad at me."

I felt my cheeks color. "You're sure?"

He frowned at me. "Yeah. Why?"

I groaned. "I think…I think she thinks we slept together."

He was confused. "She does? How?"

"I bumped into her, when I was leaving your room. She…she didn't say much, but she was mad."

His frown deepened. "Well shit. But what's she mad about? She broke up with you. Even if we were together, it wouldn't be like you were cheating."

"I know. And I don't know. Hell, Frank, I've stopped trying to figure it out. I just want this whole damned ordeal to be over." I shook my head. "But I'm sorry you got roped into it."

"It's not your fault, Kay."

"Still, I'm sorry. About all of it."

He held my gaze for a moment, then nodded. "Me too, Katherine. But come on. Let's go get some breakfast."

CHAPTER THIRTY-TWO

We weren't able to begin the id swap until just before noon. We'd run into a series of freighters and transports heading back to Union territories.

Now, though, the skies were clear. No one was in sensor range, and our window of opportunity was open. "Okay," Drake said, "you tell me when, Kay. I'll swap the chips."

I nodded. "Give me a minute. I need to cycle the module." I started the flush sequence and waited as the device powered down. "Ready," I said.

"I'm ready."

The last light flickered and went dark. "And – go!"

"Chip extracted," Drake said. We had about fifteen seconds of downtime to swap out the first card and run the second. If the system booted without id's in place, it would send a malfunction alert to the nearest Union station – and we'd have a lot of explaining to do. "Inserting chip now. And, she's in."

"Module powering up." I frowned at the screen, waiting as the seconds ticked by. It flashed the bootup sequence, and as *authenticating identification codes* came onscreen, I held my breath.

Then the monitor read, *ID confirmed*, and I loosed a nervous laugh. "Welcome aboard the *Lady's Reign*," I said.

Drake whooped, and Maggie nodded. "Good work. Let's run through the rest of the checks, though, to make sure we're set."

Swapping out the chips was the quick part. This, on the other hand, took the better part of the afternoon. We needed to verify that the new profile had replicated to the rest of the ship. We also needed to verify that the *Lady's Reign* stats matched ours.

Maggie's contact had secured codes for a compatible freighter, but, of course, they hadn't been tailored to the *Black Flag*'s particular setup. Now we had to find the discrepancies and update them. This, at least, could be done without triggering any kind of attention from the Union. Captains were within their rights to modify their ships as they saw fit, provided they stayed within the parameters of their class of vessel.

So in the course of an afternoon, the *Lady's Reign* lost an aquatic transport bay, gained two cargo bays, and adjusted the ship's complement. If we ran into a patrol and they pulled our records, of course it wouldn't stand up to scrutiny. But a noninvasive scan from a passing vessel would show that our ship was nothing more or less than what she purported to be.

And, more importantly, when we entered Deltaseal airspace, everything would check out.

There was one further bit of excitement for the afternoon. That was Henderson's transfer. He'd been confined to sickbay these last two weeks, first in an induced coma in the regen unit, and then cuffed to a bed.

Now, though, Fredricks deemed him well enough to head back to his own cell. "If you don't get him out of my medbay, Captain, I'm going to kill him myself," he'd warned.

Under escort, he was marched back to the brig. And after two weeks of flight, this was interesting enough that the entire crew turned out to watch. "I don't know what you're planning, Captain," he told Maggie, "but I promise you, you will regret it."

"My only regret, Mr. Henderson, is that we didn't put a bullet in you."

"That's a problem that can be rectified," Frank observed.

"And you," Henderson said as he passed me, "I would throw myself out the nearest airlock if I were you, little miss Kate. Once the Conglomerate gets their hands on you – and I promise you, they will – you will repent the day you were born. No one crosses the Conglomerate and walks away."

I saw Maggie's jaw clench and felt Frank stiffen beside me. I, though, was not particularly phased by his threats. "You crossed me first," I reminded him icily. "Maybe you should have thought twice about that, Henderson."

He snorted, and Corano marched him past. Once he'd gone, Frank laughed appreciatively. "You see his face? He did not like that you weren't taking his shit."

"You shouldn't antagonize him," Maggie said. "You don't need to make yourself a target."

I frowned. "Make myself? I've been a target ever since I stepped onto this ship. Probably before, but certainly since."

She seemed annoyed with my response. Her tone was sharp. "Piss him off if you want, Katherine. That's your call. All I'm saying is, Henderson is dangerous."

"It's a little late to be worried about that, isn't it, Magdalene?" I shot back.

She held my gaze for a moment, and neither of us spoke. Neither did anyone around us, either, until Frank cleared his throat and offered in conciliatory tones, "I still say we should space him."

Maggie's jaw tightened, and she shot him – both of us – a scowl. She didn't say anything further. She just left.

The crew dissipated with her, a few throwing curious glances my way. Only Frank remained when the others had gone, and he sighed. "Well that was fun."

"Hell, Frank. I can't wait to get off this damned ship."

The days passed slowly after that. The skies were quiet, and there was little to do. We'd already wrapped up the final repairs. Now all that remained was the waiting.

Henderson went on a short lived hunger strike two days in. He stopped eating for a day and a half, but when no one seemed to care, he gave it up.

We were about two days from Deltaseal, and I was just getting ready to turn in, when I heard Sydney's voice outside my door. "Unauthorized entry. Please state your business."

"Uhh…I want to talk to Kay?" This was Ginny.

"Answer within acceptable parameters. You may proceed."

Oh Syd. I hadn't asked him to screen my visitors – this was another of his own schemes – but he seemed to be relying on self-identification to ascertain their motives. I shook my head, determining that I needed to take a look at his programming when I had a chance, and headed to the door. A knock sounded just as I reached it.

Ginny started when, a second after she knocked, the door slid open. "Kay."

"Hey Ginny. What's up?"

"Some of the crew are getting together in the mess hall for drinks. To toast the mission. The captain gave us the go-ahead and David's bringing out some of the top shelf. You want to join us?"

"Oh. Tonight?"

"Yeah." She grinned. "Magdalene didn't want us dealing with hangovers when we reached Deltaseal space."

"Ah." I glanced back at my bed, and the pajamas I'd laid out on them. It wasn't like I had anything planned. "Sure, why not?"

"Cool. We're going to be meeting up as we can – I think some of the guys have already started drinking. So come as you're available."

"I don't know, Ginny. My calendar's so packed, I may not be able to squeeze it in between all the nothing I've got planned."

She laughed. "I still have to try to convince Kereli. But then I'll be there too."

I headed back inside to double check my hair. I'd been loafing around for the last hour, and figured it probably needed a touch up.

It did. Then I headed out of my room. Sydney was manning his post as self-appointed sentinel. "Shall I accompany you, Katherine?"

"Nope."

"I may be of assistance."

"Assistance? You can't drink, Sydney."

"Precisely."

"That's the point of the get together."

"It is my observation that the presence of alcohol in group settings usually leads to intoxication and compromised decision making."

"Well, you're not wrong, Syd. But I don't think anyone would thank me for bringing an eight-hundred-pound babysitter to crash the party."

"Perhaps not. But their expressions of gratitude are not relevant to my mission."

"I suppose not. But you're going to have to stay all the same." He began to offer an objection, and I interrupted, "But I promise not to misbehave, mother."

"Mother? I am not your mother, Katherine."

"I know, Syd. I was being sarcastic."

"Oh. Why?"

I sighed. "I'll explain later."

"Very well. I await your explanation. Sarcasm is another human trait that eludes my algorithms, so I anticipate the opportunity to increase my understanding."

"Alright then," I said. It might not have been his intent, but the fact was, Sydney was making a good, stiff drink sound better by the minute.

CHAPTER THIRTY-THREE

For once, David did not disappoint. He really had rolled out the top shelf alcohol. Most of the crew was here, at one table or another. Maggie was a few tables away with Kereli and Corano.

After my first few sips of whiskey, her presence didn't bother me much anymore. I was, slowly, making my way through the rest of the glass. Frank was teasing me about my cautious pace and laughing rather more than usual. "Don't want a repeat of the sunrise incident, eh?" he whispered, nudging me.

"You won't see another sunrise if you don't shut your mouth, mister," I warned.

He laughed – giggled almost – into his glass, and I laughed at the sound. "Jesus, Frank. You're drunk. How much have you had?"

"That's his third bottle," David sighed.

"Bottle?" My eyes widened. "Of whiskey?"

Frank raised it in a mock salute. "And every drop has been appreciated, I assure you."

David shook his head. He was, it seemed, in too good a mood to quarrel. A little disapprobation would have to suffice.

Fredricks was staring into his glass, his arm wrapped around Ginny. That development was something of a surprise to me. But, then, I'd spent the last three weeks moping. It was inevitable that I'd missed things. "So, what do you think you'll do with your cut?"

Ginny snuggled into his embrace. "I don't know. Probably put a down payment on a ship of my own. One of those one-man rigs."

"And leave *Black Flag*?" Fredricks asked. "Leave the crew?"

She grinned up at him. "Well, I could always wait, I suppose. Save up a little more."

He squeezed her. "Or at least wait until you can afford something that'll need a medic."

David rolled his eyes. "Oh God. Not you two too. It's like a damned virus going around. And the whole crew's catching it."

"Fortunately for you," Frank offered, "your winning personality has inoculated you. You're safe from harm."

"Thank God for it," he nodded sagely. "I don't care how good the sex is. It never ends up being worth it in the end. You're better off paying for it: at least then you get to set the terms up front."

We all groaned. "Jesus," Fredricks said. "That was definitely TMI."

He shrugged, though, and downed his glass. "Just telling it like it is."

Ginny shook her head. "What about you guys?" she asked of Frank and I. "What are you going to do with your money?"

"Well," Frank snorted, "we know what *David's* going to do with his."

I almost spit out a mouthful of whiskey at that.

"Some of it, anyway," the cook agreed.

Ginny cringed again. "Anyway…Frank, what about you?"

"I don't know." He shrugged. "Maybe buy a place of my own."

"That sounds nice," I nodded. "On Kudar?"

"Oh hell no. Nothing that puts me that close to my family. I need a galaxy between us at least."

I laughed. "Just as long as you don't end up getting one of those floating monstrosities like Henderson's."

"I don't know…it could be fun. Spend my time looking down on everyone."

David groaned. "You're a doctor, Fredricks. Can't you do something about that brain damage?"

"What about you, Kay?" Ginny asked. "Will you be living among the stars with Frank, looking down on everyone?"

"Me?" I blinked.

"Oh, I think they're going to have other things to occupy their time," Fredricks grinned. He pecked at her ear. "Speaking of, what do you say we take this party off the deck?"

"I thought you'd never ask," she smiled back at him, while David mimed gagging.

I pushed myself out of bed with an effort the next morning. I didn't have a hangover, but I felt unrested. I'd fared better than a lot of the rest of the crew, though. Drake was in the mess hall, eyes closed, coffee mug in hand.

David glowered at my "Good morning." And his scowl only deepened when I glanced around, wondering, "Hey, where's Frank?"

"I make food, Kay. I don't babysit gorillas."

I said no more, taking my plate and heading to our customary table. Lately, Frank and I had dined alone. Maggie hadn't joined us since Kraken's Drop. Some days, she didn't even eat in the mess hall at all, just grabbing a plate and returning to her ready room. Now and then Ginny or one of the other crew would spend a meal with us.

Today, the table felt positively empty, and, somehow, Frank's absence made me think of Maggie's. *Goddammit.* I toyed with my breakfast casserole. It was some fashion of reconstituted egg bake, full of fatty meat and starchy potato pieces.

Ginny and Fredricks came in a few minutes later, arms wrapped around each other and giggling. *At least Kraken's Drop worked out well for someone*, I thought. It was an unlikely pairing in my mind. He had always seemed so dour and absorbed in his work; she was shy at first, but bubbly and happy. I would not have guessed they'd have connected.

But then, what the hell did I know about love? Not a damned thing, obviously.

The doors slid open again, and I was relieved to hear Frank's voice, "Ah, breakfast!"

"I found him, Kay," David called. "Unfortunately."

I flushed. In a minute, plates and coffee in hand, Frank joined me. "Sorry I'm late. I take it you were looking for me?"

"I thought you must have still been in bed with a hangover, is all."

He laughed. "Kudarians don't get hangovers."

"Lucky for you."

He glanced around us, and then lowered his voice. "Actually, Kay, I got called into the captain's office."

I felt my heart skip a beat. "Maggie?"

He nodded. "You know why?"

I shook my head. Maggie had been standoffish to Frank since Kraken's Drop. I knew she blamed him, in some inexplicable way, for our separation. And I hated the idea that his friendship with me was hurting him. "Why?"

He grinned at me. "To ask if she needed to find another helmsman."

"What?" I blinked. "She's not…firing you?"

"No, nothing like that." He leaned in closer. "Our conversation last night, Kay? She heard us talking about the house, you know, like Henderson's. She thought we were going to move in together."

I flushed again. "She did?"

He nodded.

"What did you tell her?" I wondered. My heart was racing with embarrassment, with fear, with…I didn't even know what.

"The truth." He glanced askew at me, with fond eyes. "That as much as I might want that, you carry a torch for her."

"You didn't?" I could feel my face burn hotter.

"I did. And I told her…well, we had a good chat."

"Oh Frank. What did you do?"

He took my hand in his. "What neither of you had the good sense to do, Kay. Cleared the air."

"Oh God." We were so close to being done, so close to going our separate ways forever. I had reconciled myself to that, or nearly had done so. I'd given up on the idea of Maggie feeling anything for me. And now? Now, every damned, stupid, futile hope flooded back.

"I'm tired of seeing you miserable, Katherine. I told her that too. I don't know if it'll do a bit of good, but she needed to hear it, if nothing else."

"What did she…say?"

"Not much." He glanced up at me. "To be honest, I don't know how much got through to her. I don't know if she's too damned stubborn to hear what I said. But she looked like she might have taken some of it to heart."

I dropped my eyes to my plate, studying the lumps of egg absently.

"Are you mad at me?"

"No, Frank. Just…I don't know what I want. Part of me hopes she heard every word. And part of me…well, hopes she ignores it all, so this can just be over."

CHAPTER THIRTY-FOUR

I didn't see Maggie that day, though – fool that I was – I looked for her at each meal. When dinner rolled around and she didn't even show up to the mess hall, I figured I had my answer. She wanted it to be over too. She wanted to move on.

I stopped by Fredricks' office on my way back. He and Ginny were there, looking rather flushed when I entered. "Uh, sorry to interrupt."

They exchanged a glance and a smirk, but he was all professionalism as he answered, "No problem. What can I do for you?"

"You got something to help me sleep?" We were arriving at Deltaseal the next day, and I needed to be rested for that. "Nerves about the mission."

He glanced me up and down. "Sure."

"Everything okay, Kay?" Ginny asked.

"Of course."

"You and Frank have a fight or something?"

I felt my cheeks color. "God, no. Why does everyone think we're a couple?"

Fredricks shrugged. "There's nothing to be embarrassed about, Kay. Human-Kudarian pairings aren't common, but – biologically – we're one hundred percent compatible. Human-Kudarian children are healthy. There-"

I held up a hand. "Thanks, doc. I'm not embarrassed. We're not a couple. We're just friends."

He and Ginny exchanged glances. It was clear they didn't believe a word of it. "Okay," he said mildly. "My mistake." He handed me a hypo. "This'll help you sleep. Adjust the dial here-" He broke off to tap a tiny wheel on the side of the device. "To set the number of hours. It's in two-hour increments. So if you want to sleep for eight hours, choose the fourth setting."

I nodded. "Thanks."

"Of course."

"Well, I'll let you two get back to 'work,'" I grinned.

"I don't know what you're talking about," Ginny smirked. "We're just friends."

Fredricks' hypo worked. My rest was long, deep and dreamless, and I awoke feeling refreshed. My mood was a little better too. I'd already accepted the inevitable, and for however briefly I might have entertained ridiculous hopes the day before, well, I was back to reality now.

We started the morning with a briefing in Maggie's ready room. We went through the plan again, rehashing every step from what we'd do when we entered Deltaseal space – *send the identification codes, wait for authorization to proceed* – to what we'd do when we left – *take out the targeting system, blast off.* None of it was new. We'd been over this plan time and time again, looking for flaws, searching for points of failure, planning for the unexpected. We were as ready as we would ever be.

We were ushering out when Maggie said, "Katherine, could I have a minute?"

I glanced up. She was still seated at the head of the table, and her eyes returned to her notebook when mine reached her. "Uh…sure."

Frank's eye caught mine as he left, and he flashed me a reassuring smile. I didn't feel reassured. Maggie was studying her page with an effort that did not seem natural. But her countenance was lowered. I had no idea what she was thinking.

My own heart hammered so heavily I was surprised the crew couldn't hear it. *It's probably something about Deltaseal*, my mind argued. *Just business.* I took a breath, trying to steady my nerves. *What if it isn't?* Then, I remembered her weeks of cold shoulders. *Don't be stupid, Kay. That's over.*

When the door slid closed and the last crewmember left, she glanced up. "Take a seat, Kay. Please."

I moved to a chair several spots down from her. Her brow creased, but then she got up, leaving those notes she'd been so intent on, and sat beside me.

"Thank you," she said, studying her hands, "for staying."

"You're the captain."

She glanced up at that, meeting my gaze. "I…I didn't ask you to stay as the captain, Kay."

There it was again, that thunder in my ears, in my chest. "Oh."

"I…I talked to Frank."

"I know."

"Oh." She seemed nonplussed. "Then…then you know what an imbecile I am."

"Maggie," I said, "tell me what's going on. Please. I…I can't keep guessing."

"I'm apologizing, Kay."

"Oh. Okay." I sucked in a breath of air to steady my nerves. It was less than I'd hoped for, much less. But at least I knew where I stood. "Okay. Apology accepted."

I moved to get up, but she stretched out a hand to mine. "Please. Don't go."

My heart fluttered in my chest again at her touch. "What do you want from me, Mags?"

"Diane? The woman at the bar? I…I didn't go home with her, Kay."

I blinked. "The blonde?" I didn't know her name.

She nodded, admitting, "I was going to. I thought that would help. But when you left, I…" She shook her head. "It wasn't her I wanted, Kay. It was you."

I was stunned. "God, Maggie. What are you doing? I've gotten nothing but three weeks of cold shoulders from you, and now – the day we're going to rob this damned bank – you tell me this?"

She flushed, her face turning as red as her hair. She looked miserable, and I almost regretted my angry words. "I know. I'm sorry. I just…I thought you and Frank were…well, you know."

I frowned at her, less sorry for what I'd said. "And what if we had been? You dumped me, Magdalene. You dumped me, and were all over some rando in a bar. Why the hell shouldn't I do the same?"

There was a mist in her eyes as she nodded. "I know, Katherine. You're right. I just..." She swallowed and took in a great breath of air. "When Irene dumped me, it was for a guy. A guy she'd known for years, a 'friend.' But they'd...they'd been fucking all along. When I saw you coming out of his room? You guys were such good friends, and I knew he liked you. I...well, I thought it was Irene all over again. I thought you'd lied to me, when you said you were nothing more." She shook her head. "I'm sorry, Kay. I know I was wrong. And I know my timing's shit. I just...I wanted you to know."

"Why? Dammit, Maggie, why?" This was more openness than I'd seen from her in all the time we spent together as friends, and in our brief time as girlfriends.

"Because...because I still care about you, Katherine. And I know maybe I blew my chance. I know I don't deserve another. But I don't want to go out there today knowing that you hate me."

"I could never hate you, Magdalene."

"Could you ever forgive me?"

I studied her, the ruts under her beautiful green eyes, the flush of color in her pale cheeks. Forgive her? I guess I'd already done that, hadn't I? My heart was full of nothing but warmth and concern. "You know I will. But I can't keep going back and forth." I took her hand, and looked her straight in the eye. "You need to make up your mind, one way or another, Magdalene Landon. Because if you do this again, I don't care how much it breaks my heart, there will be no more second chances."

CHAPTER THIRTY-FIVE

She'd cried in my arms after that, and I felt the last vestiges of my anger wash away with her tears. I'd never seen Maggie so raw, so vulnerable, so trusting before. I knew it cost her in pride.

When her tears dried, she told me of her conversation with Frank. "He told me I would have to find a new helmsman," she laughed, "if I didn't get over myself."

"He said that?" Frank had told me bits and pieces of what had been exchanged, but not this.

She nodded. "Yes." She ran a hand down my cheek. "He said he couldn't stand to see me breaking your heart."

I felt my cheeks flush. I could only guess how much such a speech must have cost the Kudarian, when his own feelings were so entwined in the mix.

"He called me a coward." My eyes widened, but she smiled. "And if it had been another situation, I would have put him in medbay for it. But he was right, Katherine." She moved her lips to mine, kissing gently. "I have been a coward. I've been so terrified of repeating the mistakes of the past that I couldn't see the blunders I was making in the present. But no more."

"Tell me about Irene," I said.

There was confusion in her features, but then she nodded.

"Alright. What do you want to know?"

I shrugged. "I don't know. How you met. What made you fall for her."

"We met on a job, working a freighter. The *Outlander*. I was crazy about her from the first time we met. She was beautiful and confident and smart. She had a kind of aura about her, that drew you in. It took me almost a whole run to work up the courage to ask her out, though."

"Really?"

She nodded. "We dated for three months. I was in love." She smiled. "She was not. I asked her to marry me, and she said yes. I still don't know why. It lasted for just over two months." She shrugged. "And I woke up one morning to find her stuff gone, and a note. It wasn't what she wanted. She was sorry. So on and so forth.

"And I found out, after we were divorced, that she and Adam, one of our mutual friends, had been hooking up even while we were dating." She shook her head again. "And I hadn't had a clue."

"That sucks."

"Yeah." She held my gaze. "But it's no excuse for what I did to you, either."

I leaned in and kissed her. "I'll never hurt you, Mags."

"I've already hurt you, Kay," she said, and her tone was sad. "But I'm done being a coward. I want you. I want to make this work."

"Does that mean you don't want me off the *Black Flag* when the mission's over?"

"You know I don't." Her eyes were tender. "Will you stay, Katherine?"

"You know I will, Magdalene."

Our reconciliation made, we returned to the bridge. She wrapped an arm around me as we walked, and made no effort to hide it when stepped on deck.

Frank first shot us a furtive glance as we entered, as if to ascertain what had transpired, and then grinned. He seemed almost relieved. I was reminded again what a damned good friend he was.

Then, though, he turned to Maggie, and was all business. "Captain, we're about three hours out of Deltaseal airspace."

"Copy that, Frank." She pressed a button on her panel for the comm. "How's it going, Kereli?"

"It's 'going,' Captain. Are you ready?"

"Me?"

A sigh came over the comm. "We discussed this already, Magdalene."

"Alright, alright," she grimaced. "I'll get changed too."

"Good."

"What's that about?" I asked after she disconnected.

"Kereli says I need to 'look the part.'"

"What does that mean?"

"Apparently," she said, wrinkling her nose in distaste, "no self-respecting Esselian would be seen with me. Not without a makeover."

I snorted. "They'd be so lucky."

She smiled at me, then punched the comm again. "Corano?"

"Here."

"You ready?"

"Almost, Captain."

"Okay. Meet on the bridge when you are."

"Copy that."

"Well," she sighed, standing, "I suppose I better get this over with. Time to go put on a dress."

"Be brave, Captain," Frank smirked. "You'll pull through."

"I advise you to hold your tongue, Frank. Or we'll be swapping roles."

He laughed. "I'm game. As long as you got a dress in my size."

"I said roles, Frank. Not clothes."

"Come on, where's the fun in that?"

She shook her head but paused by me. She brushed my hand with her fingers and lowered her voice. "You want to come with me? Help me find something?"

I felt my heart tremble a little. "You sure that's a good idea?"

"Probably not," she grinned. "Do it anyway?"

I should have said no. My head was already reeling, and I was having a hell of a time concentrating on the mission. But, of course, I said, "Alright."

"Good."

"Not to ruin anyone's plans…but we are on a schedule," Frank reminded us.

I flushed, and Maggie rolled her eyes. "Come on," she said to me. "You can help me with my hair."

She slipped her hand into mine, and we walked back to her room. "So how dressed up do you have to be?" I asked. She and Corano were playing the role of Kereli's mates. Esselians didn't have a concept of marriage, exactly. Each male and female was head of their own family unit, and could be a member of as many units as they liked. Occasionally, partners would combine units – that is, all the partners in both units would be bound to all the partners in the other. But it was far from uncommon for mates to have mates of their own, who in turn would have more mates of their own.

The living dynamics of this sounded complex enough to my human ears. Adding to the equation that, while there was theoretically no upward limit on the number of mates an individual could accrue, Esselian society had a very fixed hostility to separations, and it all seemed a bit too much trouble to be worth it. Hell, I could barely keep up with one relationship.

Maggie, meanwhile, was nodding. "Apparently, she's expecting me to be rather done up. Esselians are very particular about the presentation of their mates. It is a reflection on them, and the other party's perception of their relationship."

"Ugh." I shivered. "That sounds like it would get almost competitive."

"Yes. Kereli says it sometimes does, between two partners

and between tertiary partners."

"Well," I needled her, "that's what you get for cheating on me with an Esselian matron."

She laughed. "That is a fine way to start a relationship, isn't it?"

"Not even an hour in, and I find you with another woman." I shook my head. "What *am* I going to do with you, Magdalene?"

CHAPTER THIRTY-SIX

Maggie pulled a dress out of her closet. "Ginny lent me this."

I laughed. "Don't you have any dresses of your own?"

"Just a few sundresses. Alas, not what this mission calls for. What do you think? Is this okay?"

She held Ginny's dress up in front of her. It was a slim, belted black pencil dress, somewhere in that perfect sweet spot between sultry and all-business. I nodded. "I think Kereli's about to be the luckiest damned Esselian alive."

She rolled her eyes but smiled. "Alright, I'll get it on."

I turned to give her privacy, feeling terribly out of place all of a sudden. I heard her clothes hit the floor, piece by piece.

"You can look, Kay," she said, and I started at the sound of her voice. She was near me, very near.

"What?" I cast my eyes in her direction, and there she was, a few steps away. I glanced aside as quickly, but not before I saw enough to make me flush. She was wearing nothing but a bra and panties, and she looked better than I'd imagined.

"What's wrong?"

"Wrong? God, Mags, I'm supposed to be concentrating on

this damned mission. Not…not you."

"We've still got time," she said. I felt her hand on my chin, turning my face to hers. "Plenty of time."

I gulped and met her eyes. They were smoldering with desire. "Oh God, Maggie, what are you doing?"

She touched her lips to mine, gently at first, then with more urgency. "Anything you want, Katherine. Anything at all."

My last resistance faded. The mission was a million lightyears from my mind. All I knew, in the moment, was that I wanted her, needed her, more than I'd ever wanted anyone. I kissed her in return, reaching for her bra clasps. She pulled my jacket off, and then my shirt.

Piece by piece, we unwrapped each other. I trembled as the air hit my naked body. I felt a bit ridiculous to be standing next to her. She was firm and flat where she should be, and full and round in all the right places too. I was less toned, skinnier and flabbier.

She didn't seem to mind. She wrapped me in her arms and guided me back to the bed, kissing me as we went.

She was strong; very strong. And feeling the muscles in her back tense, feeling the strength of her arms as she lifted me onto that bed, made we weak with desire. "Oh Maggie," I said.

She hovered above me, drawing a hand over my stomach. My body screamed at her touch. "Well, Katherine?" She pecked at my lips playfully, teasingly. "What do you want?"

I reached up, wrapping an arm around her and drawing her to me. "Goddammit, Mags, what I've wanted all this time: you."

She didn't tease me after that. My body didn't need teasing. Neither did hers. We spent a long while exploring and re-exploring our need for one another, and satisfying it.

I was less certain in my lovemaking than she, but she guided me to where she needed me to be. There was something almost as satisfying in watching her pleasure, in knowing that I could bring her to such moments of ecstasy, as in my own.

Almost, but not quite. Maggie found her way around my body quickly, and once acquainted – well, it was a hell of an acquaintance.

Still, eventually our time together ran out. "I need to get going, Kay."

"I know. I wish we had a week."

She grinned, drawing her fingers over my stomach so that my skin danced under her touch. "Just a week?"

I kissed her. "It's a good start, anyway."

She got out of bed, and so did I. One by one, the garments we'd discarded were retrieved and put back in place.

"Do me up?" she asked, once she'd slipped the pencil dress on.

She pulled her hair out of the way, and I obliged, kissing the back of her neck as I closed the zipper. The fabric ensconced her as it closed, conforming to her curves and dips. "God you're gorgeous, Mags."

She turned around, wrapping her arms around me, the greens of her eyes sparkling as the hair fell back around her shoulders. "I'm not sure what you think all this flattery's going to be able to get you," she murmured, "that I haven't already given you."

I grinned, running my hands down the length of her back and derriere. "More of the same sounds good to me."

Maggie smiled too, putting a kiss on my lips. "Let's go rob this place, Kay. So I can have you to myself again."

The crew was assembled when we reached the bridge. Frank rolled his eyes at both of us. "Oh, look at that. They *are* alive."

Kereli threw a critical glance over Maggie, then nodded. "You'll do."

It was my turn to roll my eyes. Mags was stunning in the figure-hugging dress and knee-high boots. Her hair was pinned back in a bun, with tendrils of red spilling out here and there. She damned near took my breath away.

"Our standards would be lower," the Esselian was continuing, "for a human anyway."

"Thanks, Kereli," Maggie laughed. "You look good too."

She was dressed in a more traditional ensemble. She wore a loose dress of embroidered green and blue silks, tied at the waist with a black sash, and a headdress replete with sparkling gems of an alien composition. She looked every bit a wealthy Esselian matron, the powerful head of her family unit. From the disdainful cast of her eyes to the upturned tilt of her nose, she lived and breathed her role. Gia Areli, a woman of great wealth and exotic tastes, was born.

Corano's ensemble was a homage to his Tulian ancestry. Tiny braids of his silver hair tied the rest into place, so that it stayed back behind his ears. He'd donned a jacket of silver-embroidered, jet black fabric, and black trousers and boots to match it. He seemed almost an elf, out of some old Earth high fantasy story, rather than a flesh and blood man.

And he was every bit as aloof as I would suppose an elf might be. He looked Maggie over and pulled a face. "That's not very traditional, Captain."

"I'm not an Esselian," she reminded him. "Or a Tulian."

"Still. Esselians value tradition."

I scoffed. "Kereli isn't playing the most traditional of Esselians, Corano."

He considered. "That is true." He glanced back at her. "Your…unorthodox appearance might be useful, in the circumstance."

Kereli agreed. "Considering the character of Gia Areli, I would concur. I believe she would place a higher value on some assets than others, in choosing a mate. And I believe you have highlighted the appropriate ones, Captain."

"There you have it, Corano: I'm Gia's exotic alien squeeze. You and me both."

He frowned at this characterization, and Kereli rolled her eyes. "Proving, I suppose, that money cannot compensate for a lack of taste and judgement."

CHAPTER THIRTY-SEVEN

Drake and I fitted Corano, Kereli and Maggie with tiny, hidden cameras. Now, I was at my workstation. "Alright, going live in three…two…one." I pressed the button. Three separate video feeds popped up on monitors around the bridge, each from the perspective of one of the three. "Houston, we are 'go'," I declared with a smile.

"That, I assume," Kereli asked, "is good news?"

"Yup. Means we're good to go. Video feeds are working."

"Excellent," Maggie said. "Good job you two."

"Captain, we're being hailed," Frank interrupted.

I sucked in a breath. I was situated out of view of the cameras, so I could work without being spotted. Maggie and Corano stepped aside too, and Kereli settled into the captain's chair, crossing her legs. "Bring them up, Mister Frank."

A man's face appeared on screen, framed with a buzz cut and square jowls. "Incoming ship, this is Commander Johnson with Deltaseal Air. Please identify yourself."

Kereli smiled. "Good morning Commander. I'm Gia Areli of the *Lady's Reign*. I believe you have our identification codes."

"Copy that, ma'am. How can we assist?"

"I have an appointment with the bank manager. A Mister Wyman, I believe."

Johnson glanced down at his screen, then nodded. "Affirmative. I have you in the roster. You are cleared to proceed, Lady's Reign. And welcome to Deltaseal."

I don't think anyone breathed until the transmission ended, and then we all released a sigh of relief. "Okay," Maggie said, "we didn't get blown out of the sky. That's the first hurdle down. Oh, and you were great, Kereli. *I* almost believed you."

The Esselian nodded graciously. "Those credits aren't going to earn themselves, Captain."

Mags grinned. "No they're not. Step two. You ready, Kay?"

"Roger that, Captain," I declared, with far more levity than I felt.

"Good. Get started."

I was logged into Henderson's device. Now that we were in Deltaseal airspace, I browsed to the planet's network. "Alright. Here goes nothing."

"You've got this," Frank reassured.

"Let's hope your confidence is well placed, Frank. If they catch me, we're going to be in a world of hurt."

He shrugged. "If they catch you, they'll shoot us down before anyone knows what happened anyway."

"That's the spirit," I sighed. "Thanks."

He grinned. "I do my best."

I was navigating through the security alert directories. There were a lot of familiar faces there. Mine, of course, was one. But Maggie and the crew of the *Black Flag* had been added too. The timestamp matched our first call with Henderson. *Good old Andrew, as efficient as ever, I see.* "Looks like Esser added most everyone on the crew roster to their watchlist when he found out you picked me up." The bank's automated defense grid – turrets, battle bots, and drones – relied on the watchlist to flag potential problem arrivals for apprehension or death. In my case, I'd been flagged for termination. Maggie and the crew had been flagged for interception.

"You can remove us?"

I nodded. "In theory. Here goes nothing." I took a breath, and pressed the delete key. There were no earth-shattering kabooms, no sudden influx of missiles. I breathed out again, and Frank laughed out loud. "See? I knew you could do it."

"So we're all clear?"

"Yes," I said.

"You too?"

"I'm out of the automated system. None of the computers will recognize me. But that doesn't mean some of the employees won't. I spent awhile here."

Maggie nodded. "We shouldn't need you to leave the *Black Flag* before things go dark. But if we do, remember the wig."

"Aye aye Captain."

She grinned at my teasing tone. "All I'm saying is, human eyes are easier to fool than computers. New hair, new you."

"Yeah, yeah. I'll wear the silly wig."

"Good."

"We just received the landing coordinates from Deltaseal Air," Frank offered. "Locking them now."

We began our descent. Deltaseal was a moderate sized planet with a single primary continent spanning both sides of the equator, and a handful of smaller islands speckled throughout a vast, global ocean. Some of the smaller islands housed artillery batteries and drone launch sites. Mansions had been erected on others, reserved for visiting Conglomerate bigwigs and affiliated dignitaries.

The continent itself, though larger than whole nations on other planets, was unutilized except for the bank and a handful of staff housing units. This was by design: it would be easier to spot suspect activity when any activity was suspect.

We entered the atmosphere in a rush of fire and smoke, but this gave way to browns, blues and greens.

"Pretty planet," Kereli observed. "Too bad it belongs to these dirtbags."

It was, too. Great forests and endless plains, shimmering lakes and deep canyons, stretched across its surface.

North of the equator, on a plateau over a thundering waterfall, the untouched beauty gave way to an elegant, carefully manicured park. A series of landing pads were discreetly tucked behind rows of shrubbery and trees. A waiting passenger cart stood by to transport Gia Areli and her party down the shaded lane to the bank.

And the bank itself? It seemed something straight out of history, and yet from a catalogue of future marvels too. It was a massive stone building, some several stories tall, with marble pillars and carved friezes adorning the face. Marble statuary lined the walks and park, sometimes alone, sometimes worked into the fountains and decorative ponds. Like a palace from old Earth, in the days of kings and queens, princesses and dauphins, it proudly boasted its old-world majesty and opulence.

And yet, those delicately manicured parks and paths were patrolled by the heavy, rumbling forms of battle bots, shimmering silver in the light of Deltaseal's sun. Now and again, along with the birds and insects, a drone would flit by noiselessly, its mechanical eyes keeping an ever-watchful surveillance over the world below.

The *Black Flag* – or, the *Lady's Reign*, as she was presenting at the moment – settled into the landing pad that had been reserved for us.

We all headed, of one volition, for the airlock to see the team off. They stood for a moment at the portal. Even Kereli looked nervous. She took a deep breath, then asked, "You ready, Captain? Corano?"

"Let's do it," Maggie said.

"I am ready," the tactical officer agreed.

"Alright," Kereli nodded.

They stepped toward the door, but I grabbed Maggie's hand, pulling her toward me and kissing her. "Be careful out there, babe."

She smiled, running a tendril of my hair through her fingers, and kissed me a second time. "I make no promises. But I'll try."

Then, they stepped out. I watched her go, walking down the gangplank with the others, until the door closed, and they disappeared from view. I took a breath. They were gone. Now, I needed to return to my station.

Lost in these musings, I almost missed the openmouthed stares from Ginny and Fredricks. David was just shaking his head, a vindicated expression on his face.

I flushed. I could only imagine what they were all thinking to see me and Maggie back together, not least with Frank standing right there while we kissed. They'd decided the Kudarian and I were a couple, and nothing I had said so far seemed to dissuade them from that position. *Well, maybe that will.*

If not, well, it'd have to wait until after the mission. "Come on," I said, "back to your places. We need to monitor the feeds."

CHAPTER THIRTY-EIGHT

Kereli settled into a plush office chair. Corano stood behind her on one side, and Maggie on the other. Clay Wyman, the bank manager, smiled at them all. "A real pleasure to meet you, Gia Areli. And won't you take a seat, Mister Keliano? Miss Williams?"

Maggie – Matilda Williams, as she was known at the moment – and Corano – Keliano, as he was known to Wyman – looked to Kereli. The Esselian nodded her permission imperiously, and they took seats by her.

I watched, glancing between the three monitors to catch glimpses of all of their expressions. I was, I realized, chewing on my thumb.

Kereli, meanwhile, was speaking as Gia. "A pleasure to meet you as well, Mister Wyman. I have heard remarkable things about Deltaseal. I am pleased to see that, for once, the rumors seem to be true."

Clay smiled carefully. "I am delighted to hear it, of course, Matron Areli. Deltaseal really is one-of-a-kind, and it often surprises people to learn that that is more than marketing."

A door opened behind the trio, and Maggie turned. Her screen showed a young woman in a jacket and skirt entering the room, carrying a tray.

"Ah," Wyman said, "can I offer you anything, Matron Areli?"

"Call me Gia," Kereli said. Somehow, she managed to make it sound more like a boon granted than a friendly overture.

"Gia," he smiled. "Can we get you anything?"

"No, thank you."

He glanced at Maggie and Corano. "Would you like anything, Miss Williams or Mister Keliano?"

"A cup of tea," Corano declared.

"I'll have the same," Maggie said, adding, "With honey, if you have it."

Kereli hissed. "No sweetener, Matilda. You're trying to lose weight, remember."

I think those of us on the bridge were as stunned as Wyman appeared to be. Frank laughed out loud, and I frowned. If the Esselian's tone was anything to go by, she was enjoying her role a little too much.

"Of course," Maggie said, "you're right, Gia. I'll take mine plain."

The bank manager recovered himself quickly, nodding at Miss Kaine. The young woman busied herself with the cups. "Now," he said, "you had mentioned opening a safe deposit with Deltaseal."

"That's right," Kereli nodded.

"Well, of course we are always delighted to take on new clients. We have a number of options available. We have our standard safe deposit boxes, in the tertiary vaults. And, for the most sensitive items, we have boxes in our core vault."

"I am," the Esselian drawled slowly, as if choosing her words carefully, "a very private person, Mister Wyman. I have done my research on your facility, and I understand the safety of your vaults. I am curious about the steps Deltaseal takes, however, to ensure the privacy of its clientele."

The bank manager nodded briskly. "Our clients' privacy is as important to us as the safety of their valuables. As you know, Union law prohibits the ownership and storage of certain items. A facility inside Union space is required by law to scan any incoming deposits for contraband, illegal devices, biological remains, and so on."

"I know," she said pointedly.

He smiled. "We at Deltaseal believe a measure of trust is necessary in any successful business relationship, but few as important as between a client and her bank. For the safety of our other clients, we will scan for devices that might compromise the security of the vaults. But otherwise, we take no steps, active or passive, to monitor our clients' boxes." He spread his hands, grinning like a Cheshire cat. "One of the privileges, Gia, of working with select clientele is in being able to rely on that trust."

Maggie was watching Kereli. I could tell by the angle of her camera, and the feed we saw. The Esselian nodded with a smile. "I am pleased to hear it, Mister Wyman. I too believe trust is foundational."

"Excellent. I believe my people sent over the fees and terms?"

"They did."

"And did you have any questions?"

"I did not."

Wyman nodded. "If I might ask, do you know which vault

you would be interested in?"

Kereli snorted. "I didn't travel all the way from Alfor to settle for half measures, Mister Wyman. If I decide to open an account on Deltaseal, I expect one of your securest boxes."

"Understood."

Kereli had asked a few more questions about the bank's hours and the availability of staff. When satisfied that her property could be retrieved – "at any time, day or night" – Gia Areli was sold.

Clay Wyman prepared the necessary paperwork, and signatures were exchanged. "We'll need your biometric data on file," he said, "before you leave, to ensure the safety of your items."

"Of course."

"But I can take you to the box now if you have the items with you. We'll stop by security on the way back."

She nodded. "I do." We'd put together a stash of memory chips and a handful of Esselian gems and charms for this step. The gems were pricey, but not the kind of pricey that would justify a box like the one Gia Areli was renting. The combination of personal items and data storage, though, would be convincing to any prying eyes. At least, that was the plan. Whether it worked out or not remained to be seen.

Wyman's office was large and spacious, with marble flooring, paneled wood walls, and comfortable furniture. The lobby beyond was much the same, but on a grander scale.

There was no wood paneling in the foyer, though. Gray marble ran the length of the walls, from the deep blue marble floor to the ornate crown moldings overhead. A central crystal chandelier, as large as a passenger vehicle, hung from the ceiling, surrounded by gold-framed paintings. These were scenes of commerce and prosperity and – oddly enough – angels. At a glance, it was impressive. Anything longer than a glance, and it seemed more ostentatious and ridiculous than anything else.

A fountain sat in the center of the lobby, bubbling away. Here and there, judiciously placed potted plants and luxurious seating had been arranged to carve artificial nooks out of the space, so that waiting patrons might converse in relative privacy.

The bank manager led them past this monument of greed, and down a set of fine halls. It felt strange, in a way, to watch the bank from my current vantage. I'd traveled these same halls in person, stood in that lobby and passed those offices so many times. Now I watched them from monitors, three different views of the same, familiar surroundings.

Something like guilt played with my thoughts. I'd been one of the Conglomerate's minions not two whole months ago. My hands had been no less dirty than Wyman's. And, really, my hands *were* no less dirty than his. What I was doing now was no atonement. I was no Robin Hood, stealing from these monsters for noble reasons.

I was a thief, crossing a thief; a mob pawn, crossing the mob. *A fool.*

I sucked in a breath and stared at my screens. I found myself toying, absently at first, with the bracelet Maggie had given me. I was a fool, navigating life and the endless abyss of space blindly, stumbling from place to place and mistake to mistake. But for the first time in a long time, I felt like I'd found my north star, the Polaris in my otherwise dark night sky, to guide me to where I needed to be.

CHAPTER THIRTY-NINE

They'd traveled through a stretch of the bank, passing more waiting areas and corridors of offices. Wyman did his best to engage in small talk – the kind that was just nosey enough to be useful to him, but not so nosey as to rankle a patroness like the fastidious Gia Areli.

"I believe you mentioned your business was mining?"

"In a sense," Kereli nodded. "My interests are more diversified than that."

"Of course."

"But my initial success was in developing certain holdings on Alfor for mineral extraction, yes."

"I understand it is very difficult to get mining licenses on your home planet."

She snorted. "Only if you don't know your way around the system, Mister Wyman."

"Ah."

They reached a second lobby, this one considerably smaller than the first. A receptionist waited behind a desk and smiled a greeting as they approached. "Good morning."

"Good morning. Gia, this is Luke. He's our daytime

coordinator, and will, of course, be at your service whenever you need to access your box. Luke, this is Gia Areli. We're going to take a look at her new box."

"An honor, Matron. Welcome to our Deltaseal family."

Corano's monitor showed Kereli glancing the young man over, with a lingering, appreciative gaze. "Is there a last name that goes with Luke?"

He colored at her interest, but was all politeness as he answered, "Of course. Forgive me, I am Luke Spence."

Kereli smiled, intoning, "Well, Luke Spence, it is a pleasure to meet you."

"Likewise, Matron Areli."

"Call me Gia," she insisted. Corano made a show of clenching his jaw, and Maggie crossed her arms.

"Of course, Gia." He flushed a deeper red, and Wyman shifted uncomfortably.

The Esselian let her eyes linger on him a moment longer in a very deliberate way, then smiled again. "Well, Mister Wyman, shall we take a look at my box?"

"Of course, Gia. This way."

Maggie and Corano moved to follow the pair, but Kereli held up a hand. "You two stay." Then, she glanced back at the receptionist. "That won't be an inconvenience, will it, Luke?"

"Of course, not, Matron. I mean, Gia."

"Good."

Now, the three views diverged. Maggie's and Corano's screen

showed two different vantages of the lobby, and two different angles of Luke Spence. The young man was decidedly uncomfortable in both shots.

Kereli's screen, meanwhile, displayed her progression toward the vaults. "There's a series of biometric scanners beyond this door. The only way in is to pass them all."

"What about out?"

"What?"

"I assume we are allowed privacy with our items?"

"Oh, of course. Once you're inside, and your box is scanned as we discussed, I will wait for you outside. You can leave whenever you like. The door only requires to be pushed from the inside."

"Very well."

I turned to Frank. "Alright. It's almost showtime. You ready?"

He grinned at me. "Champing at the bit."

"Well, good. Because you're going to have to move fast. You'll have about fifteen minutes."

"Can do."

"This a suicide mission," David sighed. "There's no way we're going to make it there and back again in enough time."

"We can move the ship," I reminded him, "as soon as Deltaseal Air's eyes are off."

Frank nodded. "I'll land her right by the entrance. It'll be cutting it close, but we'll make it."

"Even with the bots and drones offline," Drake mused, "that still leaves all the personnel. Some of those tellers and office monkeys are going to have guns. And some of them are going to know how to use them."

"It's a suicide mission," the cook repeated.

"Way to stay positive," Ginny shook her head.

"Look," I said, "we've already been through this. That's the plan."

"Easy to say, since you're not the one running out there to face the firing squad."

"Right, because I'll be too busy shutting down the entire planet's defense grid."

"It is definitely a suicide mission."

I shook my head. "Get ready, David, and stop complaining."

"And if you need motivation, just think of all the prostitutes you'll be able to hire with your cut," Frank grinned.

The cook snorted. "I won't be the only one, though, will I, Mister Single?"

Kereli, meanwhile, was nearing the inner vault. I turned my attention away from this squabbling to the monitors. She and Wyman had passed through the first sets of doors and biometric scanners, and now were approaching the final door. "Well," he said, "here we are."

In the lobby, Luke was asking Maggie and Corano, "Can I get you anything while you wait? We have a full refreshment bar."

Corano glanced the young man up and down dismissively and said nothing. Maggie had been wandering around the lobby lethargically, stopping at paintings or plants in a disinterested fashion. "I don't know." She turned to his desk, and she too cast an appraising glance over him. It was much more appreciative than Corano's had been. "What do you have?"

Luke flushed again, but this time with more pleasure than he'd shown Gia Areli. "The cafeteria stocks us with a wide range of food and beverages – I can show you, if you like."

She considered for a moment, then nodded. "Alright. I am a little peckish."

"Remember what Gia said," Corano sniffed.

"Bite me, Keliano."

Luke hesitated, as if unsure of what to say. Maggie smiled at him. "Don't mind Keliano. He's a prick, but you get used to him."

"Oh…uh, this way." He gestured toward a door off the lobby, then glanced back at Corano. "You're sure I can't get anything for you, sir?"

"Quite sure."

Luke nodded and turned toward Maggie, taking a moment to appreciate the view before following her.

"We, uh, like to keep a selection of food from most of the major worlds," he said. "Since we serve a very diverse client base." They had entered a café style lounge, with several refrigerators and beverage stations.

"Very openminded of you," Maggie said. "I'm interested in Earth foods."

"Of course. Anything in particular?"

She sighed. "Carbs, if you've got them."

"Carbs?"

"You know, bread. A sandwich, maybe?"

"Oh. Of course."

"Gia won't let me touch the damned things."

He glanced up at her. "Oh. That…that's rough."

"You have no idea."

While Maggie played up her tyrannical paramour story, Corano, meanwhile, shifted nearer the vault door.

I glanced between the three monitors, and their three divergent views of the scene of the crime-to-be. Wyman had fed Kereli's valuables through a scanner, and declared them to be "ready to proceed." He'd returned the box, and said, "I'll wait for you out there, then."

"Thank you."

I took a steadying breath. "We're about ten seconds to go-time," I called.

"Here we come, money," Frank smiled.

"Here we come, Death," David sighed.

CHAPTER FORTY

Wyman passed through the doors, back to the lobby. I had about fifteen commands queued up, waiting for that precise moment. One by one, I submitted them.

With an agonizing slowness, Henderson's device spit back a progress feed. *Initiating shutdown procedures. Terminating Deltaseal Air link. Sending kill commands to drone network.*

In reality, it was only seconds. But it seemed an eternity. Finally, though, I saw the magical phrase: *all commands executed successfully.*

"We are go," I said.

At the same time, the three feeds showed the impact of my changes. The vault flickered black for half a second before its backup power came online. Wyman threw a furtive glance around, reaching for his comm. Corano, though, was waiting just outside the door for him, and a quick knock between the eyes put the bank manager onto the floor in a heap.

Luke, meanwhile, broke from his small talk with Maggie when the room went dark. Unlike the vault, the non-essential areas of the bank didn't have emergency power. "What's going on?" she asked.

"I'm not sure," he said. "Looks like we might have lost

power."

Maggie loosed a cry of alarm that was so over the top I almost laughed. He, though, fell for it. "Don't worry, Matilda," he said. The room was dim, cast only in what light seeped in from the outside. He stepped closer. "There's nothing to be afraid of. The technicians will get it figured out. Come on, let's go back-"

His gallantry was rewarded in the same way Wyman's efficiency had been: Maggie waited until he was close enough to strike, and then knocked him out cold. She took her belt off, and while Luke was still unconscious bound his hands.

Back on the *Black Flag*, Frank had already powered on the engines and got us into the air. We cut across the park, and he set down right outside the bank entrance. I shivered at the sight of a battle bot on the path down from us, frozen in its patrol. *God, I hope this works.*

If someone, somewhere along the way figured out what I'd done, and how to undo it, we were going to be in a world of hurt.

"Go, go," Frank called. "Kay, keep the place locked 'til we get home."

I nodded, but didn't look up. I was working on the network accounts, deleting the other admin users. People all over Deltaseal would be scrambling to get the systems back online. Without access to the network, that was going to be a lot harder to do.

I'd already changed the password to the local admin account, so no one else would be able to use that. Even when the system's automatic reboot happened in fifteen minutes, without a manual config update – which for obvious reasons I wasn't going to make – the password change would cripple a handful of key systems. That would buy us a little more time too.

I heard the tromping of feet, and a flurry of excited and nervous chatter behind me as the crew headed for the gangplank.

"Be careful, you crazy bastards," I called after them. "And turn your damn cameras on."

As of now, only Ginny and Drake had their feeds active.

"Aye aye, Captain," Frank's voice echoed down the hall. A moment later, though, his feed did activate. One by one, the others' did as well.

My workstation was a dizzying array of perspectives. Sixteen monitors had been set up or coopted for the purpose. Now, I had a direct feed to every member of the crew, seeing what they saw as they raced down the gangplank toward the bank.

I'd never been motion sick before, but the jostling streams before me came close to doing the trick. Still, I gritted my teeth, focusing on one screen at a time. It wouldn't do for the only occupant of our makeshift command center to be sick all over her laptop.

Despite the separate feeds and slightly different vantages, the streams all showed the same thing: the crew racing toward the bank, past a world arrested by sudden inaction. It was as if we'd paused time and unleashed our band of merry robbers.

For all of about thirty seconds, anyway. In the next thirty, all hell broke loose. The crew had just reached the top of the steps when a handful of forms emerged. I saw four at a glance, and then six.

There were a few suits and what looked like a janitor in the mix, but two were bank security. While Deltaseal relied on mechanical guards for its primary security fleet, a handful of flesh-and-blood security personnel were on staff, both as a failsafe for situations like this one and to handle more delicate scenarios. It wouldn't be good for business to subject a powerful client throwing a tantrum to the merciless, crushing appendages of a battle bot.

Fredricks spotted them first, firing four shots in the lead guard's direction. One found its target, and with a sizzle of electricity, he slumped to the ground, unconscious.

We might have been opting for nonlethal, but the screaming spray of laser energy that bore down on the crew indicated that we were alone in doing so. In this, superior numbers came to our rescue. The crew got off more shots in less time, and before the bank staff managed to hurt anyone, they'd been taken out. "Be careful, guys," I said into their comm. "There's probably more inside."

"Thanks, Captain Obvious," David returned.

"Status?" Maggie called.

I turned back to her screen. She'd left Luke bound in the other room. Corano had the bank manager's slumped figure over his shoulder, and they were heading into the vault. Kereli held the door to admit them.

"Team's incoming, Mags," I said. "They are taking some fire, but no casualties yet."

"Copy. Stay safe, everyone."

Now, she turned her attention to the vault. "You get these boxes out," she said to Corano and Kereli. "I'm going for the gold storage."

The Conglomerate's gold was stashed in the inner vault, in a chamber of its own. It was locked with a pin and protected by a palm reader. The first was easy enough, for me anyway. The pin was stored in an encrypted database. The encryption algorithm was complex, and probably would have taken months to break – if I hadn't put it in place myself.

In a sense, I almost understood why the Conglomerate wanted me out of the picture. I was far from counting the mission a triumph until we were in the air, underway. But the fact that we'd gotten as far as we had was something of a miracle in its own right. Without insider knowledge, Deltaseal was all but invincible. Not for the first time, I was struck by the irony that the insider knowledge they feared so much would never have been a problem to them had they not meant to murder me over it.

But contemplating the vagaries of fate would wait. Maggie was heading for Wyman. He was the second piece of the puzzle: the bank manager's palm print was the final authorization we needed.

He was slumped on the ground where Corano had left him. Maggie moved to hoist him up, and I jumped in my seat as the still body became, in the blink of an eye, a blur of motion. Wyman was on his feet, tackling Mags.

"Jesus," I gasped. "Fuck. Corano!"

I saw the tactical officer turn to the commotion, but my eyes were on Mags' screen. The view was harried, jumping between near and far as they wrestled and broke free. Wyman was sporting a purple welt in the center of his face, but it wasn't slowing him down. He came at her with fists swinging – and, I saw with horror, a silver blade flashing in the dim lighting.

Maggie sidestepped his thrusts, waiting until the knife passed close by to fall on his arm. She dove forward, seizing his wrist and drawing the elbow rigid with one hand as she threw her weight against his shoulder. I heard a crack of bone, and the bank manager shrieked.

Corano's screen showed a better vantage than Maggie's. He'd reached them now, but Wyman was already subdued. His arm hung at an angle that made my skin crawl.

She was a little tussled, her bun a bit messier than before, but unharmed. I breathed out a sigh of relief.

"Don't try a stunt like that again," she told the manager, picking up his fallen blade. "Or I won't be as forgiving next time."

He offered a few choice words in response, but mostly whimpered.

"You got this under control, Captain?" Corano wondered.

She nodded. "I do. Come on, Wyman. Time to scan that paw of yours."

Frank's voice called me back to the other monitors. "Which way, Kay?"

"Uh…" I studied his screen. They were at a fork in a now dimly lit hall. I tried to picture it with the lights on. "I think you're by the stairs. So that's a right, until you hit the staircase."

"Copy."

"Wait, you *think*?" David wondered.

"Good way to spend time," Frank offered. "You should try it sometime."

I shook my head but smiled. I wasn't sure there was a scenario possible that would preclude the Kudarian finding something to laugh about.

The cook ignored his comments though. "You better not be sending us to our deaths, Kay."

I glanced back at Maggie's screen. She'd just buzzed into the gold storage. I whistled at the sight of hundreds of gold bricks, all stacked neatly in rows and columns. "Holy shit," I said into the comms, "that's a lot of gold."

"Yes it is," she responded. I couldn't see her face, but I could hear the grin in her tone. "Hurry it up, Frank. We need you here."

"Almost there, Captain."

CHAPTER FORTY-ONE

Thanks to Wyman's master key, Corano and Kereli made short work of the safe deposit boxes. The contents were dumped unceremoniously into a canvass tote for transport.

Now Kereli targeted the credit chips, and Corano joined Maggie at the anti-grav hand truck. They were loading it with matter-resynched gold bars.

"We're at five minutes and counting," I reminded everyone.

Having dispatched every one they'd come in contact with, the rest of the crew reached the vaults, knocking to be admitted. Kereli glanced up. "Get that, Corano."

He did. She, meanwhile, buzzed me. "Katherine, I believe I'm ready here."

I nodded. She'd loaded about two dozen credit chips into the vault's terminal ports. "Copy that. You've got a direct line in. You're going to want to initiate a transfer. Max these cards hold is five hundred million credits."

"Understood." She worked for a minute as the crew filed in, filling duffel bags and hauling crates away. "Okay, I've got the transfers prepped. I'm ready."

"Good. Hit 'yes' when it asks you if you want to proceed. You'll be prompted on the first transfer for an authorization code. I'll give you Wyman's. You have thirty seconds to put it in."

"Copy. Okay, transfer initialized. It's prompting for the code."

I read off the string of characters I'd pulled from Deltaseal's databases, and she punched them in, repeating them back as she went.

"Ha," she exclaimed. "It worked."

I grinned at the excitement in her tone. Kereli was a tough nut to crack, but not even she, it seemed, was immune to the lure of billions of credits. "Good work."

"Do I have to reauthorize every time I put new chips in?"

"Afraid so."

"Okay. Stay on the line, then. I'll have to get that code from you again."

"Copy."

"Kay?" Maggie's voice cut in.

"Yes?"

"First round is on its way up."

"Copy that."

"Kay?" This was Frank.

"Yes?"

"Make sure you have the damned elevator back online, or no one gets their payoff."

I glanced at the monitors again and snorted. The hand truck

he was hauling bowed under the weight of all that they'd loaded onto it, and he was hunched forward and straining just to budge it. "So much for anti-grav."

"More like," he grunted, "assisted grav. Which only goes so far. Not far enough when you have maniacs packing the damned thing."

"Stop bellyaching," Maggie called, "and get a move on it." I caught the sight of her eyes twinkling from Corano's feed. "We're on a timer, remember."

"You're not going to hold it against me, are you Kay, when I murder her?" the Kudarian wondered.

Maggie sidled up beside him. "Scoot, you big whiner." The cart moved a bit more easily as she threw her strength behind, but she was panting too as they reached the elevator bank. "We might have overfilled it," she admitted.

"Just a little," he puffed.

"The elevator is online," I said.

"Good," Maggie nodded. "Hey, Kay?"

"Yeah?"

"Tell Corano to go a little easier on the next load."

"Copy." I relayed the message, and the Esselian acknowledged.

"Waiting on that code, Kay," Kereli reminded me.

I grimaced. I'd heard her, in the periphery of my thoughts, ask for the authorization code again. I'd been too busy with the elevator to pay attention though. "Sorry, one second."

"Kay, Drake and I are heading back with packs," Fredricks put in at the same time.

"Copy." *God, if another person calls my name, I'm going to lose my mind.* I wished I'd kept one of them onboard to assist in the command center. Too late for that now, of course.

I glanced at the clock. Eight minutes and twelve seconds left. *I can get through that.*

"Kay?"

I groaned, but not as deeply as I might have. "Yes, Maggie?"

"You think you can handle this, once we get it onboard?"

"Uh…" I blinked. "How heavy is it again?"

"Heavy," Frank grunted.

"Just roll it out of the way," she said. "Into one of the storage rooms."

"Okay. Sure." I wasn't confident that I could, but I'd give it a shot.

"Good. That way, we can get back for the next load."

I glanced back at the vault. Fredricks and Ginny were taking a load upstairs. Corano had finished loading the last hand truck and was now carting it out of the vault. His, I noted, was packed considerably lighter than the rest. Which I observed to him, via his comm, adding, "Slacker."

"I work smarter, Katherine. Not harder. I am naturally faster than either a human or a Kudarian, so I will make twice as many runs as Frank and the Captain in the same time."

"A beer says you won't."

"You're on."

He passed Wyman now, whose unbroken arm they'd cuffed to a rail. "You're dead," he said. "The Conglomerate will find you."

The Esselian snorted. "You sound like Henderson. You humans: your threats are always the same."

"They could take some lessons from Frank," I laughed, remembering the Kudarian's terrifying handling of Rex.

"Now *that* would be scary," he agreed.

Wyman, who heard only Corano's half of the conversation, had gone silent. Corano moved for the elevator.

I sat there considering his words, though. The prospect of moving a cart that required both Frank and Maggie was rather daunting to me. But I too could work smarter, not harder.

I punched a button to open ship wide comms. "Sydney?"

A moment later, the robot's metallic voice answered, "Yes, Katherine?"

"Hey, Mags and Frank are bringing a cart full of – well, never mind. Point is, it's heavy. Heavier than I think I can move. Any chance you can get it to one of the storage bays for me?"

"Of course."

"Thanks, Syd. I'll meet you by the gangplank."

"On my way, Katherine."

I pressed the button to broadcast to the entire team comm network. "Hey, I'm stepping A-F-K to get the gold onboard. Anyone need anything from me before I go?" A chorus of voices chimed in, indicating that I was free to go. "Alright, Mags, I'm on my way."

“So, uh, Kay? We hit a snag,” Frank said.

“A snag?”

“The stairs. How the hell are we going to get the hand truck down steps?”

“Shit.” We’d thought of everything – every possible threat, every possible foul up. But the stairs? We hadn’t addressed that. “Leave the cart,” I decided.

“What?”

“There’s a ramp at the side, but it’s out of the way. It’ll shave a minute off our time each way. Leave the gold. I’ll take care of it.”

“You sure?” This was Mags.

“Yes.”

“Alright. Be careful.”

“It’s heavy,” Frank cautioned.

“Don’t worry.” I grinned, and my amusement reached my tone. “I’m going to be working smart. Not hard.”

“Ugh.” Maggie shuddered. “You’ve been working with Corano too long.”

“Hey,” the Esselian piped up over the comm. “What’s that supposed to mean?”

CHAPTER FORTY-TWO

"Is this all, Katherine?" Sydney asked. He'd hoisted the hand truck Maggie and Frank left at the top of the bank steps into his arm, as easily as if he was lifting a basket of laundry.

"Yes," I said. "Show off. Come on."

"Show off?"

"I'm joking."

"Oh."

"Come on, Syd. Let's get back to the ship."

"Understood." The battle bot had extended his stilts, lifting himself and his continuous track assembly off the ground. He was not as agile on stilts as he was on the track, but he managed alright. He'd gotten up the stairs quickly, and he seemed unfazed as he ambled down them with a hand truck piled in gold that reached far above his head. In fact, he made much better time than me.

When he reached the ground, he lowered himself to the track and retracted his stilt appendages. "Are you coming, Katherine?"

"I am. You get inside."

"I will wait for you." He did, and as soon as I caught up, rolled off again. We reached the ship, and he trundled into the storage room I'd indicated, dropping the cart with a calamitous crash.

I flinched, and he said, "Alright, mission accomplished. Is there anything further I can do to assist?"

"As a matter of fact, there is."

"Excellent. I must thank you, Katherine, for the chance to be of use. I have not had the opportunity much of late, and I appreciate it."

I blinked. I knew his gratitude was a programmed response – *it is, isn't it?* – but it seemed so genuine I couldn't help but be touched. I was anthropomorphizing him, I knew. But I said, "Of course, Syd. Thank *you.*"

"My pleasure. Now, what other tasks did you have in mind for me?"

"More of the same, actually. They're bringing more carts."

"Excellent. I shall fetch them for you."

"Thanks Syd." I buzzed into the comm network. "Alright, the gold is stashed."

"What the hell?" Frank wondered. "How did you manage that?"

"I told you: work smarter, not harder."

"That's the spirit," Corano agreed. "Speaking of, I've got another *opportunity* for you. I'm leaving my hand truck on the steps."

"Copy."

"Got to get back there and earn my beer."

"Hmph," I snorted. "Good luck. Maggie's going to run

circles around you."

"I'm going to what now?" her voice buzzed over.

"I'll tell you later. Just get that gold up here, babe. Or I'm going to owe him a drink."

"Okay," she said warily.

"Don't bother, Captain. You will lose."

"Hey," Drake's voice reached my ears. He was huffing up the gangplank, bowed under a heavy duffel bag. "You got the robot carrying stuff?"

"Yup."

"Good thinking."

I grinned. "I thought so."

"You think you can lend him to us?" David grunted. He was a few steps behind the engineer.

"Sorry, he's got more carts to handle."

"Anyway," Frank called over the comm, "your fat ass can use the exercise."

He glowered as Drake and I laughed, but seemed to be panting too heavily to offer a retort. They took their leave, and I returned to my station in the command center.

"How much time do we have left, Kay?" Maggie called.

"Umm…" I glanced back at my clock. "Shit. We're down to five minutes and forty seconds, people."

"Alright, last haul," she said. "Whatever you've got loaded, get it up here. Now. We need to be on the ship and underway within four minutes."

A slew of *copy*'s and *roger that*'s sounded.

The seconds ticked by slowly after that – and, somehow managed to race by at the same time. One by one, the crew made their return trips. Sydney rolled along at a rapid pace, ferrying carts of gold back to storage just to head out for more.

Frank returned with a minute to spare, covered in perspiration. Corano and Kereli were right behind him. Maggie waited outside on the gangplank, keeping an eye out for any lingering Conglomerate employees, and ensuring that we didn't miss anyone.

Sydney rolled in with his last load, declaring, "The Captain informs me that there is no more to fetch, Katherine."

"Excellent – thanks, Syd."

"You are welcome."

Ginny and Fredricks were the last to return, with Mags right on their heels. "Alright," she called as soon as the gangplank was retracted, and the door sealed. "Let's get in the air, Frank."

"Copy that, Captain."

"Corano," I asked, "you got those missiles locked?"

"Of course."

I nodded. Until the clock ran out, I was left with little to do but monitor the situation. I felt a bit like Sydney at the moment, in standby mode while everyone else had tasks to keep them busy. Except, unlike my battle bot, the anxiety of *what-if*'s were creeping into my head as I waited.

What if the reboot starts early for some reason?

What if we don't reach atmosphere in enough time?

What if I can't trigger a second shutdown in enough time?

Maggie took her seat behind me, and I turned to flash her a smile. She was grinning ear to ear. Rather than fretting like I was, she was exhilarated. She caught my eye and smiled a little wider. Then, she turned to her tactical officer. "Alright, Corano, as soon as we're in range, fire."

"Copy."

The *Black Flag* lifted off, leaving the bank and quiet park, full of its mechanical sentries arrested in their patrols, behind. Once more the plateau and the waterfall came into sight, growing smaller and smaller as we rose.

"First round of missiles deploying in three…two…one," Corano called. A hiss sounded as the armaments were sent on their way. I pulled the tracking camera up on one of my monitors. A dizzying blur of motion showed the missiles racing toward a mainland battery of artillery. At first, the cannons seemed tiny and far away; but they grew, enveloping the screen, and then, very suddenly, all was black.

"Direct hit," Corano declared. "Weapons destroyed."

"Good job," Mags nodded.

The ship pulled up further, and the bank vanished from view. All that remained was the green and blue of the continent below, growing smaller by the moment.

"Deploying second and third rounds now."

Again, I watched the missiles' progress. Corano was targeting two island stations. One was another ground to air defense system. The other was a drone launch station. His targeting was exact. The missiles raced to their destructive ends, and he confirmed what my black screens already hinted: "Targets destroyed."

"We're about to break atmosphere," Frank advised.

"Copy."

"We've got twenty-five seconds left," I observed. I managed to keep my tone calm, but my anxiety was spiking again. Twenty-five seconds was not much time to get in range of Deltaseal Air and disable it. Twenty-five seconds was not much time at all.

"Copy," Maggie said. Otherwise, we were all silent, waiting, watching.

The seconds ticked by as we climbed higher and higher. *Twenty. Fifteen. Fourteen. Thirteen.*

I almost jumped in my seat when Corano said, "Missiles deployed."

Ten. Nine. Eight. Seven. I chewed at my thumb, staring at a feed of the last missiles racing for Deltaspace Air's cannons. *Five. Four.* My screen went dark, and everyone – everyone – on the bridge sighed a breath of relief.

"Deltaseal Air defense destroyed," Corano confirmed.

CHAPTER FORTY-THREE

It was smooth sailing after that. As a parting gift, I shutdown the systems a second time. Another fifteen minutes without power would mean tracking and pursuing us would only be that much harder.

That's when the celebrations started on the *Black Flag*. There'd been whooping and cheering, of course, but once the clock reset, the nervous tension that had been building so long was released in a torrent. Maggie said a few words of congratulations for so many jobs so well done. Then she crossed the bridge to wrap me in her arms and give me a smoldering kiss. "Damn," I said, catching my breath.

David made a gagging sound. This time, Ginny and Fredricks were too preoccupied with similar interests to pay much attention. The rest of the crew discreetly averted their attention.

"You were great, Kay. Amazing. I still can't believe we got away with that."

"It was your idea," I reminded her.

She didn't argue, but her eyes were full of an appreciation that made me preen, and blush a little too. She held me for a moment longer, then returned to her seat. Still, now and again, I'd feel her eyes on me, or catch her glance.

We flew for a few more hours under the name of the *Lady's*

Reign. But once we were sure no one was in pursuit and we were well beyond the reach of scanners, we set to work swapping out id codes again.

It took a while, but soon enough the *Black Flag* was back to her old self again and the *Lady's Reign* disappeared into the void of space. Then began the task of really examining our haul.

It was less a task than a pleasure, but it was still hard work. In our haste, we'd deposited our haul haphazardly. Sydney had added to the general confusion by dumping hand truck after hand truck full of gold into the storage rooms.

Now, the tiny gold bars had to be collected, stacked and counted. We hadn't had time to touch the regular gold. Everything in our storage was matter-resynched gold. In a sense, in its current state, it was worthless. The resynch process changed its molecular structure, compressing it for transport. It would have to be passed through a synchronizer before it was actually gold again. But because it was one synch away from being gold, the current state didn't matter much to buyers.

Credits were more straightforward. Kereli had cleared the Conglomerate accounts of as many credits as she could move to chips. There were dozens of them, all maxed out with half a billion credits each.

I whistled at the size of the crate she'd accumulated. "You could live relatively comfortably for the rest of your life on a handful of those. Imagine what you could do with a whole box?"

"There's seventeen of us," Kereli reminded me. "It'll go a lot less far."

"Still," I said, "once we add the gold? We're going to be rich."

She smiled. "Yes. Yes we are."

"Like we hit the jackpot," I said.

"I'm still reeling from the fact that we pulled it off," Maggie admitted.

"You thought we wouldn't be able to do it?" I was a bit incredulous. She'd been so confident, so sure. Had she really been harboring doubts all along?

"In theory, of course. But I can't believe we got away with *so much*. I mean, there's a thousand factors – what they've got on hand, what complications you run into as you're hauling it…it can all change your final numbers. And this? This is a hell of a lot of money."

I nodded. We'd talked about trillions of credits before, but that had been in the abstract. Now, as we counted the gold and credits, it seemed tangible. "A hell of a lot of money." I still wasn't sure I'd entirely wrapped my brain around the enormity of it.

By time we'd gotten everything counted, the day had run long. Not that anyone minded. We were still running at fifteen-shots-of-espresso levels of energy. "Okay," Maggie said. She'd called us all together in the mess hall, and we'd broken out the top shelf again. A few of the guys were several glasses in already. "Are you ready for this?"

A chorus of impatience matched the question, and she smiled. "Okay. At current transfer rates, deducting for resynch fees…and keeping in mind that I'm not counting any of the jewelry from the safe deposit boxes, since we need appraisals on all of that…"

"Get to it, dammit," David said.

We all laughed, for we were as impatient as he was. "One

trillion, one billion, and fifty-four thousand credits."

A round of cheers broke out.

"Which brings our individual shares to forty-six billion, nine hundred and twenty-one million, eight hundred and seventy-seven thousand, five hundred and thirty-one credits." She grinned, adding. "And a quarter."

"What about Kay?" Drake asked.

"What?"

"She's getting a quarter of the whole pot, isn't she?"

Maggie nodded. "That's right. Those were our terms: a quarter for Kay, and the rest split evenly between us."

"So how much is that?"

"That's about two hundred and fifty billion credits."

Frank whistled appreciatively, raising his glass. "Don't forget the little people, Kay, now that you've made it to the top."

Drake, though, frowned. "So more than five times what any of us earned."

"That's what we agreed to," Maggie said.

He nodded. "I know. Just seems crazy when we were the ones taking fire."

"Without Katherine's efforts, we wouldn't have survived long enough to land," Kereli observed.

"And Deltaseal's fleet of battle bots and drones would have reduced us to bloody stumps even if we had," Corano added.

"I'd say that's money well earned," Ginny agreed.

David shrugged. "And forty-six billion credits is hardly chump change."

Drake nodded slowly, staring into his glass, and it seemed the point had been resolved. In truth, I felt a bit embarrassed about it. I'd negotiated that rate before – well, before *everything*. Before I'd gotten to know the crew. Before I'd fallen for Mags. Before I realized that I wasn't dealing with cutthroats at all, but a group of people I genuinely esteemed.

"Tomorrow," Maggie was saying, "we'll start working on the deposit boxes. There's a ton of stuff in those totes. Some of it-"

Drake downed his glass, mumbling just loud enough to be heard, "Guess it pays to fuck the captain."

We all went silent. My face flushed, and one of Maggie's eyebrow arched upward. "Say again, Mister Sage?"

He met her gaze. "You heard me, Captain."

"It's not like that, Drake," I protested. "We made the deal long before I even liked anyone here, much less – well, that." Hell, it had taken literally my entire time on the ship, until this very day, before I'd gotten to "fuck the captain." Not that he needed to know that; but it did drive home the unfairness of the charge.

"Come on," Fredricks sighed, "don't be like that, man."

Maggie, meanwhile, was holding his gaze. "You knew the terms before we were half an hour off of Trel. If you had a problem with them, that was the time to mention it."

"Maybe my eyes weren't open to what was really going on," he offered.

"You're drunk, Drake," Frank said. "Shut your stupid mouth before you say something you'll regret."

"Have to agree with dumbass there," David chimed in, jutting a thumb in the Kudarian's direction. "A deal's a deal."

Maggie and Drake, though, were sitting in place, eyes locked. He was sullen and – Frank was right – drunk. She was livid, her eyes blazing like an avenging angel from some old painting.

Granted, I might have been a little biased in my observations. But the enmity between them was clear enough. "Listen," I said, "we can just split our take – all of it – seventeen ways. Forget my quarter. I'll take an equal share."

Drake started to agree that this was the only fair solution, but Mags cut him off. "Bullshit. I don't renege on my deals. A quarter is what we agreed to. That's what we're doing." She added with a pointedness that seemed to undo everything I'd been trying to accomplish, "This is my ship, and I'll be damned if I'm going to start breaking my word."

Drake's jaw clenched. So did hers. Then, though, he laughed. "Goddamn, you all are uptight." He shook his head, pouring another glass and downing it in one gulp. "Can't take a joke."

He hadn't been joking. I don't think anyone believed that he had. But a few nervous chuckles met the proclamation. "You got me," Fredricks said. "You definitely got me."

"Me too," Ginny agreed.

"Just don't make it a habit," David added. "We've already got to put up with Frank. I don't think the ship could survive another so-called comedian."

CHAPTER FORTY-FOUR

The exchange had put something of a damper on our mood, but, with the alcohol flowing freely, it was forgotten soon enough. We went through a first round of bottles, and David fetched a second. When we went through that, he wasn't to be budged. "I'm not getting up until I finish my glass. I'm not a damned servant."

Maggie giggled at his grumbling, and I giggled at her giggle. It was light and free, and happier than she usually allowed herself to be, openly at least.

She was adorable.

"Oh God," Frank shook his head. "I'm going to be the only sober one left on the whole damned ship. You're all drunk."

"I'm not drunk," I protested. "On the way, yes. But not there yet."

Maggie grinned. "Give me the key, Dave. I'll get it."

"Here." He tossed her the key, and leaned back in his seat. His point – whatever it was – had apparently been made.

She caught it and got to her feet. "I'll be right back. Any special requests?"

At this point in the night, we were less picky than we had been at the beginning. The responses were tepid. It seemed anything upwards of thirty-proof was going to be a hit. I watched her go, and then turned back to my glass. It was mostly empty.

Impulsively, I pushed to my feet and followed her into the galley. She'd reached the liquor cabinet and was in the process of selecting bottles. "Hey," I said.

She glanced back at me and smiled. "Hey, sexy lady."

I grinned. "Need help?"

"Sure." Then, she pulled a face. "Careful, though. We don't want anyone thinking you're raiding the liquor store. Perks of fucking the captain and all that."

I shook my head, moving closer to her. I took her hands in mine, studying them for a moment. Then, I flashed an arch smile. "If he only knew how long you made me wait for that, eh?"

She blushed. "Don't remind me."

I laughed. "I don't know. I think you deserve to be reminded, now and again, after all I suffered." Then, though, I sobered a little. "I did mean it, though, Maggie. If it's going to cause problems, I can split my take."

She shook her head now, rather adamantly. "No. We made a deal, Kay."

"I know. But that was before I knew you guys. It was before…well, before I knew you, babe."

She pulled one of her hands from mine to caress my cheek. "And that, my Katherine, is exactly why I can't let you do it."

"Why?"

"Because you earned your money. And I won't use *us* as a reason to guilt you into losing it."

"Babe, it's not like that."

She shook her head, though. "No, Kay. A deal's a deal. You keep your share." She leaned in to peck me on the lips. "Please?"

I made a point of sighing to make my discontent known, but I was done arguing. The truth was, she probably could have convinced me to jump out an airlock by turning those gorgeous green eyes my way and asking nicely. The kiss was just the proverbial nail in the coffin of my resolve. "Fine."

"Good." She turned back to the liquor. "Now what should I take?"

I shrugged. "I don't know." I shot her a sly glance. "I'm ready for bed, myself."

She laughed. "Are you, Katherine?"

I nodded.

"Well, it's been a long day."

"It has."

"And I could tuck you in."

"Ohh, I'd like that."

"Alright. Let me get a few more bottles for the table, though. Then we'll get you to bed." She grinned impishly. "You know, it'll be the first time I've slept with a billionaire."

I snorted with laughter. "Me too, actually."

"On the other hand…I do seem to have a habit of chasing rich women." She turned from the liquor cabinet again, wrapping her arms around me and kissing me playfully. "First Gia, now you."

"Well, *I'll* at least let you eat carbs," I declared.

She laughed. "Good. I made the right call, choosing you then." Her fingers trailed up my back. "Always go for the girl who lets you have carbs."

My skin burned at her touch, even through the fabric. I brought my lips to the delicate skin of her neck, saying between kisses, "But it's still a 'no' to honey."

She smiled impishly and brought her lips to my ear. "That's okay. I've got something much sweeter in mind anyway."

I shivered at her words, at her breath on my ear. "Oh God, Maggie. What the hell are we still doing here?"

"Good question."

We didn't stay much longer. We brought out an armful of booze, and while the rest of the crew spent their night drinking, we spent our hours more pleasantly engaged.

She stayed the night, and I woke the next morning to find myself still wrapped in her arms. It was surreal, at first. I'd spent so many days, so many weeks, pining for her; and here she was, in my bed. In my arms. Close enough to feel her breath on my skin, to smell the traces of perfume and sweat from the day before, to watch the rise and fall of her chest as she slept.

I had enough money coming to buy my own moon and build a palace on it. But I didn't care for any of that in the moment. I'd hit the jackpot, alright, and it had nothing to do with money. I'd hit the jackpot when I'd managed, somehow, to matter to Maggie Landon.

She woke shortly after me, and I blushed. I'd been watching her sleep absently, lost to the beauty of the moment. "Hey," she said.

"Hey."

"Did you sleep well?"

I grinned. "Better than I have in a long time."

It was her turn to blush. "I didn't mean that."

"I know. And yes, I did."

"Me too." She smiled. "But dammit, babe, this is a tiny bed."

"I know," I agreed. "I really need to file a complaint."

"What asshole," she teased, "assigned you this berth anyway?"

"The captain," I reminded her.

"Oh. I should have a word with her."

I laughed. "You do that."

She kissed me. "I will." Then she sighed and yawned, pushing to her elbows. "But I should get up. I'm already supposed to be on the bridge."

"Come on," I said, tugging her back gently, "everyone else is going to be hungover as hell. No one's going to notice if you're late because they will be too."

She grinned, plopping backward. "And what if we run into trouble, and no one's on deck?"

I rolled over and pushed myself up so that I hovered above her, face to face. "We'll hear the alerts, same as anyone else." I kissed her. "We got through the night just fine on autopilot. We'll survive a little longer."

She wrapped her arms around me, pulling me toward her.

"That's terribly irresponsible, Katherine Ellis."

"Then let's be irresponsible, Maggie."

She brushed aside a lock of hair that had slipped over my face and smiled as she caressed my cheek. "Alright. Irresponsible it is."

CHAPTER FORTY-FIVE

Kereli was on the bridge when we arrived, and so was Frank. The latter was asleep at his station, though, and remained sleeping for the better part of an hour.

Kereli nodded a good morning, and then went back to a puzzle she was working on. Maggie and I sat talking in low whispers for a bit. Eventually, when she was content that she'd done her duty by making an appearance on the bridge, we and the rest of the crew trickled into the mess hall.

Here, we saw more faces than we'd encountered on deck. Most of them were a little grey, a little bleary-eyed, and a little weather-beaten. "I'm glad we stopped drinking when we did," Maggie confided with a grin.

I nodded. "Looks like this party went on for quite a while."

There were still empty bottles on some of the tables. Everyone seemed to have fanned out to avoid them as they nursed cups of coffee.

We headed for the line. David was visible, working away over something. There was no food ready yet, though. "Morning," Mags said.

He glowered at us. "Keep it down."

"Uh, morning," she repeated in a low whisper. "What's for

breakfast?"

"Food."

"Okay. You need help, Dave?"

He stared up at her suspiciously. "What?"

"If you need to take a morning off, I can fill in."

His expression lightened, and he seemed to genuinely consider it for a moment. Then, though, he shook his head. "I got it, Captain."

She nodded. "Alright. But if you do – I'll be out there, drinking coffee."

He smiled – actually smiled – and said, "You and the rest of the crew."

Maggie grinned. "It was a hell of a party."

"Yeah. It was."

We grabbed a coffee and found a table. "He takes his job as seriously as you do," I observed.

I'd been largely kidding, but she nodded. "We got a great crew here, Kay."

We spent a few minutes sipping our coffee and chatting. Slowly but surely the aromas of food wafted into the mess hall. It was Drake's approach that really got my attention though. The engineer had been at a back table and had shot a furtive glance in our direction only once. Otherwise, he'd ignored us. Now, though, he walked over to our table.

"Captain," he said, "Kay."

"Morning Sage," Maggie greeted. Her tone was cordial but not warm.

"Look, I need to apologize. I guess I was an asshole last night."

She nodded. "You were. But, apology accepted."

He glanced at me, and I said, "Same. It's all good, Drake."

"Thanks. I don't remember too much of what was said, but they-" This was said with a jerk of the thumb toward the rest of the room. "-tell me I was quite the jerk. And I'm sorry about that."

Maggie nodded. "It's okay."

"Thanks, Captain." He glanced down at his empty coffee cup. "Well, I better get a refill if I'm going to make it through today."

It took a few hours for everyone to get back on their feet. The crew, Fredricks informed us all sagely, was getting too damned old to party like that. "Other than me, of course."

Eventually, though, the day proceeded as normal. We pulled out the safe deposit box totes after lunch, and sorted the goods by type. There was a slew of jewelry, some of it ancient by the look of it. There were also photographs and data cards. Some seemed to be intended for blackmail purposes. There were photos of senators with mistresses and governors with paramours.

Not everything was so tame, though. Some of the images depicted crimes, some rather grim crimes. There were dead bodies and all manner of assaults in progress. Maggie shook her head. "Those'll go to the police," she decided.

"There's going to be a lot more on the data cards," Corano

observed. "Print photos are very old school. But I'll bet most of the digital storage is for stuff like this."

Maggie nodded grimly. "I'm not sure I want to even see what's on it. And yet, if it's evidence of crimes – especially crimes like these – we shouldn't just sit on it."

"We could just ship it all to the cops," Frank offered.

"There'll be a lot of collateral damage from that," she said. "A lot of this stuff could ruin a career, but it's not harming anyone." She picked up an image of a senator from one of the Dacu sector planets, his arm wrapped around a young woman. "Like this crap."

"Still," Corano mused, "I don't want to be the one who has to go through those chips."

"No," she agreed. "Me either."

In the end, the decision was made to hold off on making a decision. "We'll figure it out," Maggie declared. "Either way, we won't let these dirtbags get away with it."

A postponement of the difficult question meant we could savor the more palatable aspects of our haul, though. And there were lots of those.

We'd lifted some incredible pieces from the troves of the Conglomerate's spoiled scions and wealthy partners. There were bags of rare gems and boxes containing exquisite jewelry. There were artifacts, too, from cultures all over known space. Kereli found a pair of earrings of jade-colored stone, carved with old world Esselian symbols. "These are from the first dynasty," she marveled. "It is prohibited for private collectors to own these."

"I doubt most of this stuff was legally acquired," Maggie observed.

"No. But these are the heritage of my people, Captain. These belong in one of Alfor's cultural preservation sites. Not a lockbox."

Maggie nodded. "Well," she said, "I think, in cases like that, we return them."

Kereli nodded. "I concur."

Corano chimed in, "Me too."

"Is there some kind of reward?" David wondered.

"No. But it's the right thing to do."

The cook frowned. "I'm all for doing the right thing…but how much money are we talking here?"

"Come on, Dave. We're privateers, not grave robbers."

He sighed. "Dammit, Cap…you're right."

"Are we going to sell this all off?" Fredricks wondered. "Or just divvy it up?"

Maggie shrugged. "We could do either, I guess. It'll take awhile to move some of these pieces for a good price. If someone would rather try to move it on their own, I have no problem with that."

"We'd have to have them appraised first," Drake said.

"Alright. But, my point is, I want this one." Fredricks held up a necklace sporting a silver Valarian diamond surrounded by emeralds.

"Good choice. Definitely brings out the color in your eyes," Frank agreed.

The comment brought a roll to those eyes, but was otherwise

ignored. "Deduct it from my share. I'd just rather keep it than sell it."

"I have no objection to that," Maggie agreed.

"Me either," Drake added. "As long as it comes out of your cut."

Fredricks nodded. "Of course. Mind if I take it now, though? I'll hand it over for appraisal, of course, when the time comes."

"Well, we know where to find you," she grinned. "I'm not worried."

"Thanks, Captain."

He pocketed the piece, and waited a few minutes. Then, he got up. "Well, I should probably go check my office. See if anyone needs me."

Maggie smirked, and I laughed, intoning in a voice that approximated the ship's automatic paging system, "'Medical emergency in engineering.'"

He flashed a grin as he headed for the door. "I will neither confirm nor deny anything."

"My engine tech has real work, you know," Drake said.

Fredricks ignored the comment and left. David and Drake rolled their eyes. "Just goes to show, I guess," the cook opined as the door closed, "hormones can make imbeciles of anyone. Even an otherwise sensible human being like Fredricks."

"Come on," I said. "That was sweet. Ginny'll love it."

"Then she could have taken it out of her own share," he countered sagely.

Frank shook his head. "Well damn. You're a hell of a

romantic, Dave."

CHAPTER FORTY-SIX

I was getting dressed for dinner when I heard Sydney's voice outside my door. "You may enter, Captain. Katherine has cleared you." A moment later, a knock sounded.

I laughed. "Come in, Mags."

She did, and when the door closed, turned questioning eyes to me. "What was that about?"

"Syd's my bodyguard. He's been stopping unexpected visitors and questioning them. I told him you're clear to pass as you see fit."

Her eyebrows were raised. "A bodyguard? You really think that's necessary?"

I grinned. "No. But Syd does."

She shook her head and laughed. "Okay." Then, she glanced me over. "Wow. I am way underdressed, compared to you."

I flushed. I was wearing a plush, bell-sleeved sweater and a pair of business casual pants that fit just snug enough around my butt to look nice. It was the closest I had in my trunk of job site clothes to sexy, and when I was with Mags, I felt like being sexy. "I thought, with what David was saying, it might be nice to dress up. If you think it's too much-"

"No, not at all." She smiled, stepping closer. "You look

damned nice, as a matter of fact."

I grinned. "Well, I figured we might as well celebrate. Anyway, this is one of David's special meals, remember?"

He'd resolved earlier to treat us all to culinary sensations worth remembering. "I don't suppose I'll cook for myself very often once we're off this ship," he'd said, "now that I'm so damned rich. So you all better work up appetites for the next few days, because I'm going to be cooking up some treats." When Frank had groaned, he'd snorted. "I mean it. Not even a Kudarian's palette will forget these culinary sensations."

"I'm not sure if that was a promise of good things to come, or a threat," she said, laughing.

"I'm assuming good things."

"Alright," she nodded. "Then I'll be optimistic too."

I wrapped an arm around her. "Good. Now, I'm ready. How about you?"

She nodded, and we walked, arm in arm, out of the room. Sydney greeted us with a, "Good evening, Katherine. And another good evening to you as well, Captain."

"Evening, Syd," I said.

Maggie smiled askew at me. She thought I was mad for carrying on conversations with a robot, I knew. I nudged her, and she obliged me. "Hi again."

"Katherine, may I ask a question?"

"Uh…sure."

"Based on your request to add Magdalene to the trusted visitors list, in combination with your patterns of touching, your failure to observe the distance ratios humans call 'personal space', and the speech patterns of affectionate banter, my algorithms predict a ninety-seven percent likelihood that you are engaged in a romantic relationship. Is that accurate?"

Maggie's eyebrows rose again.

"Um, yes," I admitted. "But why?"

"My algorithms are adaptive, Katherine. They will adapt to adjust for this new information."

"That sounds ominous," Maggie observed.

"On the contrary, Magdalene. I only mean that – as you humans would say – 'a friend of Katherine's is a friend of mine.' Knowing the value she places on you, I shall now adjust my own."

I wasn't sure I had ever heard anything simultaneously so sweet and yet so insanely creepy. "Thanks, Syd. But don't bug Maggie, okay?" She, I thought, would be less patient with his eccentricities.

"Certainly not."

"Alright. Well, we'd better get to dinner."

"Understood. Enjoy your meal, Katherine and Magdalene."

"So I'm Magdalene now," she said, once we were a ways down the hall. "Instead of Captain?"

I grinned. "Syd's a sweetheart. Even when he's creepy."

"He's a machine."

"Yeah, but that doesn't mean he doesn't try."

She squeezed me and laughed. "Oh Kay. I should have

known letting *you* adopt a robot would be a mistake."

"If you're not nice," I warned," I'll have David teach him to cook. And Frank write in some humor algorithms."

"Oh God." She shivered. "I repent."

Most of the crew was already at dinner when we arrived. David's promise of culinary adventures had, I think, evoked a kind of morbid curiosity in us all. The place smelled good, too.

"Is that…lasagna?" Maggie wondered.

"It is," Ginny said. She was, I noticed, wearing the necklace Fredricks had taken earlier. "He even made breadsticks."

"Holy crap," Mags marveled. "He wasn't kidding, then."

"I was not, Captain," David called. "It's not quite ready yet. But it will be in about ten minutes. Find a seat in the meantime."

We did, and I leaned in to whisper to Mags. "You know, I think this is the first time since I boarded that people have been excited to eat in the mess hall."

Dinner was as good as the aroma promised. David was not a chef extraordinaire, by any stretch of the imagination, but when he put his mind to it he was a very accomplished cook.

His lasagna was followed up the next morning by pancakes and eggs. The afternoon's soup, a Kudarian dish heavily seasoned with paprika, surprised even Frank. "This is actually good," he said, demanding of the cook, "Who the hell are you, and what did you do with David?"

"Very funny."

There was some irony to the fact that David was subjected to more teasing as his cooking improved than he ever had been before. I think it was the realization that, all the while he'd been serving such unappetizing slop, he was capable of making enjoyable food, that affected us.

He, too, seemed to relish surprising us. He'd respond to our comments with, "Told you I could cook, didn't I?"

The days passed quickly and quietly. However the Conglomerate was going to respond, now that we were back in Union space, they didn't seem in a hurry to chase us down. That was a relief.

It still left the issue of Henderson, though.

He was as bellicose as ever. He seemed to have guessed what we'd done. It was not surprising, I supposed. My involvement pointed toward Deltaseal; and our general exaltation indicated success.

"You've signed your own death warrants," he'd warn. "Damned fools. You'll beg for death before the end."

"We should space him," Frank advised. "I know you don't want to kill him, Kay, but he's a son-of-a-bitch. If he lives, he's going to put a target on all of our backs."

"They'll figure it out soon enough," I said. "We can't murder him, Frank."

"Killing a killer isn't murder. Mathematically, a negative negative is a positive. That's what killing a killer is: it's a negative negative. A positive. The world ends up a better place."

I shook my head. "This isn't math. We're talking about a life."

"An evil one, Kay."

"Still a life. He's our prisoner, Frank. If we kill a prisoner, how are we any better than him?"

Maggie pondered this for a while. "You know," she said at length, "there's probably enough evidence in the safe deposit boxes to put him away for the rest of his life. We could maroon him somewhere and get the evidence to the police. The evidence, and his location."

"He'll still get word to the Conglomerate," Frank sighed. "About us."

"We knew that was a risk from the beginning."

"It'd be much simpler to kill him."

"Yes," Maggie agreed. "It would. But…" She shook her head. "Probably not right."

He sighed again. "For all your progress on us, you humans could still learn a few things from the Kudarians."

"Like how to season human flesh?" David snorted.

"No. That clemency today leads to a new battle tomorrow."

CHAPTER FORTY-SEVEN

A quiet few days gave us the opportunity to start sorting the evidence. This was a grim business. First, I built an isolated network as we had no idea what was actually on those chips. We were dealing with some of the universe's shadiest characters. The idea that a potent virus or two might be nestled among the data stores had certainly occurred.

Then, we loaded all the chips onto it and ran deep scans. Nothing dangerous turned up, but I kept the copies isolated just in case there was something the scans missed.

Sorting through the data was not pleasant, though. There were plenty of spreadsheets of financial transactions, and the more innocuous blackmail images. But these Conglomerate types seemed to keep good tabs on each other, and there was evidence of just about every conceivable crime in these files.

Once I'd been assured that there were no viruses lingering among the data trove, I'd left off reviewing it. I knew I'd have to, eventually. But that would wait. We still had time, plenty of time to get to it.

And before then, I was happy making the most of the lull. It meant I got to spend a lot of time with Mags. Usually she was hard to pry off the bridge. Now, she didn't need much persuasion. A few check-ins here and there were all she seemed compelled to make, and I could keep her mostly to myself.

It was glorious. We spent a lot of time in bed, of course. Once introduced to her loving, it seemed I couldn't get enough of it. But we spent a lot of time just getting to know each other, too; and that was as sweet. Watching her walls come down, a little at a time, filled my heart.

Maggie talked about her time in the service, about the friends she'd made there; about the brother she'd lost. We made plans to visit Richard, the friend who had lost his husband a few months ago.

She convinced me to send my brother Jake a letter, to let him know that I still cared about him. I wasn't sure it would do much good. He'd been the one to shut that door, not me. "You can never replace family, Kay," she'd told me. And so I sent it, with not much hope of hearing anything in return.

We saw less of Frank in those days. This was by design, his and my own. His feelings for me, however good a job he did at relegating them to the background, were strong enough that seeing Mags and me together all the time had to be painful. He was a good friend, and I hoped we'd be able to remain good friends. But I didn't want to hurt him, and I hoped a little distance for a little while would help.

He seemed to think it would, because while he was as friendly as ever, he didn't join us at our table anymore. His conversations were as cordial, but they were briefer. I missed our banter, our easy chats; but I understood.

And, anyway, I had Mags to occupy my attention. Of all the things I learned about her in that brief period, that she was an ardent gamer was perhaps the most surprising. She'd always seemed a little too no-nonsense for such things.

"So there is a fun side to you after all, Magdalene Landon. It's not all just ships and business."

She smiled impishly as I examined the gaming console she kept tucked in her quarters. "Given our last few days together, I would have thought you'd have figured that out already."

"Touché. Still, video games?"

She shrugged. "It's a good way to kill the time."

"What do you like?"

"First person shooters, mostly. Military."

I rolled my eyes. "Of course, Mags."

She laughed. "Some medieval ones too."

"You any good?"

Was she ever. I considered myself a fair hand at games, once I learned the controls and mechanics. I was not accustomed to having my ass whooped so frequently, and so consistently as when we played.

She would laugh good humoredly at my frustration, suggesting, "Why don't we play cooperatively?"

"Because I'm going to kick your ass, Maggie Landon. Sir Kay is coming for you." Sir Kay was the handle I'd chosen in our fantasy-Earth based game. I was, ironically, playing as an armor clad, sword-wielding knight while she'd opted for the lightweight wizard class.

"Sir Kay's about to get spanked. Again."

We wasted a lot of hours on that silly game.

It wasn't a waste, though. Not really. It was a lot of fun, and for all the frustration of losing to her again and again, it was worth it for the satisfaction of winning now and then.

Sydney had taken up almost permanent residence outside Maggie's quarters now. There was no mystery to that. It was where I was to be found most hours of the day, if we weren't on the bridge or in the mess hall. He'd taken her almost as much under his wing as he had me. She was not thrilled by the development, and his straightforward answers did little to sell the idea to her. "Forgive me, Magdalene. I do not mean to be, as you say, 'annoying.' But it is my job."

"How the hell is advising me to drink more water your job?"

"Health is an important factor of human well-being. And a partner's well-being is an important concern in any relationship. Ergo, your health is of concern to Katherine. Katherine's well-being is my concern, and so by extension is yours."

"Sydney, don't push your luck."

"I do not understand, Magdalene."

"I think what's she's saying is she can figure out how much water to drink on her own."

"Forgive me, Katherine, but I must disagree. My scans indicate-"

"You've got to stop scanning people without their permission, Syd. That's – well, kind of creepy."

"Creepy?"

"Yes."

"Will you explain, please? I do not understand the concept of creepy."

Maggie snorted. "That's an understatement."

"Well, it means you make people uncomfortable. You do

things that are invasive."

"Like scans?"

"Exactly."

"How are they invasive, Katherine? Humans are unable to detect them. By definition, that seems the opposite of invasive."

"Well," I said, nodding slowly, "you're right, kind of. But it's a matter of trust. Nobody wants to be scanned without their consent. That's the invasive part."

"Why?"

"Why?" I shrugged. "Hell, I don't know. It just…feels wrong."

"I see. Very well. I shall ask permission before scanning people from now on. But I must advise you, Katherine, that this limits my ability to detect illness and injury."

"Understood. Still, I think it's for the best."

"Then I shall do it."

CHAPTER FORTY-EIGHT

We'd been underway for just over a week when the first inkling of trouble came. It was around two-thirty in the morning, and Mags and I were fast asleep. My comm device went off. It was the first time I'd been paged after hours, and it took me a minute to register what was happening.

Maggie groaned. "Hell. Is that me? Or you?"

"Sounds like it's me." Blinking, bleary-eyed, I picked up the device. "Hello?"

"Kay?"

"Drake?"

"Hey," he said, "sorry to wake you. But Ginny paged me, and I think we have a problem."

"A problem?"

"Yeah. We're getting weird readings from the engine. Some kind of power fluctuation. But my diagnostics aren't picking anything up, and we can't figure out what the hell's going on. I hate to ask…but you mind heading down to engineering and taking a look with us?"

"No," I said, suppressing a yawn. "Of course not."

"Thanks, Kay. I owe you."

"No problem. I'll be there in five."

"Great. And, hey, is the Captain with you?"

"Yeah."

"If she's awake, can you ask her to come down too? I think she's going to want to see this."

"Of course."

"On my way, Drake," Maggie called.

"Copy. See you in five."

"Shit," I said after we'd disconnected. "What do you think's going on?"

"No idea. But we're about two days from anything. I don't want to be stranded this far out of the way."

"Especially not after pissing the Conglomerate off."

"Exactly," she nodded.

We were dressing as we spoke, and I glanced up to see her pulling her hair into a rough ponytail. Her brow was creased, and there was a worried look in her eye. "Hey," I said. "We'll figure it out."

She glanced over and smiled. "I know. I just…it's weird. The timing. Those data cards you loaded…you made sure it was on an isolated network, right?"

"Of course." I was emphatic, but the truth was it had been the first thought to flit through my mind. I had made sure – I'd double and triple checked. But still, niggling doubt played at my thoughts. *What if I missed something? What if there'd been a virus or some kind of malware that's now on the core servers?*

She, though, nodded. "Alright."

We finished dressing and headed out. Sydney was waiting, and whirred to life as the door opened. "Good morning, Katherine. Good morning, Magdalene. You're up early."

"Morning Syd. Got to run, though."

"Ah, I am pleased to hear that you are implementing my wellness plan."

"Uh…right." I was in too much of a hurry to bother correcting him. "See you later."

"Happy jogging, Katherine."

We didn't actually run, but we did move at a quick pace toward engineering. "If we do end up needing replacement parts or something," I said, "and we don't have what we need onboard, we should change course right away."

"Yeah. I don't want to wind up adrift."

"No. That would-" I broke off suddenly, my motion arrested mid-step. We'd just rounded a corner, a little way down from engineering; and I was staring into the business end of a pistol. "What the-?"

The pistol's owner, a burly man in nondescript clothes, was a stranger to me. He grinned.

Maggie, meanwhile, moved forward. But another pistol-wielding stranger had his weapon trained on her. "Uh uh, Captain. Don't make me use this on you."

"Who are you? What the fuck's going on?" I demanded.

"Slater sends his regards," my intruder said. And a moment later, a burst of energy ripped through me.

I woke on the bridge, in a heap of bodies. It took a few seconds for me to get my bearings, but when I did, I felt a surge of panic swell in my chest. "Maggie?" I pushed up, shifting the dead weight of limbs off of me. "Maggie, are you okay?"

"It's yourself I'd be worried about, if I were you, Katie."

I shivered at the voice – Henderson's voice – and turned my eyes from the bodies around me to him. "What the hell?"

It was the Conglomerate client account manager, alright, standing free on the bridge with a handful of roughs on either side. And he was smirking ear-to-ear. "Good to see you too."

I swallowed the fearful knot that materialized in my throat. "What the hell's going on? How'd you get out of the brig?"

He shrugged. "With the help of a few friends. You've made enemies, little Katherine. Not just with the Conglomerate."

I felt a chill run up my back. I remembered the man who'd stunned me in the hall earlier. I remembered his words. *Slater sends his regards.* "Slater?"

He nodded. Satisfaction oozed out of his expression. "That's right. You make a habit of not playing nice, I guess."

"How the hell did they get onboard?" There was always someone on watch. Even if they'd fallen asleep at the controls, no one could board the *Black Flag* without either breeching her or being admitted. And, asleep or not, we'd have heard if we were under attack. We all would have.

"Well, that'd be me," a voice sounded behind me.

I started, drawing out of the pile of bodies to get to my feet. Then I turned. "Drake?"

The engineer shrugged, almost apologetically. "In the flesh."

I could see him there, and hear him. He'd admitted to his role already. Still, I was stunned. "You? You sold us out?"

"I made a smart business decision," he said. "I struck a deal with the Conglomerate."

The call, then, had been fake. The engine trouble, the mysterious readings he and Ginny couldn't decipher, had just been a ruse to lure us out. I glanced down at the pile. Ginny was there with everyone else, her chest rising and falling in her imposed sleep. She'd been another pawn in his treachery. "But Drake…why?"

His eyes flashed. "Because I'm no fool, Kay. I know what's going on here. And I don't want to spend the rest of my life on the run from the Conglomerate. This way, I get what's owed me. And I don't have to live my life looking over my shoulder."

CHAPTER FORTY-NINE

One by one, the crew woke. Maggie was livid. I could see the flash of anger in her eyes, the set of her jaw. But she was mostly quiet.

Frank, on the other hand, was vocal in his threats of retribution. He'd been the one on watch, and before Slater's ship had shown up Drake hit him with enough energy to put him out of commission for the duration of the takeover. He was visibly singed, and seemed to be in pain. "I'm going to eat your damned heart," he warned Sage. The engineer just rolled his eyes.

Meanwhile, the business of unloading our stolen goods was underway. Slater's men went back and forth, hauling gold and credits from the *Black Flag* to the *Sea Witch*. We'd robbed thieves, and were in turn being robbed by thieves.

Maggie waited until Drake was talking to Henderson before whispering in a low tone, "Hey. Where's Sydney?"

The two turned back to look at us, and Henderson laughed. "You can forget the battle bot, Captain."

I felt my heart sink. Had they somehow reprogrammed Syd? Had Drake figured out a way to get around my lockdowns, into his interface? Had they turned Syd? "What did you do?" I demanded, turning my eyes to the engineer.

He laughed now too. "Not much, actually. You might have

shut us out of the bot, but his artificial intelligence isn't that intelligent."

"What do you mean?"

"I mean, all it took was telling him you wanted him to guard a room full of empty bank boxes. And he rolled on, happy to oblige." Drake was grinning at his own cleverness.

"That's why you called Maggie and me down to engineering." I felt, somehow, more betrayed by the realization. The page, the urgent call to engineering, had been about getting us away from Sydney. He'd sent us in one direction, and the robot in another.

He nodded smugly. "Of course. No sense taking on a battle bot if I don't have to."

"You son-of-a-bitch," Frank fumed.

"Oh shut up, Kudarian," Henderson sighed. "It's only because of Drake that you're still drawing breath. If it was my call, you'd be dead. The lot of you. But you in particular."

The minutes ticked by. Captain Slater stepped onto the bridge a few times to converse in hushed tones with Henderson. He was rather as I imagined he might be. His features were pleasant enough, I suppose, but there was a hardness, a coldness, to them all that sent a shiver up my spine.

I didn't notice it at first, but the second time it happened, I did. Maggie moved in front of me when Slater or his men were on deck. It was a subtle shift, just a pivot here, a half step there. But it was unmistakable.

Frank, too, seemed to pick up on it. He started to inch himself to the foreground.

I felt at once relieved and mortified. Other than the comment about making enemies, no further allusions had passed about what transpired on Yukon Station. But it was foremost in my mind. The choice of Slater, the captain whose crewmen had tried to abduct me and had answered for it with their lives, was deliberate. Was this, a double cross and robbery, the extent of the revenge they had planned? Somehow, I couldn't see Henderson or Slater walking away at that.

The fact that Maggie and Frank were reacting as they were meant they couldn't either. And that terrified me.

I sat there, for those long minutes, wondering what lay in store. I remembered Henderson's words to Frank, that we'd all be dead if not for Drake. Was it possible that he'd negotiated our safety into his bargain? We'd flown with this man, Maggie and the crew for longer than me. We'd faced danger together. It would be one thing to rob us. Surely, my mind argued, he wouldn't do more?

Then again, I wouldn't have thought he'd betray us at all. He'd known the terms of the deal from the beginning. They'd never changed. And yet the lure of more had been enough to turn him. I didn't know what Henderson had promised, but I did know that Sage had a price, and the Conglomerate man had found it.

What Drake would do for his thirty pieces of silver remained to be seen.

We didn't have long to wait. Slater's crew was efficient at transferring their stolen goods. Before an hour passed, the *Black Flag* had been stripped of all her bounty. Now a handful of Slater's men stepped onto the bridge, all brandishing weapons.

"Get them to the storage room," Henderson said. To Maggie, he smiled, "Can't have you pursuing us, Captain."

The men with guns obliged, marching us single file from the bridge toward the storage room where we'd stashed the gold. It was just across from the gangplank, and as we crammed inside, some of Slater's men retreated to their own ship, taunting us about our losses as we went.

My anxiety had been in overdrive as we marched, but it started to wane as the bodies crowded around me. They intended to lock us in, as they'd locked Syd up. It'd take a while to get out. We'd have to figure out a way to override the locking mechanisms. I was completely unfamiliar with that aspect of the systems, so it would be a challenge.

But they hadn't killed anyone, and they seemed intent on leaving us alive.

I was just starting to breathe easy when Henderson and Slater stepped into view. "Oh, not you, Katie," the former said.

My heart skipped a beat, and I froze in place. Maggie pressed closer to me.

Henderson, though, was training a gun on us. "Come on. Get out of there."

"What are you doing?" Frank demanded.

He smiled. "I've got a score to settle with Miss Katherine." He glanced, now, at Slater. "And so does my friend here."

"Like hell," Maggie said. "You got your gold. Get the fuck out of here, Henderson."

His eyes flashed. "I'm not negotiating, Captain. You're lucky I'm not taking you all back. You've got Sage to thank for that. But this bitch played with fire. Now she's about to get burned."

"Over my dead body," Frank growled.

Henderson shrugged, loosing a beam of electricity at Frank.

The Kudarian shivered and collapsed to the ground. I screamed.

"We can work our way through all your friends, if you want," he said. "Or you can come with me."

I shuddered, fear fixing me in place. "Please," I mumbled, "don't. Drake, don't let them do this."

The engineer glanced away, and Slater laughed. "Honey, I've got a whole crew itching to get even with you for Biff and Wade."

"And my people are going to want to have a chat, when they're done," Henderson smiled.

Still, I didn't budge. The Conglomerate man sighed, pointing his gun at Fredricks. "Shall we take out the doctor next?"

"Go," Maggie said.

"What?" I was thunderstruck.

"Go with him, Kay."

I glanced at her. Her eyes were cold and fixed straight ahead. She wouldn't look at me. "Maggie, you…you can't be serious."

"They're going to take you no matter what. Don't get my crew killed for nothing."

I blinked. "But Maggie…"

"Come on, Captain," David urged. "You can't send her out there."

She, though, put a hand on my back, and shoved me forward. I stumbled, catching my footing a moment before I faceplanted. "Go."

Henderson grinned. "That a girl."

I felt panic swell in my chest, panic and pain. "Maggie," I begged. "Please." On some level, I knew there was nothing she could do. We were all unarmed and surrounded by men with guns. But the thought of what awaited onboard the *Sea Witch*, and – if I survived long enough – back in Conglomerate hands terrified me to the point of unreason.

Slater laughed again and stepped forward. He wrapped his fingers around my arm, squeezing tight as he yanked me forward. Pain stung me as his fingertips bit into my flesh. "Drake," I said again. "Please."

"Drake's got his payoff, Katie. He's got what you were going to get." Henderson shook his head. "He's not going to throw that away for you. Are you, Drake?"

The engineer glanced up now, from him to me, and then back to him. He shook his head. "No."

"See?"

"Come on." Slater jerked me forward again.

"Wait," Maggie said, stepping after me. Henderson trained his gun on her, and she put her hands up. "Just…just let me say goodbye."

The Conglomerate man exchanged glances with the pirate, and then smirked. "Alright."

Maggie reached me, wrapping me in a hug and kissing me fervently. I was too numb to respond. "I'm sorry, Kay. I'm so sorry. But I have to think of my crew."

Henderson laughed. "That's what you get, Katie, for trusting a pirate."

"Don't worry, Captain," Slater added. "My men'll make sure

she's not lonely."

"And maybe you'll think twice in future about crossing the Conglomerate, Magdalene. Remembering all Katie's about to suffer for her sins."

Maggie's eyes were watering as she released me and turned back to her cell.

"Get her onboard," Henderson instructed.

I felt Slater dragging me toward the *Sea Witch*. But I was still watching Maggie. I'd half expected her to do – something. I wasn't sure what, but she was Magdalene Landon. Fearless. Brave. Resourceful.

Only now, she'd turned her back on me. "Maggie," I said again. My voice was low and raw, shaking with terror like a child's. She kept walking, back toward the storage room. Tears welled in my eyes. "Maggie."

Then, all at once, she darted for something. I saw Henderson move his gun after her. I didn't know what she was doing, but I knew, instinctually, that she was in danger. I leaped for him. Slater's fingers bit deep into my arm, but he hadn't expected this. I broke from his grasp, colliding with Henderson a second later.

Maggie, meanwhile, had reached her destination. It was the control panel for the storage room adjacent to our cell. She pressed the button, and as the doors slid open, I understood. There, in standby mode, was Sydney, guarding over the empty totes where Drake had left him.

CHAPTER FIFTY

"Sydney, help Kay," Maggie screamed.

The robot whirred to life, spinning on his track. Slater and his remaining goons wasted no time. They opened fire on Syd.

Henderson socked me, with his free hand, in the face, and trained his own gun on the bot. I fell backwards, stunned, onto the ground.

Maggie, meanwhile, darted through the crossfire, throwing her body over mine. Beams of light flashed overhead. The sizzle of energy weapons impacting with the ship, the screams of the injured, sounded all around. She remained unmoving throughout, her form pressed over mine until the shots stopped.

Only when the crew rushed to us, and Sydney trundled over inquiring, "Katherine, are you harmed?" did she release me.

I sat up, stunned. The deck was covered in blood and fragments of human bodies. Slater and Henderson and all their men were reduced to bloody pulps. Drake, too, lay in a pool of his own blood.

"Syd," I said, "you killed them all."

"Affirmative. May I scan you for injuries, Katherine?"

"Sure," I said. I was too numb to object. I turned to Maggie now.

There were tears in her eyes, and she pressed a hand against my cheek. "Kay. Oh Kay."

"Hey," Fredricks said, "I don't mean to interrupt reunions or anything like that, but there's still a ship full of Slater's men attached to us."

Maggie dried her eyes and pushed to her feet. In a moment, she'd closed the gangplank. "Kereli," she said, "get us away from the *Sea Witch*. Corano, go weapons hot. Kill those fuckers."

"What about the money?" David protested.

"Fuck the money. There's too many of them to take his ship. And I'll be damned if they're getting away."

She reached out a hand to pull me to my feet, and I accepted it. "Come on, Katherine. Let's make these bastards pay." Then, she glanced back at Fredricks. "Doc, take a look at Frank. See if – well, if there's anything we can do. I'll be down as soon as I can."

"Syd, are there any more of those guys on the ship?" I asked.

"No."

"Okay." I followed Maggie now, running to the bridge.

Sydney rolled along behind us informing me that I was unharmed. "I do detect elevated heart and respiration levels, and an influx in stress hormones. But these fall within expected parameters of human physiological responses to near death."

I was shaking and barely heard him as he droned on. Still, after the last few minutes, having an eight-hundred-pound robotic bodyguard on my heels was something of a relief.

Kereli slid into Frank's station when we reached the bridge.

"All systems go, Captain. Give the word."

"Get us away from the *Sea Witch*. Corano, you ready?"

"Copy."

"Fire at will."

The *Sea Witch* was a midsized, gun heavy cargo ship, fairly evenly matched with the *Black Flag*. Her crew, though, seemed not to realize the full extent of everything that had just occurred.

Kereli pulled away from the pirate ship before it had even raised its shields, and Corano declared, "Weapons locked. Waiting until we're at a safe range. And, missiles away."

I watched the ship grow smaller as we put distance between it and ourselves. I watched our missiles race toward her. And I watched them hit, tearing her into pieces. I watched the *Sea Witch* reduced to a cloud of fragments and debris.

"Target neutralized."

"Good job, Mister Corano. Are we clear? Any other ships in the area?"

"Negative, Captain. We are alone."

"Thank God."

I, though, was too numb to celebrate. I stood staring at the wreckage and blinked, trying to wrap my mind around everything that had just happened. Drake had betrayed us. Drake was dead. Slater and Henderson were dead.

Frank was dead.

I started as I felt an arm wrap around me. It was Maggie. "Kay, are you alright?"

"Mags." I turned to her. "I don't know."

"Oh, babe." She wrapped me in a hug. "I'm sorry I had to scare you like that. I needed to get to the door, though."

"How'd you know Syd was there?"

"He told us. Drake did. Remember? He said he had him guarding the empty bank totes. We'd put them beside the gold. When I saw the locked door – I figured that's where he had to be."

"Oh."

"I'm sorry, babe. I know – how terrifying that was."

I leaned into her arms. "They're all dead."

"Yeah, Kay. They're all dead. You're safe."

"Oh Maggie." I was shaking again. I felt like crying.

"Hey," she said, "let's get you to Fredricks."

"I'm fine."

"Let's go anyway. Kereli, can you take over?"

"Copy."

"Good. Corano, full alert. Get Ginny down to engineering, to make sure that son-of-a-bitch didn't do anything to this ship. David, I want you to get a team together for cleanup."

"How'd I pull the short straw?"

"Just do it, Dave." She ran through a checklist of commands, holding me all the while. Then, we stepped off the bridge, heading for medbay. We took the long way around, avoiding the hall replete with blood and bodies.

"Frank's dead," I said.

"I'm sorry, Kay."

"He died trying to protect me."

"He was a good man."

"You could have died too."

She nodded. "I would have, babe, before I let them take you."

I stopped, glancing back at her. Her eyes were moist again, and she didn't try to hide her tears from me. The sight, somehow, undid me. "Oh Mags." I buried myself in her embrace, and she pulled me tight. I could feel the tension in her shoulders, in her arms. We stood there for a moment, her sobbing quietly and me sobbing loudly. "I was so afraid."

"Me too."

"When you pushed me, I…" I couldn't finish the sentence. It had felt like a knife through the ribs, straight to my heart.

"I'm so sorry, Kay." She pulled back, her cheeks glistening with tears, and looked me in the eye. "I needed you to go, so I could follow. It was the only thing I could think of that would protect you, without getting everyone else killed in the process. Can you forgive me?"

I nodded. "Of course I do, babe. You saved my life. There's nothing to forgive."

"I wish," she said, her tone raw, "there'd been a better way. I'm sorry."

I smiled through my tears, tracing my fingers up her chin to her cheek and brushing her tears away as I went. "Forgive me for doubting you?"

"I needed you to doubt me, in the moment. Your fear is what sold Henderson."

"Still…I should have had more faith in you."

She smiled. "After my track record, I'd question your judgement if you had, babe." Then, she grew more serious. "But I'll never let anyone hurt you, Kay. Not while I'm still drawing breath."

CHAPTER FIFTY-ONE

Red-eyed and puffy-cheeked, but wrapped in Maggie's arm, I walked into medbay. I damned near fainted at the sight that waited.

Frank was there, a scowl on his face as his feet dangled over the bed.

"Frank," I said. "You're alive."

He glanced up, his expression brightening. "Kay. You're alright."

"I told you she was," Fredricks sighed. "Hey! What are you doing? Get back here."

But Frank wasn't in a listening mood. He'd pushed to his feet, and stumbled across the space between us. I went to meet him, wrapping him a fierce hug. He returned it with an equal fierceness.

"Frank," I said when I released him, "I thought you were dead."

"The reports of my death have been greatly exaggerated," he grinned.

Fredricks sighed. "Unfortunately, the sense of humor is as strong as ever."

"But what are you doing here? You okay?"

"I'm fine."

"She was pretty shaken," Maggie explained. "I wanted her to see Fredricks. I didn't realize…well, when we didn't hear anything, I thought…"

He nodded. "That was my fault. I'm afraid I kept the doc busy."

Fredricks rolled his eyes. "I almost sedated his dumb ass. He kept insisting that he had to get back on duty."

The Kudarian shrugged. "What's a little minor singeing when the ship's under attack?"

"It wasn't minor. That second blast was meant to kill you."

"Yeah, but Henderson forgot he was dealing with a Kudarian. Not a puny human."

"You listen to the doctor, Frank," Maggie said. "You've got to take care of yourself."

"Yeah, yeah."

"And the first doctor's order is, get back on that damned table," Fredricks put in.

Frank rolled his eyes. "Alright, alright." Then, to me, he said, "I'm glad you're okay. Doc tells me we owe that to the robot."

"And Maggie," I said.

He nodded. "Well, whoever. I'm just glad."

"Thanks, Frank. And thanks for – well, getting yourself shot for me."

"Course."

"Back on the table," Fredricks demanded. "And you two get the hell out of here, so he'll cooperate."

I didn't end up needing to go back to medbay. Once I'd had a chance to catch my breath, I was okay. Shaken, scared, and jumpy now and then; but okay.

Maggie seemed to have developed a kind of sense for when I needed her touch most. I'd find an arm wrapped around me, a hand on my shoulder, a kiss on the cheek. She was sweeter, more open, more sensitive than I'd ever known her to be. And though I didn't tell her – she wasn't ready to hear it, I knew – I was falling in love with her, one tender moment after another.

I wasn't the only one on the crew who had been shaken, though. We'd all been through hell. I was shocked enough by Sage's betrayal, but the rest of the team had spent years working with him. My surprise was nothing compared to theirs.

Pulling the brig security logs only worsened matters. Drake had been talking to Henderson since the beginning. It wasn't until we actually pulled the Deltaseal job off, though, that his conversations took on a more sinister bent.

He'd resented my larger share. His eyes, once fixed on those dollar signs, seemed blind to everything else. And, little by little, the video showed him succumbing to Henderson's persuasions.

In a sense, I pitied Drake. He reminded me of myself, not so long ago. Henderson's flattery, his friendliness, his charm: I'd fallen for them all too, hadn't I? I'd been motivated by desperation, while Drake was drawn by greed and envy. But the tactics he'd employed were all the same.

David, though, of all of us seemed the most aggrieved. "That fucker. Now no one gets anything. And you know what that means, don't you? It means I'm stuck in the galley. Instead of hiring a cook of my own."

"No call girls, either," Frank smirked.

He just nodded, though. "If he wasn't dead already, I'd kill him myself."

We were left with a lot of *what-ifs* and very few good answers. What if I'd split my share after all? What if we'd reached out to Drake, when we knew he was angry? What if…?

Would any of it made a difference, or would Henderson's promise of two hundred and fifty billion credits have turned Drake's head in the end anyway?

"It's water under the bridge," Maggie said. "We'll never know, and it doesn't pay to guess."

There was one area, though, where we were allowed some small measure of satisfaction. That was the data trove we'd copied from the safe deposit boxes. The contents of those boxes had been destroyed, along with all the gold and credit chips. And Drake had erased my copies of the data.

But he'd missed my redundant drive. He'd missed my backup.

"Send it to the Union military and police," Maggie decided. "We can let them sort it out."

"That should keep the Conglomerate busy for a long time," Frank agreed, "with all the dirt they kept on each other."

It was true. Their 'insurance policies' against one another would prove their undoing. There was enough in those files to put most of their high-ranking and mid-level operatives behind bars for the rest of their lives. And that was without the inevitable plea bargains, before people started turning evidence.

I sent the files, and then we washed our hands of the matter. "It's out of our hands now."

Once that was done, once the ship's diagnostics proved that she was clean and clear of sabotage, once the dead bodies had been disposed, and once I'd checked Sydney for any damage, we met in the mess hall.

We were drinking top shelf again, but the mood was very different this time. "Well," David sighed into his whiskey, "we're poor again."

"So much for my ship," Ginny agreed.

Fredricks squeezed her to him. "At least we all made it out alive."

She smiled. "That's true."

"And it was nice seeing someone shoot Frank," David agreed. "Silver lining, and all that."

The Kudarian frowned at him. "It wasn't nearly as painful, believe me, as the idea of choking down your cooking for the rest of my working life is."

"Sorry that we didn't end up with anything out of it," Maggie said.

"It was a risk from the beginning, Captain," Corano offered. "We all knew that when we signed on."

"And we didn't lose anything," Kereli agreed.

"A little pride, getting played by a member of my own crew like that," Mags admitted.

"A lesson in humility benefits us all now and again," the Esselian declared sagely. "And I do believe Drake Sage gave us all one."

"And on the bright side," Corano added, "we took care of Slater's crew. That was long overdue."

"Yes," she agreed, squeezing me to her. "It was."

"And," I added airily, as much for Maggie's sake as my own, "now there'll be no more talk about getting rid of Syd. Not after he saved the day like that."

A few groans met this declaration. "I suppose not," Corano said. "It is useful to keep a battle bot onboard."

"Can you at least train it some manners?" David sighed. "Like, to keep his big, dumb frame out of hallways?"

"How else is he going to get around, Dave? He can't teleport…"

"I don't know. I'm just tired of running into him."

Frank had been ignoring this exchange, and now he glanced up, as if breaking from his thoughts. "So what's next, Captain?"

"What do you mean?"

"Well, now that we didn't strike it rich…what's our next mission?"

She laughed dryly. "Well, there's always passenger runs. Cargo runs. We can see if Union command has any bounties out. What are you all in the mood for?" The question was answered only in grumbles. "I don't know, Frank. We'll figure it out tomorrow," she decided.

CHAPTER FIFTY-TWO

We didn't drink much that night. We weren't celebrating, and no one seemed to want to suffer the hangover for a pity party. I went back with Mags to her room, and Sydney followed us. "Katherine," he said, "I have a request."

"Sure, Syd. What's up?"

"I believe I could contribute more to the ship than I am currently authorized to do. I would like permission to prepare a proposal for you, to extend my usefulness to the crew and to yourself."

I glanced at Maggie, and she shook her head, ever so faintly. I grinned. That was her *Oh God, what are we about to get ourselves into* shake. Not the *No way in hell* head shake. "Alright," I said. "Prepare your proposal. I'll look at it tomorrow morning."

"I will, Katherine. And thank you."

I was probably nuts. But there was, I could swear, a note of real enthusiasm in his metallic voice. "Of course. And Syd?"

"Yes?"

"I never thanked you for saving my life. And the crew's. Thank you."

"It was my pleasure, Katherine."

We reached her room, and bid Sydney a good night. "Good night to you both as well. As your people say, 'sleep tight, and don't let the bed bugs bite.'"

"Thanks Syd."

When we were inside, Maggie turned to me. "Katherine?"

I glanced up at the sudden seriousness of her tone, and the use of my full name. "Yes, Magdalene?"

She smiled at my teasing. "We'll be near Echo Station soon. And now that the Conglomerate is going to be dealing with the fallout from Deltaseal…well, I guess what I'm saying, it's probably safe for you now."

I blinked. "And?"

"Well, if you want to leave, I will take you wherever you want to go. It doesn't have to be Echo Station, of course. But…" She was fidgeting nervously.

I took her hands in mine. "But?"

"If you wanted to stay…well, the *Black Flag* needs a new chief engineer, if you're interested."

"Does she, now?" I smiled.

She nodded, then sucked in a breath. "But…but that's not really what I'm asking. I mean, if you want the job, it's yours. But…what I'm really saying is, I want you to stay, Kay. With me. If you want to stay, of course."

"Of course I want to stay, Maggie." Could she doubt it? Could she doubt how much she meant to me? "Anywhere you are, babe, that's where I want to be."

She smiled, relief spreading on her features. "Good.

Because…well, I'd sure as hell miss you, Katherine Ellis."

I brushed my fingers through her hair, leaning in to kiss her. "I'd sure as hell miss you too, Magdalene Landon. So it's a good thing I'm not going anywhere."

ACKNOWLEDGMENTS

Many thanks to my beta readers and editors, and to everyone who let me bounce ideas off of them during the creative process.

ABOUT THE AUTHOR

Rachel Ford is a software engineer by day, and a writer most of the rest of the time. She is a Trekkie, a video-gamer, and a dog parent, owned by a Great Pyrenees named Elim Garak and a mutt of many kinds named Fox (for the inspired reason that he looks like a fox).
You can follow Rachel on Facebook at:
https://www.facebook.com/rachelfordauthor/

She is also on Twitter @RachelFordWI and Instagram @RFord191

AN ASK

If you liked what you read, please consider leaving a few lines on GoodReads and Amazon to let me know! Thank you so much!

Printed in Great Britain
by Amazon